Home

Dawn Kimberly Johnson

Dreamspinner Press

Published by
Dreamspinner Press
4760 Preston Road
Suite 244-149
Frisco, TX 75034
http://www.dreamspinnerpress.com/

Home

Cover Art by Paul Richmond   http://www.paulrichmondstudio.com

ISBN: 978-1-61581-589-0

Printed in the United States of America
First Edition
September, 2010

eBook edition available
eBook ISBN: 978-1-61581-590-6

To my mom, Donna.
Thanks for putting up with me.

Chapter 1

"YOU'RE shaking." Alec, panting and painfully hard, pulled back from Eli so he could look into his eyes. "We don't have to do this now."

"Don't stop," Eli pleaded, equally breathless and pained. "I want this… want you." He hooked his left leg around Alec's waist to keep him close and reached out for him. His fingers played in Alec's wavy black hair, traced his jaw, and brushed over his lips as he grinned up at him through heavy-lidded, passion-drunk eyes.

They had met in late summer and had been *officially* together for only a few weeks, but all the back-and-forth desire in the months before Eli decided to take a chance on the handsome, persistent American author—that was part of their relationship, too, a part of their history. Alec had gradually drawn Eli out of a darkness sparked by the murder of his partner, an attack he'd witnessed and that had nearly claimed his life as well.

But now they were facing another hurdle, another step forward, because all the kissing, breathless groping, and hand jobs just weren't cutting it any longer. There was a lot of need for something more built up in both of them—a need to be even closer. With their housemates either out of town or spending the night elsewhere, Eli and Alec had separately come to the same decision: tonight they would make love for the first time.

After a romantic dinner out, a long conversation filled with nervous laughter and secret glances, and a short walk through the chilly air of their tiny neighborhood park, they had stumbled through the front door grabbing frantically for each other: kissing desperately, pulling at their clothes, knocking into the hall table, and upsetting the tchotchkes. But after dropping and almost tripping over Eli's cane, they'd forced themselves to calm down and slowly, carefully ascended the stairs—choosing Alec's attic room over Eli's on the main floor. Up there the morning sounds of the house wouldn't reach them, and they could pretend the rest of the world didn't exist for that much longer.

They had begun with the familiar: Alec half on top of Eli, kissing him, rubbing him through his jeans, and Eli clinging to him, grinding upward against him, tangling his fingers in Alec's hair. But then, seeking skin-to-skin contact, Alec had reached beneath Eli's shirt and, as usual, when his fingers moved up Eli's torso, Eli went rigid and gasped, involuntarily inching away from his touch. Alec had slowed his eager hands until Eli settled—until, grinning and ashamed, he scooted close again.

"I'm sorry," Eli whispered.

"It's okay. It's okay," Alec repeated softly as they slowly undressed each other. But now, stripped bare and embracing, panting, with condoms and lube at hand—*Alec* was the one who wasn't okay. He had put on the brakes, worried that Eli wasn't ready for this.

"I don't want you doing this just because you know I want it. That's not good enough, not reason enough."

"Alec, look at me." Their eyes traveled down to their duel erections. "Don't I look ready?"

"I can take care of that without—"

"I want you inside me," Eli growled, reaching down between them and gripping Alec's cock possessively.

"Eh-Eli—" Alec's eyes closed for a moment. "Uh-okay."

"It's been two years," Eli said, his voice softening. "You're the first man I've kissed since Bennett was killed." His large blue eyes bored into Alec's gray. "Can't I want you and still be nervous?"

Eli reached up and gripped the back of Alec's head, pulling him into a kiss that shook them to their toes. When they parted, Alec couldn't speak. His hand fumbled over the surface of the nightstand on his left, his eyes never leaving Eli's as he found the condoms and lube.

He squeezed a generous amount of lube onto his fingers and smiled down at Eli, who grinned back, just before he reached out to switch off the light.

"Wait," Alec said, uncertainty tainting his voice.

"I trust you know where everything is?"

Alec laughed softly. "You can be certain of that, but I want to watch you." Eli's smile faltered, and he withdrew his hand. After a moment of watching the uncertainty on his boyfriend's face, Alec reached out with his left hand and switched off the light. Eli's arms and legs were immediately around him, squeezing him and throwing him off balance a bit. "Slow down," he blurted out, laughing. "I need to get my bearings."

As his eyes adjusted to the low light from the streetlamps below filtering in through his windows, Alec smiled at hearing Eli's playful chuckle from the darkness. He could feel hands caressing his back, lips kissing his neck and chest, thighs tightening around his waist, the hair on Eli's legs tickling his sides and lower back, and their cocks brushing and bumping against one another. His disembodied lover was eager, hot, and squirming beneath him.

Alec lowered himself over Eli, kissing him as his left hand stroked Eli's hair. Then Eli's hands left him, his right patting out to his side in search of the condom packet. When Alec heard the package ripped open, he rose a little so Eli could reach his erection and roll on the condom.

"You're good at that."

"I can do it with my mouth too."

"You'll have to demonstrate that sometime," Alec said as they closed their embrace again.

"Uh-uh. Once we get our results back, we won't need these anymore."

"True," Alec said as his slick fingers danced around Eli's entrance, causing his body to jerk involuntarily. "But I still want you to show me."

"I promise I will—*uh!*" Eli arched off the bed as Alec penetrated him with two fingers, curling upon entry.

Eli's whole body tightened around Alec in a spasm and shuddered. Alec didn't try to move again until Eli relaxed, largely because Eli had a death grip on the back of his head. He could hear Eli's rapid breath as his boyfriend panted against his neck.

"Sorry," Alec whispered, feeling Eli's body slowly unclenching around him. "Got a bit overeager." He wished he'd gone more slowly; after all, it'd been two years, and he wanted this first time to be perfect. "Eli?"

"*More,*" Eli whispered as he tangled his fingers further in Alec's hair.

Alec grinned and began to work his fingers inside the man. He could now make out the vague shape of Eli beneath him but none of the visual detail—only an occasional glimpse of his parted lips as he gasped, his head turning back and forth on the pillow. Alec quickly withdrew his fingers and applied more lube to his condom-sheathed cock as he spread Eli. He pressed the head against Eli's opening and pushed forward gradually.

Eli seemed to stop breathing. For that matter, so did Alec at the sensation of heat enveloping him, squeezing him, pulling him in deeper. Once buried to the hilt, he withdrew again and pushed forward harder.

Eli whispered, "Yes," spurring Alec to find a rhythm and intensity comfortable for them both—one he could maintain for a good while. He threw Eli's left leg over his shoulder but allowed his right leg to rest lower on his thigh as he pushed into Eli over and over. His hair hung in his eyes, and his skin grew slick with sweat. And not simply from the physical effort, but also from concentrating, trying to prolong the glorious sensation of being sheathed within the man he loved. When Alec was close, he reached for Eli's cock to bring him along, but before he could lay a finger on him, Eli came, screaming his name, his inner spasms bringing Alec right along after.

After his tremors subsided, Alec allowed Eli's leg to slide from his shoulder and collapsed on top of him, both of them gasping for air. He carefully removed the condom and tossed it—he hoped—into the wastebasket by his bed before rolling off his boyfriend and onto his back next to him. His right leg lay across Eli's left as he stared into the darkness and tried to make out the details in his ceiling.

When Eli's breathing began to settle, Alec stirred. "I'll get you something to clean up."

But Eli's hand shot out and held him down. "Got it." Alec got a vague impression of him leaning off the side of the bed and grabbing some discarded article of clothing off the floor to wipe the come from his chest. "See… all clean."

Alec's laughter was silenced as Eli rolled over and kissed him, wrapping him up in his arms. Surprised to feel Eli begin grinding against him again, Alec broke the kiss and asked, "Really?"

"Good… more."

"Ah." Alec reached down and began squeezing Eli's bottom. "Should I take it as a compliment that you've become virtually monosyllabic post-coitus?"

"Big words good," Eli whispered, and Alec could hear the smile in his voice.

He kissed him accordingly.

JERKING awake much later, Alec stretched languidly and yawned, reaching for Eli for a third time. But that side of the bed was now cool and vacant. He sat up abruptly, hoping Eli had not tried to navigate the stairs on his own. But then he saw the light from his bathroom and heard the shower. He climbed out of bed and padded naked across the carpeted floor. The bathroom door was ajar, steam swirling out to greet him.

"Eli?" he called as he pushed the door farther open and stepped into the small room. There was no tub, only a tiny sink and vanity, a toilet, and a glass-enclosed shower. That's where he found Eli, standing beneath the hot spray, his face buried against his arm as he leaned against the tiled wall, weeping. His other hand hung limply at his side, holding a soapy loofah.

Alec went to him, carefully opening the shower door and slipping in behind him. He flinched as the hot water stung his skin and embraced Eli right at the moment he became aware Alec was there.

"Oh, I'm… I'm ok-k-kay," Eli said, quickly wiping his eyes. Alec hugged him back against his chest, kissing his neck and swaying with him. "It's just… I… uh, I—"

"Shhh, now. It's going to be all right," Alec whispered as he took the loofah from Eli, wrapped his arms around him again, and continued swaying—while Eli continued to fail at stopping his tears. Alec hoped with everything in him that what he'd just told him was the truth.

Eventually Alec wet the sponge again, worked up a fresh, hot lather, and began to wash his lover. He turned Eli to face him and began with small, gentle circles on his chest. His fingers brushed lightly over the scars where a rib or two had punched through years ago, and for a moment, Alec became lost in reading Eli's skin like a relief map of his past, which is what scars really are. Eli didn't flinch as Alec caressed a rough line of skin where a surgeon had entered to stop his internal bleeding.

They captured each other's gaze, and Alec briefly wondered about the scars he couldn't see. He continued his work with the loofah, expanding his strokes to include Eli's arms, neck, shoulders, and back. Neither of them spoke again, and by the time Alec ran the sponge over the rough, puckered skin of his boyfriend's right leg, Eli's sobs had quieted.

Chapter 2

ELI sat up on the bed, rubbed his eyes, and yawned. He held his mop of dark brown hair out of his eyes and glanced at the clock face. *Bollocks!* He was running behind everyone else, so he quickly scrounged up some sweatpants and a T-shirt, grabbed his cane, and then went into his bathroom to splash some water on his face.

Looking in the mirror, he tried to recall the dream he'd been having. He smiled, realizing it had been about his and Alec's first time. But even as the edges of the dream began fading and blurring, he clung to the memory of that walk the two of them had taken in the freezing November air and the heat they'd generated in bed that night. Something had happened after, later that night, but it skirted away from him as he tried to catch the memory.

He went back into his bedroom to slip on some shoes and smiled at the sunshine and fresh April breeze pouring through his window. The sounds of activity outside reminded him that the others had been up for some time already. Tony and Lyle were moving out today, and he didn't want to miss their send-off.

Reaching the front doorway of the house, Eli cringed as he watched Alec and Dray preparing to lift a bureau into the rented truck.

"Ready?"

"Lift with your legs."

"One, two… lift!"

"This cannot be good for my back," Dray said as he straightened up and walked backward, bearing his half of the weight. Alec remained on the ground, lifting the bureau above his head.

Convinced he could hear Alec's muscles screaming, Eli bit his bottom lip, fearing permanent damage to his man. He smiled. *My man.* Alec's shirt was wet at the pits and chest, with sprinkles of moisture on the back, and his dark hair hung stringy and dripping on his head. After the bureau's four feet were firmly on the truck's bed, Alec hopped aboard and helped Dray carry it deeper in and secure it for the trip to their friends' new flat.

The two of them were out of sight for only a few moments, but it was long enough for Eli's suspicions of what Dray might be trying with his boyfriend to nearly flare into action. He stopped himself. He trusted Alec, and they'd obviously been working together for hours without his supervision.

Still, he fidgeted uncomfortably as he waited. *I forgot you were going to be here, Mr. Jenkins.* Dray had been pursuing Alec relentlessly since meeting him at their annual Last Blast campout the year before.

The two men reappeared, Alec looking no worse for wear, and he hopped deftly to the ground and grabbed a bottled water, while Dray remained above, leaning against the inside of the truck and chatting amiably to him.

Panting from the exertion—or, as Eli suspected, for show—Dray stared down at Alec like a starving man looks at a cheeseburger with the works. Eli glanced at his boyfriend and knew he didn't see it. Alec looked at Dray, at his casual body language, at his easy, relaxed demeanor, and saw only that. Eli's eyes narrowed as he watched Dray. *He doesn't feel you watching him from the tall grass, you arrogant tosser.*

"You stare any harder at Dray, and he'll burst into flames," Ilsa whispered in Eli's ear, startling him.

"I'm… n-not." Eli fought hard not to blush, but it didn't work.

Ilsa eyed him skeptically. "*Riiiight.* And I'm not an ample, sexy sistah from Louisiana." Eli smiled against his will. "Finish this for me," she said, passing him a mug of hot coffee as she dug her keys out of her pocket. "There's iced tea in the fridge, if anyone wants any. And there's casserole left over from last night." She kissed him on the cheek. "See you tonight." She skipped down the front stairs and went to her car. "I hope they keep the party going until we get there, because I'll be too tired to start it up again when I arrive." She dropped behind the wheel and was gone before Eli remembered to wave.

He sipped the coffee and returned his attention to Alec and Alec's stalker. Dray gripped the top of the truck with both hands, stretching, elongating his perfect torso and giving Alec an eyeful. A fine sheen of sweat coated his dark skin, most notably his shaved head, as he continued to smile down at Alec with that electric smile of his. His jeans were just tight enough to accentuate his package, while not hindering his activities.

He leaned down suddenly and snatched Alec's water from his hand, then proceeded to gulp it down as Alec watched, apparently enraptured. Eli's grip tightened on his cane. He swore he could see Dray's throat working, even from this distance. Dray drained the bottle dry just as Alec glanced toward the house, catching Eli's eye. They exchanged smiles. Dray followed Alec's gaze and frowned slightly, tossing the empty bottle over his shoulder and into the back of the truck.

He gripped the red fabric handle of the sliding door and, after giving the contents one last look, leaped to the ground, pulling the door with him. It sounded like a gunshot and reverberated throughout their neighborhood, announcing that someone was leaving.

"I think that's it," Tony said. Eli turned to see him in the hallway, struggling with two canvases as he shoved two huge suitcases ahead of him with his knees.

"That's it, huh?" Eli asked, laughing. "Are you certain?"

"Had a bit of a lie-in this morning, eh?" Tony asked as Eli joined him, draining his mug and setting it on the hall table before grabbing hold of one of the suitcases. "Don't bother with that. You'll hurt yourself."

Eli's expression darkened briefly, but he leaned on his cane before lifting the case effortlessly. "I'm a lot stronger than I was last year." Eli turned away from his friend. "I've been working out regularly." He carried the bag to the front door but paused, momentarily befuddled by the stairs he couldn't manage.

"I bet you have," Tony said as he watched Alec running toward them.

"Hey, I got these," Alec said, relieving Eli and Tony of their burdens and running back down the stairs with the bags toward Tony's car.

"He seems to have an alarming amount of energy," Tony said, peering at Alec's rather fit, retreating form before pulling out his sunglasses.

Eli went a bit pink, but he had no intention of sharing any

intimate details with the artist. And it was probably best that Tony not know that he and Alec had fucked in nearly every room in the house since getting together last November—a feat difficult to accomplish with three other housemates who followed hectic, unpredictable schedules.

He recalled one particularly passionate, impromptu encounter on the floor in front of the very sofa where Alec had first put the moves on him. That first time, they'd just come back from a day of Eli showing Alec around Soho, but, being too filled with heartache and fear, Eli had put a stop to Alec's advances. Most recently, it was Lyle and a drunken Tony who had given them pause.

Eli grinned as he remembered that night: him moaning and quivering beneath Alec as his boyfriend thrust into him, their skin slick as he clawed enthusiastically at Alec's back and thighs. Then suddenly, Alec had frozen and—before Eli could groan his objection—covered his mouth, silencing him.

Eli had tightened his legs around Alec's waist as he stared up into his handsome face, his black hair partially obscuring his gray eyes as they remained fixed on the front entryway. Eli craned his neck to see what was so interesting and quickly realized that Alec had heard a key in the door and was hoping that if they remained still enough, quiet enough, perhaps whoever was entering the house would simply walk right past them.

They did: a drunken Tony, being steered toward the stairs by a sober Lyle, and never once glancing into the living room to their left. The light in the entryway ended just before reaching the lovers as they lay naked on the hardwood floor, now breathing shallowly and locked in the most incredible, intimate embrace as they watched their housemates intently. Alec's hand slid off Eli's mouth, but then Tony had started singing—badly—and both of them began to giggle. Alec covered Eli's mouth again and buried his face against his lover's neck to muffle his own laughter, which had only served to tickle Eli further.

Once their housemates had staggered up the stairs to their room, their laughter had quieted, and Eli reached up, sweeping the hair out of Alec's eyes so he could look into them, but his gaze quickly fell to Alec's mouth. Rewarded with a warm smile that silently asked, "Where were we?", they kissed tenderly, and Eli stroked Alec's back in silent encouragement while flexing his inner muscles to awaken his partner's flagging erection.

Alec rose up on his forearms, ran his fingers through Eli's unruly hair, and began to move again. Eli had tightened his legs around Alec's waist and reached for his thighs, trying to pull him even closer, even deeper inside him, and soon after, Alec had to silence a very vocal, enthusiastic Eli with a kiss.

"Are you listening to me?"

"Huh?" Eli asked as he unconsciously rubbed his hipbone and considered talking to Ilsa about getting carpet for the living room. "S-sorry, Tony… you were saying?"

"Where did you go just now?" the artist asked, his eyes narrowing.

"How's the new car running?" Eli asked, switching to Tony's favorite topic—Tony.

The artist's first show had made him a tidy sum, pulling forth uncharacteristic generosity and netting a flat-screen television for the house. The proceeds from Tony's second and most recent show, however, were all for the artist himself and sat at the curb in the form of a cobalt-blue sports car.

His boyfriend, Lyle, thought it was ridiculously impractical and went entirely too fast.

Tony adored it.

"My baby purrs like a kitten," he said, smiling and putting on his sunglasses.

Alec reappeared. "Can I take those for you, Tony?"

"Uh, no thank you, Alec. I've got them." The three of them fell silent and looked at each other. "I guess… it's time to go," Tony said.

Eli felt his entire body tense as Dray rejoined them and threw his arm possessively around Alec's shoulders. "I'm all set," he said brightly. "Just need you to lead the way, Mr. James."

"Lead the way?" Tony asked. "You found us the place. You know exactly where it is."

"He just wants you to thank him again," Eli said. He graced Dray with his chilliest smile and got as good as he gave. Eli and Alec tried to hug Tony at the same time, collided, and then took turns.

"Ooh, man sweat. Yum," Tony said. Alec smiled crookedly as he moved free of Dray to stand next to Eli, he and Tony trading places. "I guess you two will be all alone in the house until Ilsa finishes at the restaurant." The artist grinned wickedly. "Whatever will you do?"

"Listen… are you sure you want to deal with a housewarming the same day you finish moving in?" Eli asked.

"It does seem like a lot to take on," Alec added.

"No worries," Tony said. "If anyone can pull it off, Lyle can." He started down the steps. "He's Mr. Organization, remember?" He walked to his car and carefully, almost tenderly, placed his canvases in the passenger seat. For a moment, Eli thought he might buckle them in. The engine roared to life, and Eli could see his smile from the front steps. Tony pulled the car in front of the truck and waited.

Eli had unconsciously hooked his thumb in the back belt loop of Alec's jeans, and now his fingers snaked under Alec's shirt, his nails trailing a path through the sweat dripping down his boyfriend's back. Alec visibly shivered, and Eli smothered a chuckle as Dray stood before them in the doorway, completely unaware of their intimate contact.

"Alec, you coming along?" Dray asked.

"I understand there's a small crew waiting to help with the unloading," Eli offered.

He and Dray locked eyes for a few heartbeats.

"Uh… nope, Dray," Alec said, breaking the stalemate. "There should be plenty of help waiting for you over there."

Dray sighed. "Well, I guess I'll see you tonight."

"Yes, *we'll* be there." Eli's smile held no warmth for Dray, and as they looked at each other again, he felt his gut twist, but Dray only chuckled, turned, and headed for the truck.

"Bye, Erby," he shouted back over his shoulder. Eli raised his cane as if to whack Dray on his bald head with it, but Alec stopped him, as he knew he would.

"Hang on," Alec shouted after Dray. "The door's not locked." He ran down the stairs and to the back of the truck to secure the door latch. Dray joined him there, and they looked it over together.

Eli watched them, keenly aware of every flirtatious action on Dray's part: touching Alec's shoulder, laughing, leaning toward him.

Dray had gone after Eli's last boyfriend, Bennett, and it was no fun seeing him repeat this behavior with Alec. He had a thing for Americans. Eli smiled. *I guess I have a thing for them too.* He was convinced Dray only offered to help with the move so he could put his perfect, strong, healthy, beautiful, black body in Alec's vicinity, or, at the very least, within his line of sight.

Tony honked his horn, and Dray removed his shirt from his back pocket, sliding it on and preparing to leave. *That's right. Cover up, you fiend.*

Chapter 3

ALEC waved goodbye to Tony and Dray as they drove off, heading for the new flat. He glanced at the darkening sky and wiped his brow. With the humidity they'd had today, he wouldn't be surprised if a thunderstorm hit before the party.

"Looks like a stor—"

Eli was gone. The front door of the house stood open, but there was no sign of his boyfriend. A chill ran through him, and he approached the house hoping that Eli wasn't having another fit about Dray's attentions.

As a psychologist, Alec knew the two of them, as a couple, was a process. Some days Eli was eager, passionate, funny, and ready to take on anything. But the days following one of his nightmares were another story. Directly after a nightmare, Eli would allow, even welcome, Alec's comfort. Clinging to him in the sweaty sheets, Eli would cry and mumble apologies, and Alec would hold him, speaking softly until he stopped shaking and fell back to sleep. But when the sun rose, Eli withdrew, became quiet, surly, or quick to temper. Add to that his venomous attitude toward Dray and any attention Alec might pay to him, and navigating their relationship could, at times, be treacherous.

Alec shut and locked the door behind him before walking slowly down the hall toward Eli's room.

"Eli? Where are you?"

"In here."

Alec entered the bedroom and, not seeing Eli, continued to the small bathroom within. He found Eli on his knees, leaning over the tub, shirtless and swirling his arm in the water. "What are you doing?"

"Drawing you a bath."

Alec spotted a small box of Epsom salts next to Eli on the floor. "I love the way you say 'bath'," he said, watching him from the door.

Eli looked up at him and smiled. "Alec, we've been together nearly a year—"

"Five months is not 'nearly a year'."

Eli ignored the statement. "You're surrounded by people day in and day out who say 'bath' exactly the way I do."

"I like the way *you* say it." Alec smiled and continued to watch him: on his knees, shirtless, bent over the rim of the tub in sweatpants and—he was certain—nothing else. He felt something in his lower gut quiver, and his smile grew.

"No," Eli said without turning around. Alec stopped smiling as his boyfriend looked at him sternly, slowly getting to his feet and limping toward him. "Get undressed." Eli held Alec's gaze as he came closer, and then, setting his cane against the wall, he lifted Alec's shirt and began unbuckling his belt.

Alec quickly finished removing his soiled shirt, tossing it over his shoulder onto the bedroom floor before kicking off his sneakers. His breathing caught when Eli placed one palm on his chest, spreading the fingers in the light dusting of hair there before slowly drawing them down Alec's front.

"I want you to climb in that tub and soak," Eli whispered as he leaned in, sending a thrill through Alec by taking a nipple between his lips and licking the salty sweat from it.

"Uh, just s-soak?"

"Yes." Eli moved to the other nipple, slowly circling it with his tongue before nipping it gently with his teeth.

Alec felt his cock jerk, coming to life as he eagerly reached for Eli, hoping to pull him in for a kiss, but the maddening man pulled away. "I think I'm getting mixed signals," he said, laughing.

"No, you're not," Eli assured him.

Remaining skeptical, Alec allowed Eli to pull his pants and briefs down in one, quick, easy motion, the fabric deliciously raking Alec's cock and making him shudder. The grin on Eli's face as he watched Alec's erection bounce back up and stand at attention only excited Alec more. Eli stepped closer so the head grazed his own fuzzy abdomen, and Alec's eyes fell shut from the contact, a stupid grin spreading across his face. He quickly stepped out of his clothes, leaving them in a pile at their feet, and even though what he wanted most was to take Eli in his arms, he obediently walked over and carefully climbed into the steaming water, hissing as it stung his skin.

"Jesus! You're trying to boil me."

Eli chuckled. "You'll get used to it. Now sit."

He slowly, agonizingly lowered himself into the water. "There's not much in here," Alec said in dismay, looking at the pitiful amount of water that didn't reach as high as he'd like.

"It'll rise once I'm on board." That caught Alec's attention, but Eli simply knelt down by the tub and smiled at him. "Good?"

"It would be better with you... 'on board', as you say," Alec whispered, his eyes half-closing as the hot water soothed him. "What?" he asked, catching the sudden frown on Eli's face.

"I forgot the...."

Their eyes searched for and landed on the sponge simultaneously. It was above them in the soap rack, and Alec moved to get it, but Eli stopped him, expertly using the tip of his cane to knock it into the water—followed closely by a bottle of aloe body wash. The sponge landed with a quiet plop, but the body wash sent a shower of water into the air and onto Alec's face, while also drenching the front of Eli's sweatpants and throwing both of them into a fit of laughter.

Eli captured the sponge, squeezed a healthy amount of soap on it, and quickly worked up a lather. Eli began dutifully washing him, and Alec relaxed, watching his boyfriend's face intently, even though the man wouldn't meet his gaze. As Eli covered him with lather, Alec compliantly raised his arms, turned, or leaned forward at the correct moments without being told. He hadn't had a bath like this since he was six.

"What are you smiling about?" Eli asked, still not looking directly at him.

"This reminds me of an old rhyme my stepfather told me once."

Eli paused and looked at him skeptically. "Is this a dodgy rhyme?"

Alec laughed. "No! It's from an old episode of *Sesame Street*... you have that here, right?"

Eli nodded and resumed his washing. "In some capacity, I think so, yes."

"The rhyme was supposed to teach kids the days of the week. Uh...." Alec looked at the ceiling and thought for a moment. "Poor Solomon Grundy, he washed the left side of his face on Monday, he washed the left side of his neck on Tuesday, he washed his left arm on Wednesday, so on and so forth."

"Cute."

"Yeah, but he only had seven days of the week to work with and ended up remaining half-dirty." Alec chuckled softly, and Eli smiled. "I remember thinking that some bits had been left out of the equation."

"Yes, the best bits," Eli said as he reached Alec's waist in his endeavors. "But as a children's show, I'd hardly expect them to address those bits."

"Hey, I was six or seven, and *I* knew they'd left something out."

"What? Your favorite toy?"

Alec guffawed, but then he grew very serious. "Now that you mention it, I was fairly fond of it." Alec laid his head back and closed his eyes in anticipation. "Speaking of—"

But Eli's sponge deftly skipped his crotch and moved to his thighs and legs. Alec glared at him, affronted, but his boyfriend only grinned, clearly amused with himself. Alec gyrated a bit in the tub, trying to escape his discomfort and get Eli's attention.

"You worked hard today." Eli submerged the sponge in the water to rinse it.

"I guess so."

"You must be very sore from all that lifting and carrying."

"A bit."

"Straining those muscles."

"You bet." Alec flexed his bicep impressively but then pulled an exaggerated *Ouch!* face.

Eli smiled. "You're probably worn out."

"Uh-uh." Alec made a grab for him, but Eli dodged it, instead squeezing the sponge out over his head, rinsing him. Alec sputtered and shook his head violently, sending a shower of water and soap all over them both. When he managed to open his eyes again, Eli stood next to the tub, laughing. He'd shed his sweatpants, revealing a beautiful, stiff cock of his own—and the angry dark scar that ran the length of his right leg.

Alec had seen it many times over the past five months and knew the feel of it under his fingers as well as he knew the scent of his lover's skin, the weight and pulse of his cock in his mouth, the change in his breathing when he was close to coming, and the taste of him.

"Sorry, love."

"No you're not," Alec said. "Are you going to get in here or not?"

"Of course… I have to wash your hair."

"Fuck my hair." He reached out and helped Eli step gingerly into the tub, where he straddled Alec's legs. The water level rose a good bit, but Eli didn't look interested in moving any farther up Alec's body. "You could come a little closer," Alec encouraged.

"You'd like that, wouldn't you?"

"Very much," Alec said, his voice lusty and deep. He didn't want to play this game anymore. He didn't want to wait any longer. Eli came closer, carefully positioning himself almost right where Alec wanted him—*almost*.

Alec gripped his bottom to pull him closer, but Eli resisted.

"No."

"Good Lord, you're killing me," Alec groaned. Eli chuckled, placing a dollop of body wash in his hand and aggressively working it into Alec's hair. He could feel himself relaxing against his will as Eli massaged his scalp. "I was worried you were angry with me," Alec said softly.

"Huh?" Eli continued massaging, and Alec's eyes grew dreamy, a sloppy grin crossing his lips.

"After the others left, I looked for you, but you were gone."

Eli paused, looking into his eyes. "You mean because of Dray?" Alec nodded, and Eli resumed his efforts. "I didn't need to see him putting the moves on you, so I came in to get this *baahhth* ready." Alec matched Eli's grin, taking hold of his cock and stroking it. Eli's hands faltered, and his eyes closed as he briefly lost his balance and leaned into him.

That did it.

Alec wrapped his arms around his boyfriend, pulling him in tight against his chest and kissing him. Eli's cock was pinned between them, and Alec's bumped deliciously against Eli's bottom, pulling happy gasps from both of them. Gripping him firmly, as if he feared Eli would slip away again, Alec nibbled at his neck, jaw, and earlobe before again taking his mouth desperately, his forcefulness creating a surge of bathwater that spilled onto the bathroom floor.

"Oops, sorry," Alec said, pulling back for a look at the mess they'd made, but the half-open eyes, dreamy expression, and crooked grin on Eli's face gave him pause. Eli startled him when he suddenly grabbed Alec on either side of his soapy head and kissed him deeply. When they parted he could see in Eli's face that he, too, was tired of playing this game.

Eli rubbed himself urgently against Alec's abdomen, unconsciously seeking the friction as Alec slid his middle finger past his own lips—an action that caught and held Eli's attention. After licking, sucking, and coating his finger, he withdrew it, but Eli was quick to take it into his own mouth. Alec grinned as he watched his boyfriend suck on his digit. Suddenly Eli released Alec's finger and leaned forward, offering himself, letting Alec know he was ready, and Alec responded, reaching behind Eli, spreading, and entering him with one slick finger.

"Ahh," Eli breathed into Alec's ear, his hot breath making Alec shiver. Eli sat back, his eyes falling closed and his head tilting forward as another finger worked into him. Slowly finger-fucking him for a moment before adding a third, Alec's cock twitched and jumped when Eli's lips parted, his grip digging into Alec's shoulders to steady himself.

Alec savored his changing expressions. Watching Eli like this was a true treat, because so often they'd made love in darkened rooms or in shadow. He knew Eli didn't like to be watched, but he couldn't get enough of looking at him—not since the first day he'd seen him on the street in Soho. Now if only he could get Eli to open his eyes, if they could only look into each other as they moved together, it would be perfect.

Alec removed his fingers, and Eli eagerly took hold of him, getting in position to lower himself gradually onto Alec. He could feel Eli's inner muscles straining, resisting, then relaxing, taking all of him inside. The slippery, tight heat made Alec dizzy.

"Look at me, Eli," he whispered, trying to steady his breathing. He reached between them, taking Eli in hand and stroking him. Eli didn't open his eyes, but he placed his hands on either side of the bathtub for purchase and began to ride Alec slowly, lifting himself up—almost to letting Alec slip free of him—then slowly sinking back down. Alec closed his eyes, the sensation overwhelming him.

His surroundings faded, until the world existed only where they made contact: Alec pulsing within Eli and relishing the intense heat and tightness of him, their lips and tongues meeting and dancing, their hands gripping and caressing, each losing himself in the feel of the other.

As their rhythm became faster, Eli tangled his fingers in Alec's hair, raking the soap out of it. But Alec, frustrated by Eli's refusal to look at him as they made love, drove upward into him suddenly, making Eli cry out in what looked to be more surprise than pain. His eyes went startle-wide as they bored into Alec's for a moment, but then Eli buried his face against Alec's neck, and soon after, they came—shouting out in unison. Afterward they clung to each other, now hotter than the rapidly cooling water surrounding them, and waited for their hearts to slow. Eli's mouth found Alec's, and their tongues played off each other at a more leisurely, sated pace.

Eli lingered, sucking Alec's bottom lip as they parted. "Let's go to bed," Eli said, smiling against Alec's neck. "I could use a nap before the party."

They drained the tub, showered off, and tossed extra towels on the floor to soak up the flood they'd caused before walking back into the darkening bedroom. Alec toweled off quickly, vigorously drying his hair. Then, feeling eyes on him, he turned to catch Eli admiring his behind.

"Hey, there now," he warned, and Eli chuckled.

"Sorry, just taking in the view."

Alec dropped onto the bed, and Eli came almost close enough to touch but stopped, looking around the room.

"Are we just leaving our clothes everywhere, then?" he asked.

Alec leaped forward and grabbed him, pulling him close and rubbing his face against Eli's abdomen, the hair there tickling his face. He kissed the scars on his ribs, and Eli shivered.

"Fine by me," Alec said as he dropped back flat on the bed, pulling his lover down on top of him. "It's not my room."

Eli's cane clattered against the bed frame and hit the floor. "Hang on!" he shouted. Alec flipped them so Eli was pinned beneath him. "I thought we were taking a nap."

Thunder rumbled over the house, and the sky darkened even more as Alec's hands moved over Eli's tight, fit, smaller body, sliding up his thighs.

"We will, but first you have something I want."

Eli grinned and scooted away from him, moving higher on the bed. "You're an optimistic bloke, aren't you?"

Alec took hold of him before his head could reach the pillow and began stroking him back to life. "Oh, I'll get you there. Don't you worry."

They could barely see each other now, but Alec knew where everything was located and took just the head of Eli's semi-hard cock in his mouth, swirling his tongue over it and smiling at the smoothness of it. He licked the slit, and Eli's thighs quivered in response. He wished he could watch Eli's face. He sucked him all the way in until the back of his throat was tapped, and when Alec pulled back, he drew the tip of his tongue firmly along the underside of Eli from base to tip.

"Good Lord!" Eli clawed at the covers. He squirmed, moaned, and reached for Alec, tangling his hands in his hair. Alec toyed with his balls, alternately sucking one or the other into his mouth and feeling them tighten. Then he took the now fully hard length of Eli in his mouth again. His head bobbed up and down, sometimes rapidly, sometimes so slowly it seemed as though Eli's cock went on forever. Eli made plenty of noise but no sense whatsoever. None, that is, until he began panting Alec's name and whimpering.

That's when Alec knew Eli was close—when he began to whimper. Alec reached out and found Eli's left hand as it searched for his, and they held onto each other as Eli came. His customary volume made Alec thankful the house was empty. He swallowed what little Eli had following their escapade in the tub and then rested his face against Eli's hip. Alec grinned sleepily as Eli's fingers relaxed in his hair, ending their sometimes painful tugging to play lazily in his damp curls. And though he was drifting off, he heard his boyfriend whisper, "I will gut Dray Jenkins if he comes near you again."

Chapter 4

"ARE we taking one car?" Alec asked.

"No idea," Eli said as he straightened his tie in the mirror. His eyes—for the thousandth time—flicked to his unruly hair, and he sighed in dismay.

Alec leaned out the bedroom door. "Ilsa?" Silence. *"Ilsa!"*

Upstairs, her door opened. "What?"

"Are we taking one car?"

"Yep. Mine. Almost ready."

"Good to know." Alec joined Eli at the mirror. He had showered in his own bathroom in the attic but joined Eli downstairs in his room to get dressed for the party. They did a lot of that—split their time between their rooms. Eli's ground-floor room was too small for the two of them. Alec's attic room was much bigger, but stairs were not Eli's friends.

"She always drives. She can't drink." Eli ran his fingers through his own hair in the hopes of taming it. "Almost time for another trim, I think."

"It grows so quickly." Alec looked Eli over and tried to help beat his hair into submission.

"The only way to control it is to keep it short." He turned to look at Alec, enviously perusing the man's beautiful head of hair. "Why is it your hair can be so long and luxurious," he asked, turning back to the mirror, "but I have a fright wig growing out of my skull?"

Alec laughed. "I think I have some Latin or American Indian ancestors, although Mom would never admit it."

"So you're suggesting I have a clown or a Tasmanian Devil as an ancestor?" Eli asked, his reflection raising an eyebrow at Alec.

"Well," Alec said, embracing him from behind and staring at their reflection, "you are pretty vocal during sex."

"Hey!" Laughing, Eli smacked Alec's hands away.

"Ahh, you're just a hairy, sexy beast. Accept it. Besides, I like tugging on your hair. Keep it longer. Just add some product."

Eli glared in the mirror. "It's product-resistant." They both laughed.

"Why are you wearing a tie?" Alec asked.

Eli sighed. "I don't know." He loosened the tie and removed it.

"You look great. What's with all the fussing?"

"I don't know."

"Well, stop it. You'll be the best-looking man there." He kissed Eli's neck.

Eli laughed, extricated himself, and reached in the closet, removing a light-green shirt. "Tony's invited a lot of his new gallery mates, and they can be a harsh crowd." He held the shirt up just under his chin and examined his reflection.

"I've never seen you afraid of anyone." Alec took the shirt from him, put it back in the closet, and handed Eli his sport coat.

"I'm not afraid. I just don't know what we'll talk about." He turned to look at Alec. "You're an author, a psychologist, you teach at the university. Me? I interpret for the deaf." He crossed the room and grabbed his cane. It was Alec's first gift to him, and it still held its luster, largely because Eli rarely used it. "Maybe I should take the other one," he said, looking it over.

"Why?" Alec glanced sideways at the ugly, worn, hospital-issue cane Eli had been using for nearly three years as it rested near the headboard.

"It's a lovely walking stick," Eli said as he leaned on it, checking himself out in the mirror. "I wouldn't want anything to happen to it." Alec stared at him, and Eli smiled. "I'm thinking I might have to beat Dray off of you." He repeatedly slapped the head of the cane into his palm, gauging its heft. "He wants you bad."

Eli's gaze caught Alec's in the mirror, and Alec looked genuinely perplexed.

"And?" Alec grabbed his jacket off the bed. "I don't *want* him." Eli didn't say anything. "You know that, right?" Eli pulled on his own jacket as Alec went to him. He took hold of him and turned Eli to face him. "Tell me you know that."

He knew it, certainly he did, but Dray had a way of— "I know it," Eli said, kissing him.

"What I know," Ilsa said, appearing at their door, "is that Casey will go ballistic if we're not on time picking her up."

Eli joined her, extending his arm for her to take. "Let's go, my dear."

They walked away, and after a few moments of thought, Alec grabbed their gift and followed.

ILSA double-parked and hustled out of the car to collect Casey. Once alone, Alec turned to Eli in the back seat. "You weren't serious about Dray back there, were you?"

"Of course not." Eli's face was cast in shadow, so Alec couldn't see his expression, but he could hear in his voice that he was lying.

Alec sighed and glanced out his window. He watched Ilsa helping Casey descend the front steps of her apartment building, carrying a very large gift.

"What's the deal with those two now?" he asked.

Eli looked at the approaching couple. "Casey's in love, and Ilsa's losing the fight not to be." He grinned at Alec. "But I doubt it will last."

"Why?"

"Look at how Casey's walking in those heels."

Alec looked. "So?"

"Does she walk like a woman who normally dresses like that?"

Alec thought the young nurse looked spectacular in her tight red dress and black heels, if a bit unsteady, but that could be attributed to the unwieldy present and the old steps.

"Uh... well...."

"She's playing a part," Eli said. "She's trying to be the woman she *thinks* Ilsa fancies instead of just being herself."

Alec could see that Ilsa's face was glowing as she looked Casey up and down. "It seems to be working." He got out of the car and took Casey's gift so she could replace him in the passenger's seat.

"Thank you, Alec." She reclaimed the gift and placed it on her lap. Alec got into the back seat next to Eli, and Ilsa slid back behind the wheel.

"Casey, you look gorgeous," Eli said.

"Right back at you, babe." She favored him with a dazzling smile and flushed cheeks.

"I second that," Ilsa said, leaning over and kissing Casey. "You look spectacular."

Casey smiled, placing a hand on Ilsa's thigh and squeezing. "So do you, dear."

The only illumination in the car came from the dashboard and a streetlight, but Alec could swear there was eyelash fluttering going on in the front seat. He shared a glance with Eli, and they smiled.

Chapter 5

THE new flat looked spectacular considering Tony and Lyle had completed their move just six hours before. Tony was right. As an estate manager, Lyle was Mr. Organization. He'd planned out their gradual move over two weeks. First, he cleaned the flat from top to bottom, without Tony's help. Then he painted. Tony picked out the paint but didn't lift a brush.

Per Tony's tastes, most of their furnishings were new, sleek, and stylish, but Lyle had secured a few special items through his estate work—classic pieces that would never go out of style. He was on hand to direct the delivery crews while Tony stood by flirting and offering cool drinks to the sweaty, burly men. Lyle loaded up his car with small loads from Ilsa's each day. Then he unpacked, unwrapped, and placed everything before crashing for the night and doing it all over the next day. Tony handled relocating all his canvases and art supplies from Ilsa's basement to a studio he'd rented downtown.

Upon entering the flat, the first impression was breathtaking. Alec stood transfixed for a moment as he and Eli followed Ilsa and Casey through the door. The welcoming main room—with its warm, golden-hued hardwood floors and coppery-brown walls—framed a stunning view of the London skyline through massive windows, which made up the far, back wall. Deep red drapes hung to the floor, complimenting the dark, chocolate brown, modern Italian furniture.

For the most part, the room was populated by beautiful, talkative men—young and older. But sprinkled here and there among them were a few straight couples, lesbian couples, and a variety of singles. Surprised by how many people he didn't recognize, Alec's eyes darted over the guests' faces. Living with Tony and Lyle, he thought he'd come to know most, if not all, of their friends. But apparently those friends had brought friends to the party.

Gifts were snatched from the hands of those entering and passed over the heads of the partygoers to a far corner of the main room, for opening later. Waiters in white jackets moved effortlessly among the guests, bearing trays littered with tantalizing nibbles. Soft, unobtrusive music added a sexy vibe to the gathering, and everyone was smiling and talking and laughing. This party was clearly a success.

Alec leaned close to Eli's ear. "Remind me, exactly how much money is Tony making with his painting?"

"A good amount, but he comes from money." Eli turned and looked up at him. "He just rarely touches it." He straightened Alec's collar and smoothed his jacket as Alec smiled at his unconscious, affectionate actions. "He's not very close to his parents and wants to make his own way with his talent." Eli looked into his eyes and blushed when he caught Alec smiling knowingly at him.

Alec's eyes lingered on Eli's features for a moment and then were drawn up and across the room to a frantically waving woman with a long, straight braid of black hair down her back. Lynette Maza was one of several deaf students Eli interpreted for, shadowing her around campus and to her classes.

"I think someone is trying to get your attention," Alec said softly.

"You have it, love."

Alec kissed Eli's forehead, took him by the shoulders, and turned him around to face in Lynette's direction. His hands still on Eli's shoulders, Alec felt the tension leave Eli's body. Now he'd have someone to chat with and wouldn't feel at such loose ends.

"Back in a tick," Eli said, and he was gone before Alec could ask him to tell Lynette hello for him. Ilsa and Casey wandered over to the bar for a drink, and Alec found himself alone—for about five seconds.

"Alec," Dray said, sidling up to him with a heart-stopping smile on his handsome face. About an inch or two taller than Alec, the man looked stunning in a perfectly tailored dark gray suit and no tie.

"Uh, hello, Dray."

"Where's Eli?"

Alec pointed. "He's over there with a friend of his."

Dray didn't bother looking. "What do you think of this flat, eh?"

"Haven't seen too much of it yet. Just got here."

"You know," Dray said, sipping his drink and gazing at him over the rim of the glass, "there'll be a few more units ready for occupancy in a month or so. It's a new building, and they'll probably go quickly."

Alec laughed. "Are you getting a commission or something?"

"Maybe." Dray smiled coyly before looking Alec up and down. Alec felt his face grow warm and fought the urge to cover his crotch protectively.

"Well, Eli and I aren't look—"

"Really? Remind me. Isn't he on the ground floor, and you're in the attic?"

"Yes."

Dray allowed his gaze to drift around the room as he took another sip. Alec just stared at him, waiting for elaboration that never came. He decided to change the subject. "Thanks for your help today."

"Oh, you're welcome. Glad to help."

"How did the unloading go? Any glitches?"

"I don't know. There was plenty of manpower here when we pulled up. No need for me to strain myself further." Dray's gaze locked on his, hazel eyes twinkling seductively. "Can I get you a drink?" he asked, stepping closer.

Alec backed away. *This man has no concept of personal space, and... and he smells very good.* "No, thank you. I was just about to get drinks for us... uh, me and Eli. Have fun." He walked away quickly, but he felt Dray's eyes on him. Alec joined Casey and Ilsa at the bar, where Tony was busy being delightful and productive with the liquor.

"What can I get you, Alec?" he asked.

"Guiness for me and a red wine for Eli, please."

"Done and done."

"Where is he?" Ilsa asked, and Alec pointed.

While he waited for their drinks, he watched Eli and Lynette engaged in an animated discussion. Their signing was fast and beautiful to watch. He could read some of it, having been with Eli long enough to pick up some British Sign Language. The tiny amount of American Sign Language he knew was so different that it did him little good with their conversation.

It impressed him that Eli knew both, but he likened it to someone knowing two or more spoken languages. You learn it, and you simply speak it when necessary. Eli seemed to make the transition effortlessly. Alec reminded himself to push Eli for some more instruction, because whenever the two of them scheduled a practice session, it wasn't long before their hands were doing things other than signing.

Alec grabbed his beer and carried the wine to Eli.

"Thank you."

"You're welcome."

Alec smiled at Lynette, set his beer down, and signed very slowly, *Hello, L-Y-N-E-T-T-E.* He didn't look at her but instead watched his fingers as he signed the correct letters.

Hi, A-L-E-C. How are you?

Good. Thank you.

"Sorry I ran off," Eli said.

Alec kissed him. "No worries."

Lynette waited for Alec to refocus on her. *A-L-E-C, meet my boyfriend, J-I-M.*

Alec smiled apologetically. He'd only caught his and Jim's names, but he easily guessed what was said.

Nice to meet you, J-I-M.

"I'm hearing," Jim said with a smile.

"Oh, yes? Sorry." Alec retrieved his beer.

"No need to apologize."

Eli put down his wine to sign the conversation for Lynette and translate for Alec, if need be.

"How do you know Tony and Lyle?" Alec asked.

"I'm an art student working part time at the gallery where Tony had his last show."

Lynette grinned brightly. *Tony thinks J-I-M cute.*

Jim frowned at his girlfriend's explanation, and Alec and Eli laughed. Then Alec noticed Jim looking past him, over his shoulder. "Why does that bloke keep looking over here?" he asked. Eli and Alec turned simultaneously and caught Dray watching them. He flashed them a brilliant smile and a wink before returning to his conversation, and Alec felt his face grow hot. He looked quickly at Eli.

"Because he's hot for my boyfriend," Eli said.

"Eli—"

"It's true! He won't take 'no' for an answer." Eli grabbed his wine and took a sip. Pausing, he looked at Alec. "You have told him 'no' recently, haven't you?"

Alec remained silent.

"Alec?"

"He hasn't asked me anything!"

"A simple 'back the fuck off' would suffice!"

Though she couldn't hear them, Lynette could certainly read Eli's face and body language. She and Jim shared a worried glance.

Alec sighed and smiled tolerantly at Eli. "Consider it done, babe." He leaned in and kissed him softly, instantly making Eli feel like the jealous idiot he was.

Eli looked at the floor in shame. "I'm sorry."

Chapter 6

"AND this is the master bedroom," Lyle said, sweeping his arm wide. Alec and Casey were enjoying a tour of the flat, "oohing" and "ahhing" appropriately. Alec had found the kitchen décor cold—primarily stainless steel appliances, white tile, and glass. There was sparse seating—just enough room in a breakfast nook for two to read the paper, share coffee and croissant, and gaze out on the city.

He could imagine how the morning could breathe warmth into the room, but at night it was not a place for guests to gather and chat. Only the waitstaff buzzed in and out, as it was the staging area for the food and keeping the party well lubricated. With their white jackets, the kitchen took on the appearance of a sterile environment.

Now this bedroom is an entirely different matter. It had a similar color scheme to the main room: the walls were alternately a warm fawn and berry, the linens gold-toned, and the furniture a deep, rich brown. There was a simple, geometric, wheat-and-gray area rug extending out from under the bed. The rest of the floor was hardwood, like the main room.

"There's an Asian feel to it," Casey said.

Lyle seemed pleased by her observation. "Yes. The colors and clean lines." He looked around the room, nodding. "I wanted something peaceful, tranquil," he said, looking at them, "considering the chaos of our lives outside these walls."

"Estate sales wearing you out?" Alec asked.

Lyle rolled his eyes and smiled. "I love the items we handle. You see some of the most amazing pieces, and bringing them out into the open after decades behind closed doors is a wonderful experience." He absently ran his finger over a nearby chest of drawers and checked it for dust. "Especially when they catch that one special buyer's eye and end up in a new, loving home," he continued, peering more closely at the dark wood and swiping away a smudge, "where they'll be properly cared for." He sighed heavily and looked back at his guests. "The families—they're another matter altogether, with all their bickering and sniping." He rubbed his temples.

Alec saw Casey peering at the ceiling above the bed and followed her gaze. "Lyle, what are those… are those *hooks* in the ceiling?" she asked.

Lyle's doe-like brown eyes widened. "Er… um—"

A crash from the main room, followed by gasps and raised, concerned voices, ended their conversation abruptly. The three of them hustled back to the front of the apartment. Alec saw a young waiter with short red hair standing stock-still in the middle of the room, his eyes fixed on the floor as the headwaiter and an assistant hastily cleaned up the mess from a dropped tray of *hors d'oeuvres* at his feet. Lyle rushed forward to help.

"I'm so sorry, Mr. Davies," the headwaiter said. "I don't understand—"

"Don't worry about it, Jacob," Lyle said as he scooped up the few remaining canapés, crudités, Bruschetta, and cold cuts. "It's just a dropped tray. It happens." The items were quickly collected, placed back on the tray—the assistant rushing into the kitchen with it—and the floor swabbed clean. It was like it had never happened—except for the staring guests and the trembling waiter.

Jacob stood and sighed, glancing apologetically at Lyle again and taking hold of the young waiter's arm. "Come with me, Michael," he said quietly, but the young man refused to move. "Michael?" He tugged on his arm again. "What is it?" he hissed into his ear. Michael would not budge. His gaze remained glued to the floor as the music continued to play mindlessly in the background and some of the guests went back to their conversations. Many did not, however. "You're making a spectacle!" The headwaiter tugged again, but to no avail.

He and Lyle looked at each other, and Lyle turned to look at Alec. They were at a loss. Alec could see Tony approaching the stalemate, and then he caught Eli's eye from across the room. Eli shrugged. Alec promptly handed his drink to Casey and stepped forward to join the three men.

Speaking softly, he said, "Michael, my name is Alec. Will you come with me, please?" He thought he saw tears on the man's cheeks.

"We can find a quieter place and talk, if you like." He hooked his arm with Michael's, clasping the man's hand between his own, and then took a step. Michael's eyes followed the movement of Alec's foot, and then his own foot shuffled forward to join it. "Here we go." Alec patted the hand in his.

The two of them walked slowly, side by side from the room.

"The bedroom?" Lyle asked softly. Michael immediately stopped walking and began to tremble. They were standing just outside the door to Lyle's office.

"Let's go in here, huh?" Alec said, turning them to the right. Lyle opened the office door and flicked on the light. Alec and his charge shuffled into the small, brightly lit room, and Alec deposited Michael on a low, light-green loveseat. However when he attempted to reach for the desk chair, he was brought up short by the painful grip Michael had on his hand. "It's okay. I'm not going anywhere." He looked to Lyle pleadingly. He rushed in and brought the chair to Alec before leaving them alone and closing the door behind him.

"TONY, get away from there!" Lyle hissed.

The artist jumped and, momentarily befuddled, spun around, his blond ponytail whipping out behind him as he searched for the quickest route away from Lyle's office door—where he'd been nonchalantly trying to overhear Alec and the young waiter. Eli, Lyle, and Casey giggled quietly as he rushed by them toward a small group of his gallery friends.

Eli looked at the clock over the bar. "They've been in there quite a while." The others nodded and sipped their drinks. In addition to Alec and Michael, they'd lost several other guests. Lynette and Jim had left for the airport to pick up Jim's mother, who was coming for a visit. Lynette was terrified she wouldn't pass muster with the woman, but Eli had talked her down and prevented her from having yet another drink. He was relieved that Dray had left with one of Tony's visiting art-critic friends, in town for a few days from Los Angeles. He and Eli exchanged parting frowns as he exited.

Eli also kept an eye on Casey and Ilsa as they warmed up to each other again after a few short, tense moments earlier. They'd lost sight of Ilsa about twenty minutes before, but she was soon discovered in the kitchen chatting with a waitress. Apparently they'd met some time ago when the young woman had applied for a hosting position at Peaches— the restaurant where Ilsa was head chef. Eli had watched Casey wind herself up in preparation for a jealous fit as Ilsa stood there, wide-eyed and tensing before the coming storm, but he quickly advised Casey that "Ilsa doesn't do jealousy." She calmed down, and Ilsa rejoined the party with her.

Jacob, the headwaiter, continued to do his job efficiently but also kept glancing at the office door, as did another young waiter—and Michael's best friend—Lincoln. The door opened, prompting Lincoln's tray of champagne to rattle frighteningly, but he steadied himself. Alec spotted Jacob in the kitchen. He caught his eye and motioned for him to come over. Eli watched the man weave his way through the guests and speak quietly with Alec. Then he went over to Lincoln, took his tray and spoke to him, the young man nodding frequently. Lincoln began quickly undoing his tie and headed toward the office where he and Alec entered, shutting the door again.

Eli watched the entire exchange and saw Jacob sigh and wipe his brow before their eyes met. The man smiled brightly but falsely at him and handed the champagne tray off to another waiter who buzzed by. Eli thought Jacob looked like he was more than ready for this night to end.

Chapter 7

ABANDONING Ilsa and Casey to the party, Eli and Alec took a taxi home. On the way, they held hands, Eli absently stroking the back of Alec's with his thumb. He kept smiling to himself, proud of the way Alec had come to the rescue, taking charge, and helping the panicked young waiter. He glanced over at his boyfriend, sitting silently next to him, apparently lost in thought, the streetlights periodically flashing across his face as they neared their destination.

"Did you have a good time tonight?" Eli asked.

"Hmm?"

"At the party… a good time?"

"Oh, yes," Alec said, turning to look at him. "Yeah, sure." He grinned and turned back to the window.

"You were wonderful with that waiter. He looked terrified."

"Thanks." Alec sighed and smiled weakly. "Some sort of panic attack." He glanced at Eli. "I never did get it out of him… what was wrong, I mean."

"At least you helped him calm down… and he seemed fine when he left with his mate."

"Yeah." Alec looked back out the window. "I just wish I knew what had set him off." Eli squeezed his hand in reassurance. "I spoke to his friend, the other waiter, before they headed out, and he told me Michael was just returning after a leave of absence."

"He'd been ill?"

"No… not physically. He wasn't really clear."

The taxi stopped in front of their house, and Eli paid the driver while Alec held the door for him. They headed up the walk together. The night was perfect—the sky clear and filled with stars, the breeze warm enough that a jacket was unnecessary—which was odd, considering the earlier storm. They'd left the lights on in the front hall, and a warm glow emanated from the windows, welcoming them home. While Alec busied himself with unlocking the door, Eli rested his cheek against Alec's shoulder, sliding his hand under his jacket to caress his boyfriend's back.

With all five of them living there, it was rare to come home to an empty house. But now that Lyle and Tony had their own place and Ilsa spent a lot of time at Casey's flat—in fact, was probably planning to do so tonight—it would be happening more frequently. Eli wandered on toward his bedroom while Alec stopped at the hall table to look through the mail he'd avoided examining earlier.

"Hungry?" Eli asked.

"Hmm? No." Alec didn't raise his head, just focused on the mail. "I'm good, thanks."

Eli watched Alec continue shuffling through the envelopes. "Me?" he said, pausing just at the entrance to his bedroom. "I'm *staaahhhving.*" He grinned at the effect this had as Alec's hands froze, his head coming up and looking at Eli just as he vanished into the darkened room. He moved quickly behind his door and waited, laughing softly to himself.

"Eli?" Alec called, but he didn't answer.

The hall light reached into his room a ways, and his weak, flickering bathroom light struggled to stay on, but other than that, the room was very dark. He waited, his heart beating a bit faster in anticipation. *Come find me, love.*

He thought he heard Alec approaching slowly. "Eli?" He was closer now, and Eli held his breath. "Where are you?" Alec stepped forward, his hands on the doorframe, prepared to flee, from what Eli could discern between the door hinges. Alec chuckled nervously. "I feel an ambush coming on." He stepped into the room.

Eli slammed the door shut, and Alec whirled around, but Eli took advantage of the few seconds it would take for Alec's eyes to adjust to even less light and grabbed him by the front of his shirt, pulling him, spinning him, and shoving him against the door.

"I thought you liked being ambushed," Eli whispered, pressing against Alec and sliding his hands beneath Alec's shirt to caress his chest. Alec moaned softly when Eli's fingers skittered across his nipples and Eli's mouth nipped and kissed Alec's neck.

"Mr. Burke," Alec panted, finding his lover's mouth and tongue. It was Eli's turn to moan, and Alec caught him by the front of his suit jacket and turned him, swiftly switching their positions and pressing *him* into the door. He winced when Alec pulled his hair to expose his neck, but he couldn't deny that the action caused his cock to twitch and swell.

He loved this back and forth, this "who's turning who on more" competition, and he loosened Alec's belt to slide his hands down the back of his pants and grip Alec's behind. Eli smiled as Alec grunted, pressing forward and trying to pin him in place, trying to keep him from escaping, but he wasn't having it. Eli broke the kiss and shoved Alec away from him. He grabbed his cane, always at hand, and pointed the tip at Alec's chest like a lion tamer with a chair, keeping his beautiful beast at bay.

Tugging his shirt free and unbuttoning it with one hand, Eli walked unsteadily toward Alec, backing him up against the bed, where his boyfriend stumbled backward and abruptly sat. He tossed the cane to the floor and straddled Alec's lap, pinning his hands on either side of his head before leaning closer and capturing his mouth for a quick, teasing kiss.

"I win," he growled.

"Mmm, you're feeling froggy," Alec said, licking Eli's bottom lip before he was out of reach again. Eli knew Alec wanted nothing more than to touch him, therefore he refused to allow it. He knew that behavior—that dance—drove Alec crazy too.

"What's froggy?"

Alec nodded. "Warm and fuzzy, sexy, amorous—"

"Listen to you and your vocab. How about horny?"

Alec laughed. "Yes... although I was going for something a bit less explicit."

"Oh come, love. You know you want to fuck me." Eli smiled wickedly, putting more pressure on Alec's hands and keeping him from moving as he slowly rubbed his bottom against his boyfriend's erection. "Say it," Eli whispered against his ear.

Alec's eyes fluttered closed, and he grinned stupidly. "I want to f-fuck you."

Eli quickly tugged Alec's shirt free of his jeans. Hands now loose, Alec went right for the bare torso he could glimpse through Eli's open shirt. He ran his palms and fingers over his hard, flat abdomen and up, across his slightly hairy chest to pinch his nipples.

Eli twitched, and Alec sat up suddenly, kissing his neck and stripping the shirt and jacket off of his shoulders. Eli finished the job, shaking his clothes off his arms and onto the floor before forcing Alec back down.

"Am I going to have to tie you down?" he whispered, gripping Alec's jacket, unceremoniously yanking it off the man, and tossing it next to his on the floor.

"Watch my buttons," Alec warned.

"Yeah, I'll watch your buttons!" Eli grabbed Alec's shirt and tore it open.

Alec squeezed his eyes shut to the sound of many tiny, tinkling impacts as the scattered buttons hit the headboard, wall, and lamp, but he was grinning.

"Why are there so many clothes?" Eli asked, chuckling as he struggled to get them both undressed. He leaned in close, breathing heavily into Alec's ear as he rubbed himself more urgently against him.

"If we d-don't slow down, I'm going to come before I'm inside you!"

"Who says you'll be inside me?" Eli reached down, finally freeing Alec's cock and gripping it possessively.

Alec bucked off the bed to follow Eli's hand. "You said s-so. *Ughn*…. You m-made me say I want to f-f—"

"I've changed my mind." Eli grabbed Alec by the hair, kissing him until he was gasping.

"What's gotten into you?" Alec asked.

"I loved watching you take charge at the party tonight," Eli said. "You were brilliant!" He squeezed Alec's cock again, and the man quivered, his eyes rolling back in his head. "And now *I* want to fuck *you*. I'll get the lube."

Alec stopped him. "What about your leg?"

Eli rolled his eyes. "I'm fine, Alec."

But Alec sat up, grabbing him and flipping them on the bed so that Alec was on top.

"Hang on!" Eli said.

"Shhsh, trust me."

Eli stilled his protests as Alec finished stripping and grabbed the lube from the bedside table. He dropped it on the bed and pulled Eli's pants off. Alec straddled him and began stroking their cocks together. Eli grinned, his eyelids nearly closing as Alec leaned in for a kiss, smashing their cocks between their bodies. The feel of skin on skin, the scent of Alec, their tongues playing off one another, made Eli's head swim, and he quivered delightedly.

During their months together, they had taken the time to get to know each other as lovers, learning what the other liked or didn't like, experimenting with positions that took Eli's damaged leg into account and might allow him to top when he got the urge. Eli heard the "pop" as the lube was opened, but he didn't feel the coolness he expected—or *where* he expected. Alec broke the kiss, and Eli watched him prepare himself to be entered.

The light from the bathroom continued to flicker annoyingly, and Eli cursed silently, wishing he had paused to screw that bulb in tighter, or even replace it. This was a moment he definitely *wanted* to watch. He grinned, his cock throbbing, as Alec worked his fingers into himself.

He shoved aside his slight disappointment; this position ultimately still left Alec in the driver's seat, just as Eli had been in charge in the tub earlier. Even so, he licked his lips, breathless, as Alec took hold of him, guided him into place, and slowly lowered himself onto Eli's shaft.

The faint light from the bathroom inexplicably stopped flickering and fell on them. And mesmerized, Eli could see the benefits: Alec's head tilting, eyes closing, and mouth opening slightly, making the loveliest O with his lips. He'd never been comfortable with Alec watching him too closely when they were together—at first because of his scars, but now for other reasons—and he found it hard to believe he looked like *this* to Alec. *I can't be this beautiful.*

Alec was hot and tight—so tight—Eli fought the urge to speed things along, not wanting to hurt him. He was patient and soon found himself buried in his lover to the hilt. He offered up his palms so Alec could balance properly. Concentrating on the other's breathing, they matched their rhythms, the two of them fucking almost silently as they gradually increased their speed.

A sliver of moonlight peeked through the window nearest the bed, revealing a fine sheen of sweat on Alec's skin, and Eli bit his lip to keep from reacting to the sight of him gasping and moaning above him. His hair hung limply, sticking to his forehead. The image of him, the feel of being inside him, the scent of his sweaty skin, and the soft sounds escaping his lips all conspired against Eli successfully keeping this up much longer. He suddenly freed one of his hands from Alec and reached for his lover's cock.

Alec's head jerked forward, and their pace increased until they were panting each other's names. Thanks to Eli's efforts, Alec came first and came hard, spurting over Eli's hand, arm, and chest. Before the tension left Alec's body, Eli stiffened beneath him, and he spilled himself inside his boyfriend. Alec collapsed on top of him, and Eli barked in surprise as the air left his lungs in a rush.

"Oops." Alec smiled and nuzzled Eli's neck. "Mmm... feels like you've been wanting to do that for a while."

"I love being inside you," Eli whispered, grabbing a fistful of Alec's hair and tugging a bit, "but you cheated."

"Huh?"

"You topped from the bottom, love."

Alec laughed. "Oh... sorry. Not what you had in mind, huh?"

"It was lovely." They kissed, and Eli patted his behind. "We should clean up." He wiggled, grimacing at the stickiness on his chest that would soon bond to Alec's if they didn't wipe it away.

"I got it," Alec said, kissing him and hopping up, heading for the bathroom. Eli stretched and sighed as he heard the water come on briefly. But then he heard the vanity being opened and Alec knocking about.

He sat up on his elbows. "What are you doing?" He didn't get a verbal answer, but after a few more moments, the light went out in the bathroom, then returned bright, strong, and steady. He smiled and flopped back down on the bed. Alec joined him seconds later with two warm washcloths, and they began cleaning up.

Eli could see Alec had something to say. "What is it?"

"I am sorry, Eli. I just thought your leg might—"

"Don't worry about that. I've been working out." Eli winked. "I'll have ya yet." Alec grinned nervously.

They finished, and Alec balled up Eli's cloth with his and, rising up on his knees, threw them all the way into the bathroom, where they smacked against the back wall and dropped directly into the clothes hamper. "Aw! I'm awesome!" He fell back down next to Eli, who embraced him.

"Yes, you are," Eli whispered, kissing him softly and smiling. Alec snuggled in close to him, and Eli pulled the covers over them.

They lay in silence for a good while, Eli absently stroking Alec's hair as he rested his head on Eli's shoulder. He tightened his arms around Alec, and his boyfriend responded in kind, the heat from his body radiating down Eli's side where they made contact. Eli wriggled his toes, which only reached to Alec's ankles, and giggled.

Alec grinned, craning his neck slightly. "What?"

"I feel so short next to you."

"I've only got you by a couple of inches, babe," Alec said, settling back into his spot and kissing Eli's neck. "You're perfect."

Eli frowned. *Not hardly, love.* He changed the subject. "You were great tonight."

Alec yawned. "Thanks. You're quite the ride yourself."

Eli laughed. "I meant at the party!" He continued laughing.

"Oh."

He couldn't see it, but Eli was sure Alec was blushing.

"I'm glad you were able to calm… Micheal…?"

"Um, yeah, but his friend said Mickey."

"Well, you were brilliant… very sexy."

"I wish he'd told me the problem," Alec said, his voice heavy with exhaustion. "But he wouldn't or couldn't articulate it."

"Talk to Tony or Lyle. Maybe you can track him down through the staffing company they used."

Alec yawned again. "Yeah, I could do that."

Eli tightened his grip on Alec again, and in his sleep, Alec responded again in kind.

THE sun smacked Alec in the face. He woke to find it spilling across the bed but mostly on his side of it. He stretched and yawned noisily, cutting it short when he became aware of a weight tucked against his side. Eli liked sleeping closer to the wall, boxed in, and since he was now on Alec's left side, he'd apparently crawled across him at some point during the night to reach his favorite spot. He suspected Eli somehow felt safer that way. Alec looked down to see him curled up near his abdomen, his mouth at Alec's ribs, making his skin tingle with each exhalation. Eli had also kicked his covers off and lay naked beside him. *Probably a nightmare.* His left arm lay across Alec's middle, and his right arm rested under his chin like a cat's paw. Alec reached down and stroked Eli's mop of dark brown hair, causing him to stir.

"Mmm… morning," Eli moaned as he slid upward to reach Alec's lips. He started to kiss him but stopped himself. "Or maybe I should say 'morning breath'." He chuckled. "Sorry."

"You apologize too much. Come here." They kissed for a long time, Eli stretching out on top of him, their hands coming together. Alec looked at how their fingers mated, fingertip to fingertip. "Eli?"

"Yes?"

"Why did you bother learning ASL when you took your gap year?"

"Mmm." Eli kissed and sucked on Alec's earlobe, and Alec shivered happily. "I already knew BSL from living with my auntie." He rose up briefly to look at Alec. "I told you she was deaf, didn't I? She's how I got interested in interpreting." He kissed Alec's cheek and the corner of his mouth. "But I figured ASL would make me more useful." He smiled brightly and gazed into his boyfriend's eyes. "You Yanks have an awful habit of finding your way over here, you know?" Alec laughed, and they began kissing again. Eli paused again, looking at him. "You want to practice the alphabet?" he asked.

Alec smiled. "How do you manage to make that sound sexy?"

Eli laughed. "I don't know, but you'll need both hands for BSL." He dove back in to kiss and bite Alec's neck.

Alec sighed and grinned. "I would love to, but I've got an early class."

Eli sighed. "Very well." He rolled off Alec, flopping onto his back next to him.

Alec tilted his head as if he were listening for something or someone. "I wonder if Ilsa is up yet." He sniffed the air for the aroma of brewing coffee or frying sausage.

"Why?"

"Because I have to get to my room to shower and get some fresh clothes, and I'd rather not startle her with my manliness."

Eli laughed out loud. "It's not like it would be the first time." Alec started to get out of bed, but Eli quickly climbed over him and, grabbing his cane, padded across the floor toward the bathroom. Alec smiled, watching Eli absently scratching his beautiful bottom as he went.

He got up and began collecting his clothes from the floor. "That's my point. I'd like to avoid doing that again." He knelt on the floor and fished his boxer briefs from under the bed. He heard Eli say something and raised his head. "What?"

Eli flushed the toilet and turned on the shower. Then he poked his head out the bathroom door. "I said, how do you propose to remedy it?" He vanished again.

Alec got up only to drop on the bed to slip his pants on. "We could get our own place... like Tony and Lyle... maybe even in the same building. Dra—uh, I'm told there will be units opening up there in a month or two, maybe sooner." He looked at the bathroom door, expecting to see Eli reappear, but he didn't. *Must be in the shower already.*

Alec held the front of his slacks together and gathered up his shoes and remaining items. He struggled to open the door without dropping anything and slowly poked his head out. He scanned the hall, listening for sounds from the kitchen, before exiting Eli's room and dashing up the stairs like "the other man" trying to avoid being caught by a jealous lover.

On the second floor landing, he slammed his toe so hard at the start of the next set of stairs that he saw stars and lost his breath for a moment. After he recovered, he continued—much more slowly and limping a bit. Having their own place where they could truly live together, could share a bedroom and home, was becoming a more appealing idea to him by the second.

Eli, however, remained frozen on the other side of his bathroom door. Alec's suggestion echoed in his head as his shower grew cooler. It had never occurred to him to leave this house. Apparently... it *had* occurred to Alec.

Chapter 8

ABOUT ninety minutes later, after hearing the front door open and close a couple of times, Eli poked his head out of his bedroom. The only noises he heard came from the kitchen and were accompanied by some heavenly aromas. He headed that way and found Ilsa and Casey leaning against the island, kissing, and Tony sitting at the kitchen table sipping coffee.

"Well, if it isn't Eli of the long showers," the artist said softly. His eyes were puffy and red, and Eli was convinced there was more than coffee and cream in his cup.

He pulled up a chair and eyed Tony suspiciously. "How are you doing this morning?" Tony didn't answer, but he squinted at Eli as if he were looking at the sun and began massaging his skull. Eli smiled. "That bad, eh?"

Ilsa suddenly realized another person had joined them and disengaged her lips from Casey's, allowing the young nurse to try her hand at flipping some chocolate chip pancakes. "Eli! Excellent!" Ilsa said.

"Shhh!" Tony said.

"Coffee, Eli?" Ilsa asked more softly. She held up the carafe while watching Casey out of the corner of her eye. Casey flipped the pancakes beautifully and beamed at Ilsa proudly, prompting the beautiful chef to begin kissing her again.

Eli grinned at them. "Ahem! Yes, please."

Ilsa poured him a cup, brought it to him, and then quickly returned to Casey's side. "Oh, I almost forgot," she said. "Alec had to rush out to class. He told me to tell you he'd see you at the gym later."

Eli frowned as he sweetened his coffee. "Thanks." He'd successfully avoided discussing moving out by lingering in his room, but they had a date at the gym to work out together and he had a physio appointment he couldn't miss.

"He tried to wait," Casey said, concentrating on the last few flips she had to do. "That was an awfully long shower you took this morning."

"Uh, yeah, sorry about that."

Ilsa went to work finishing up the sausages as she watched her girlfriend neatly stack the remaining pancakes on a plate. "Ta dah!" Casey exclaimed, causing Tony to wince.

"Very good, sweetie," Ilsa said before kissing her again.

"Are you going to feed us or just stand there snogging?" Tony asked.

Ilsa rolled her eyes and whirled on him. "Excuse me, but *you* don't live here anymore." Tony calmly sipped his cup dry and held it out for Ilsa to refill. "It's no longer my job to feed you," she said as she walked over and refilled his cup.

"Here you are," Casey said, proudly setting down a plate piled high with chocolate chip pancakes and sausages. She giggled. "I'm feeling all domestic, serving our men."

Eli chuckled at that, thanking her and pulling the plate of food away from Tony's horrified and nauseated face. Ilsa replaced it with a saucer sporting two aspirin. "Eat up, sugar," she said, patting Tony on his sensitive head.

He popped the aspirin in his mouth. "I'm going to lie down," he mumbled. The three of them watched silently as he shuffled away toward the living room with his coffee.

"What's he doing here so early?" Eli asked.

Casey set plates out for each of them and started parceling out the food. "He came stumbling through the door this morning at eight complaining that Lyle was on a cleaning spree."

Ilsa laughed. "He said he's allergic to cleaning before noon, so he came over here to be properly pampered."

Casey's pancakes were delicious, and they ate in silence for a while. Eli was aware of some foot play under the table between his two friends, but he pretended not to notice. When the phone rang, Casey jumped up to answer it, wolfing down the last of a sausage on her way. "Hello?"

"What are your plans today?" Ilsa asked Eli.

"Um...," he began around a mouth of food. He paused to finish chewing and swallow. "I have a client followed by practice with friends for my next level of certification...." His voice trailed away, and his face darkened.

"Eli?"

"Then I'm meeting Alec at the gym. We're working out together." He knew he sounded less than enthused.

"Is that a problem?"

He didn't say anything for a moment or two. "Are you really peeved at Tony and Lyle for leaving?"

"Of course not, silly!" Eli watched her viciously slice up a sausage before taking a bite of it. "I was just giving him a hard time. I still have you and Alec." Eli smiled weakly. "Why do you ask?"

"Alec mentioned—"

"I have to go, I'm afraid," Casey said, returning to the table and tearing a bit off one of Ilsa's remaining pancakes."

"Oh, sugar," Ilsa whined.

"I put my name in for extra hours if they needed, and... they *need*."

"Shower?" Ilsa asked, standing and wrapping Casey up in her arms. She nibbled her neck as her hands began to roam.

"Mmm... better not." Casey caught Ilsa's hands in hers. "I'll shower and change at the hospital." Her kiss, sweet with syrup, promised delightful things later for Ilsa, so they grinned at each other as Ilsa released her. "Maybe we could all meet for lunch? Around one thirty?"

"I might do," Eli said, running through his schedule in his head and calculating how much time was needed for each activity he'd committed to.

Ilsa appeared to be doing the same. "Mmm, better make it two," she said. "I can go into work early after."

Casey nodded and looked to Eli.

"Sounds good," he said.

"Great. See ya."

"What? No kiss?" he asked.

Casey laughed and kissed the top of his head before heading

upstairs to retrieve her clothes.

With apparent hunger in her eyes, Ilsa watched her go. "Now... Alec did what?" she asked, sitting back down.

Eli glanced at the clock on the wall and quickly drained his coffee. "Oh nothing." He got up and grabbed his messenger bag and cane. "I'd better get going."

Ilsa watched him hurry down the hall and out the door before moving to the sink to start the dishes.

LYLE rushed from the bathroom to answer the cordless phone in the great room. He tugged the yellow rubber gloves off his hands on the fourth ring.

"You've got Lyle."

"Hey there."

"Alec? How are you? I hope you and Eli had a good time last night."

"We did, Lyle. A great time. Are you busy?"

"Just cleaning. What can I do for you?"

"I wonder if you might have the number for the catering staff you used for the party."

"You planning one?" Lyle headed for his office. "I know Ilsa's birthday is coming up."

Alec could hear him rummaging through a drawer. "Oh, I hadn't thought about it, but that's a good idea. I'll speak to Eli."

"I know I have Jacob's card in here somewhere—ah ha! Got it. Ready?"

"Shoot."

Lyle read off the phone number for Catering Jake, and Alec copied it down.

"If you're not planning a party, why—"

"I'd like to check up on that waiter...."

"I see. Well, I'm sure Jacob can help you."

"Thanks, Lyle."

"No worries... uh, speaking of worries, you didn't happen to see

Tony this morning, did you?"

"He was coming in the door as I headed out."

Lyle sighed. "Okay, good. Ilsa will take care of him."

"Listen, Lyle, another thing…."

"Yes?"

"I heard there might be some units opening up in your building soon."

"That's what I hear. They're getting them ready as fast as they can. Why?"

"I was toying with the idea of maybe Eli and I—"

"That would be brilliant! Bloody fantastic… but…."

"What?"

"I guess I'm surprised Eli would want to move out."

"Oh… uh, we haven't really discussed it yet."

"Mmm-hm."

"Why surprised?"

"Well… it's just…."

"Yes?"

"Uh… well, Bennett…." Alec didn't say anything, and Lyle rushed on. "I'm sure I'm wrong. Don't listen to me. I'm silly."

"No, no you're not, Lyle. You have a point. It was *their* home… it's something to consider." It was Lyle's turn to keep quiet. "Well, thanks for the number," Alec said. "I should get off. I've got a student knocking at my office door."

"You're welcome and good luck."

Alec hung up and stared across his tiny office. There was no one at the door, no one waiting to see him. He ran his fingers through his hair and sighed.

"Bennett," he said to an empty room.

Chapter 9

AS HE ran on the treadmill, Alec's thoughts were filled with what he would say to the young waiter who had frozen up during Tony and Lyle's party. He'd called Catering Jake to track the man down right after hanging up with Lyle. It felt good to occupy his mind with something other than Bennett and the possible hold he might still have on Eli. He had never voiced it to Eli, but there were times he feared his boyfriend's reluctance to look at him when they made love was—Alec shook his head to clear it. He wasn't going there.

Just then he saw Eli passing in front of the gym windows: ball cap, head down, hand in pocket, gym bag over his shoulder, and grave expression. He looked like he was on his way to the gallows. He walked into the building and paused at the reception desk before entering the gym proper and immediately spotting and heading for Alec on the first treadmill at his left.

Alec punched the controls several times, slowing down from a full-out run to a lope and wiping his face with his towel. "Hey."

"Sorry I'm late. Things ran long."

"That's okay." He quickly kissed Eli without breaking his rhythm.

"You're delightfully sweaty." Eli smiled. "You're not working too hard, are you?"

"Nah, I'm on my cool-down. What's first for you?"

"Warm up with Devon."

Alec grinned. "Stretching in the studio?"

"Yeah. Find me when you're done?"

"You bet."

ELI headed toward the back of the expansive room, past the weight and resistance machines.

"Hiya, Burke," Carl called. He was on the abductor—in shorts again.

Eli averted his eyes, kept moving, and tried not to smile. "Hey, Carl."

On the far right side in front of a bank of windows were the free weights. He saw Dray working out over there, and they exchanged scowls. Dray's bare torso glistened with sweat as he lifted the dumbbells. Next to him were Vanessa, George, and Alan. The three of them waved with their hand weights, and Eli waved back right before disappearing into the locker room.

He worked the combination on his locker and then dropped his gear. He stripped and slipped on a pair of black sweatpants and a T-shirt. Dray came in as he tied his shoes and began massaging his leg.

"Hello, Erby." He walked by without even looking at Eli, toweling the sweat from his head, chest, and back. He stopped just before entering the shower area and began stripping, toeing off his shoes and pulling off his sweatpants until he was completely bare—a tower of perfect, fit, unblemished dark brown skin and muscle. Eli couldn't help but stare as Dray knelt and gathered his clothing, tossing the items onto the bench closest to him.

"Have you and Alec made a decision yet?" he asked as he leaned against the entrance to the showers, arms folded across his chest, completely unashamed—actually, somewhat proud.

Eli blinked. "Decision?"

"About a flat in Tony and Lyle's building. I mentioned it to Alec at the housewarming last night."

"You—"

"Told him there would be one or two units ready for rent soon. You should really get in on them right away."

Eli's expression darkened. "We haven't had a chance to discuss it yet," he said quietly. "But why would you—?"

Dray straightened and turned his back on him, walking into the shower area. "They'll go fairly quickly, just so you're aware." Eli heard the water come on. He gathered his things, shoved them in the locker, and slammed it shut. As he left the locker room, he bumped into Devon heading to the elevators.

"Whoa, there!"

"Sorry, Dev."

"You're certainly fired up today, eh? Ready to work?"

Eli smiled weakly. "Of course."

Over the next thirty minutes, Devon worked with Eli's leg, slowly warming, massaging, stretching, and getting it ready to work on the resistance machines. He talked throughout about his newest baby girl, but Eli heard very little of it. While lying on the mat and letting Devon maneuver him, Eli's mind was occupied with thoughts of Alec wanting to move out. What would Ilsa say? What did he want to do? Why had Dray brought it up? It seemed strangely helpful of him.

"Eli?"

"Huh?" He refocused and saw Devon and Alec standing above him—each with a hand outstretched to help him up.

"Where were you just now?" Alec asked, smiling and kissing him as he pulled him to his feet.

Devon handed him his cane. "Just thinking." Eli headed for the elevators.

"About what?" Alec persisted, following him.

"Devon has a brand new baby girl," Eli said, turning to Alec with the brightest smile he could manage. "Did he tell you?"

Alec stared at him for a moment before turning his attention to Devon. "Really? What's her name? Do you have pictures?"

On the ride down to the main level, Devon showed Alec and Eli several photos of his new daughter, Felicity. "It's a family name," he explained.

When they reached the main floor, they split up and headed to their respective favorite starting places. Throughout their workouts, Eli and Alec crossed each other's paths a couple of times, always pausing to share a smile, a kiss, or to show their concern or respect for how hard the other was working.

"Let your right leg do most of the work," Devon instructed as Eli got comfortable on the leg press. "Your left leg is only there to prevent disaster, yeah?"

"I remember." Eli flattened his feet against the panel and slowly pressed to lift the weight as Devon watched over him.

A FEW machines away, Alec sat on the bench press. He'd seen Eli do this workout for months now, but the weights he lifted were gradually increasing. He reclined on the bench and took hold of the barbell. He wasn't fooling himself into thinking Eli could get rid of his limp—the muscle and bone damage had been too extensive—but making the leg as strong as it could be was worth all the work.

Alec took a couple of quick, deep breaths, adjusting his grip rapidly, squaring his feet, and adjusting his back before lifting the barbell off its rack and lowering it to his chest. Just as he struggled to press it upward, he heard, "I'll spot you." He looked up to see Dray standing over him. He was freshly showered and out of his workout gear, his crotch directly in Alec's line of sight.

Alec pressed the weights up and brought them back down. "You look like you're headed out, Dray. I'm good. You have a nice day."

Dray didn't move. He simply watched Alec continue through his reps to exhaustion, and when Alec couldn't press the weight upward one more time, Dray grabbed it and helped him place it back on its rack.

"See? I came in handy, didn't I?"

Alec sat up and wiped the sweat from his face. "Yes, Dray. You were very helpful."

Dray leaned closer. "My hands are not all I'm good with."

Alec laughed and looked at him. "You're relentless." They smiled at each other, but when faced with the lustful gleam in Dray's eyes, Alec's smile faltered, and he became very serious. "I need you to hear me. I'm with Eli. I'm not interested in being with anyone else, Dray—not even you. Got me?"

Dray stopped grinning, straightened up, and examined Alec's expression for several moments. Then a slow smile spread across his face. "Got you? Not yet, Alec. Not yet." Dray winked, turned, and headed for the door. Alec watched him go with a disbelieving grin on his face—until Dray strolled past Eli, and Alec saw his boyfriend watching him—watching him smile. Alec's expression quickly changed to mirror Eli's scowl, and he got up and went to him.

"Lunch after? I know I'll be starving when we're done here."

Eli didn't say anything. He simply passed his cane to Devon and inserted his arms in straps to begin his abdominal work. Eli brought his weight forward, off the step so that he was hanging, and began slowly lifting his knees to his elbows. He was methodical, his breathing steady and deep, his eyes focused forward.

Alec glanced at Devon, who studiously counted Eli's reps and pretended not to feel the tension in the air. "Eli?"

"I'm meeting Casey and Ilsa for lunch." Eli didn't look at Alec. "You're welcome to join us, if you like?"

Alec felt the heat rush to his head and couldn't stop himself. "I'm welcome to—" He stepped in front of Eli, preventing him from raising his knees like he wanted. "I'm not playing this game with you anymore."

Eli glared at him. "Game?"

"This Dray-spoke-to-you-and-you-didn't-spit-in-his-face-so-I'm-not-speaking-to-you bullshit you've become so fond of lately."

Eli smiled. "What would you like me to do?"

"Fellas, do I need to be here for this?" Devon asked. They ignored him, so he turned his back and wandered a few machines away.

"I want you to grow the fuck up!" Eli's eyes widened in shock, and a couple of heads in the room turned toward them. Alec could see he'd shocked him. He wasn't known for his temper like Eli was. He couldn't remember the last time he'd lost control. Alec took a couple of steadying breaths. "I've told Dray, and I'm telling you—*you* are the man I want. Trust it or don't. I'm sick of the tantrums and pouting."

Eli's eyelids fell to half-mast. "I don't have tantrums," he said evenly.

"Right." Alec turned to leave, but Eli captured him, his legs encircling his waist and then tightening their grip so that Alec was pulled forward, almost close enough to kiss.

"Alec, wait, I'm—"

"Let me loose, Eli."

ALEC didn't look at him, didn't see the playful smile fall from his lips as he released him. Alec headed for the showers, and he didn't look back.

"Walking stick?" Devon was back and holding it out to Eli. With his foot he slid the small step beneath Eli's feet and handed him the stick.

"Thanks, Devon—for everything." Eli stepped down. "I'm good from here." He looked toward the showers.

"Best of luck, mate." Devon saluted him, and Eli slowly followed in Alec's footsteps.

He found him standing at the far end of the large shower room, beneath the very last showerhead. He watched Alec from the entrance; his head hung as the water pounded his shoulders, his palms resting against the tiled wall as if he were trying to shove it out of existence. He was so beautifully tan, strong, and perfect that Eli found his thoughts wandering beyond an apology. He shook his head to clear it just as Alec slapped the soap dispenser several times and began lathering up.

He watched Alec soap himself from top to bottom before rinsing and beginning again. He set his cane against the nearest locker and stripped, dropping his clothes onto the pile of Alec's by the shower entrance. He limped over to stand beside him, placing one hand on the shower wall to steady himself.

"Alec?" No response. "I'm sorry."

Alec turned to face him. "I don't know that that's enough, Eli. You always apologize, and then you do it again. This has been happening for nearly six months now. What I want is for you to trust me."

"I do—"

"No, you don't! If you did, you wouldn't flip out whenever Dray speaks to me."

"You know my history with him—"

"Despite that... despite what he tried to do to you and Bennett, he failed." Eli didn't say anything, but he looked away. "He failed then, and he's failed now." Alec went back to washing himself. "Your attitude toward him is... it's approaching irrational."

"I promise I'll do better." Inching forward, Eli moved to stand directly in front of his boyfriend, under the spray. "I trust you." He kissed Alec, pressing himself against him.

Alec responded for a moment, but then he pulled away. "No. You can't make this better by getting me off." He looked Eli in the eyes. "I'm serious."

"I know. I hear you. I'll do better… I swear."

Eli kissed him again, lingering at the corner of his lips, trailing light kisses along his jaw toward his ear, and eagerly massaging Alec's behind. Alec wrapped his arms around him, squeezing him against his rapidly responding body.

"I'm tired of being tested," Alec whispered before pushing his tongue past Eli's lips and pressing him into the wall. Eli's tummy flipped-flopped as Alec pressed his thigh between Eli's legs, lifting slightly and drawing a moan from him as he fought to gain purchase on Alec's slippery skin. "I'm sick of having to prove I love you."

Eli suddenly pulled back. "What?" His eyes searched Alec's, not sure if he'd heard what he thought he had.

"I said—"

"Uh… fellas?" Devon stood in the shower entrance, trying to look everywhere but at the two of them. "We're about to get our afternoon rush. You might want to…." He waved a hand in their general direction in an unfocused, hurry-up motion.

"Oh… uh, sorry, Dev," Eli said.

Turning off the hot water completely, the two of them quickly finished showering and rushed to get dressed.

"Thanks," Alec said as he dashed by the trainer.

"No worries, mate. I remember the last row I had with the wife—and how it ended. Thought I'd best check on you two." He watched them rush about, collecting their clothing and drying off. "Not that we don't have a few of that lot who like an audience—I just didn't think you were into that sort of thing."

"We're most definitely not," Eli said. "Cheers."

Holding hands, he and Alec exited the locker room and walked through the gym, stepping out into some welcome and rare London sunshine.

Chapter 10

THEY spotted Casey outside Covent Garden Grill. The sunlight shone off her short, blonde hair as she paced, speaking angrily into her cell.

"You promised you'd be here. We picked this restaurant to give you a break from yours." Casey listened for a few moments. "Fine!" She ended the call and turned to face her friends. "Oh, hey. Sorry about that. Ilsa can't make it. Busy at Peaches."

"Oh… sorry," Alec said.

Casey's gaze fell to Alec and Eli's entwined hands. "Let's go in, shall we?" she huffed.

The two men glanced nervously at one another and followed her into the restaurant.

ELI watched how quickly Alec was eating. He must have been hungry after his workout, because he wasn't allowing conversation to slow his intake.

"I might head to Richmond on Wednesday," he was saying, and as Eli gave him a cautioning glance, he added quickly, "Just to watch, mind you."

"Just be careful."

"I'm not even limping anymore."

Alec had joined the London Kestrels, a local football team. And during his first game, as Eli, Ilsa, Tony, Lyle, and Casey cheered madly—and his loyal, but snarky, good friend Mirabell watched, calmly chain-smoking and occasionally clapping—he had raced up the field for a goal. Unfortunately he was limping after, and Eli nearly came out of the bleachers to look after him. But Ilsa had grabbed his belt and sat him down.

"I know this is a gay- and bi-friendly league, but Alec doesn't need you fussing over him in front of his teammates," she'd said firmly.

Even though Alec was all healed in time for the following Sunday's game, he'd missed it in favor of Tony and Lyle's move. Wednesday evening was their next training session, however, and Alec was determined to make it.

"I don't want Casey to have to patch you up," Eli said, and the two of them laughed, tangling their feet together under the table. They had practically inhaled their meals, but Casey still picked over her salad, scooting the cherry tomatoes off to the side in disgust.

"Huh?" she asked, having heard her name.

Eli sipped his tea and looked at her. "Alec's team… the Kestrels? They train Wednesday in Richmond."

Casey nodded, obviously still distracted, and Eli looked worriedly at Alec.

"Are you okay, Casey?" Alec asked.

"Yeah, just disappointed that Ilsa couldn't make it."

Eli brightened. "Speaking of… any ideas how you want to handle her birthday this year? It's the first for you two as a couple."

Casey grinned, suddenly becoming more animated. "At first I thought a nice intimate dinner party would be nice… very adult and all—"

"But?" Alec asked.

"But you and I both know Ilsa would never properly relinquish the kitchen to let someone else do the cooking. And if it were catered, she'd be critiquing all the dishes." Alec and Eli nodded. "So I've decided on a big party at the house. I'll invite everyone we know and ask them to bring a dish of some kind." Casey smiled broadly at them. "She wouldn't dare critique their cooking."

Eli laughed. "True."

"Is there anything we can do to help?" Alec asked.

Casey thought for a moment. "It's still a ways off, but if I think of anything, I promise to let you know. Okay?"

"Good enough," Eli said.

Casey glanced over the remnants of their lunch. "Dessert?" she asked hopefully.

"Casey, we just came from working out," Alec said.

"And you've barely touched your salad," Eli added.

She rolled her twinkling blue eyes at them. "The point of working out is so you can eat dessert without guilt." She laughed, looking at them. "And I'm more in the mood for chocolate than salad."

"None for me, thanks," Alec said, paying his portion and standing. "I've got to get back to the university. But you stay, babe." He kissed Eli. "Stay and *indulge*."

"I think I will."

They grinned at each other. "See you soon, Casey." Alec headed for the door.

Casey and Eli watched him leave and then turned to each other, simultaneously asking, "What's up with you two?" They blinked at each other and immediately followed that with, "What do you mean?"

They could read each other very well by now. Casey had been at Eli's side during his recuperation and physical therapy. During that long, painful process, the two of them had become the best of friends. And the young nurse had fallen for Ilsa a bit more with each visit.

"Dessert?" their waiter asked, suddenly appearing.

Without even looking at the menu or the waiter, Casey asked for a warm nut brownie with ice cream, and Eli ordered peach pie à la mode.

When the waiter had gone, the two friends leaned closer, each reaching a hand across the table toward the other. "What are you talking about?" Eli asked.

"You and Alec were uncommonly lovey-dovey over lunch." Casey grinned wickedly. "Don't think I didn't notice the foot play under the table."

Eli blushed brightly. "Well, we... uh, we had an argument earlier."

"About?"

He hesitated. "I... I pitched one too many tant—I got upset over Dray and—"

The waiter reappeared, placing their respective desserts on the table in front of them, and Eli dug in immediately.

"And?" Casey prompted.

"And nothing," he said around a mouth full of peach pie and ice cream. "We made up."

"Yeah," she said, taking a bite of her brownie. "I know how nice making up can be." Her expression grew dreamy, and he wasn't sure if she was remembering something specific or if that brownie was very good.

"Your turn," he said.

"Hmm?" Casey continued savoring her brownie.

"I noticed the tension between you and Ilsa at the party and earlier on the phone."

She sighed, taking another bite of her dessert. "It's just not how I thought it would be." He just looked at her, not understanding. "I mean—hell, I don't know what I mean."

"You... you don't...." He didn't know how to finish.

"What?"

"You don't seem like yourself when you're around Ilsa, not like you are with me, with your other friends."

Casey thought about this. "I'm afraid I'm going to need an example."

"Off the top of my head... your outfit for the party last night."

"What about it? You said I looked great."

"You did! You were the best-looking bird there, but...."

"What?"

"Were you comfortable in that?"

"Clothes like that aren't meant for comfort, Eli."

He rolled his eyes. "What are they meant for, Casey? Making the woman you want think you're someone you're not?"

She stared at him, and then her eyes wandered over the remainder of her dessert. The ice cream had quickly melted, turning the once neat, perfect pairing into a delicious, sticky mess. "Been holding that in for a while, have you?"

He lowered his eyes. "I'm sorry, Casey. I just want the two of you to be happy."

She looked out the window at the shoppers strolling through Covent Garden Market. "When I first began pursuing her, I remember you warning me that Ilsa and I were looking for different things."

"And you told me you could do casual."

She turned back to him and smiled. "I thought I could, but the thought of her with anyone else—"

"Makes you want to chew through a brick?"

She laughed. "Or hit the other woman with one."

"I have a brick somewhere with Dray's name on it."

"Now, now, love. Isn't that what you and Alec were arguing about?"

He looked around the room at the other diners, spreading his arms wide. "I don't see Alec here, do you?"

They both laughed.

"What exactly is your issue with Dray?"

"He tried to come between me and Bennett, and now he's sniffing after Alec."

"But he didn't succeed with Bennett, and Alec's not interested in him." He shrugged and took another bite of pie. She watched him finish it off. "Are you sure that's all that's going on?"

"What do you mean?" he asked, looking at her sharply.

"I get the feeling there's something else on your mind."

He began to fidget. "Well… this morning Alec mentioned something about us maybe finding our own flat."

"Ooh, how exciting! Tony said there were units opening up in their building."

"So you think it's a good idea?"

Casey appeared surprised. "Don't you? The two of you on one level and in your own home." She paused, but he didn't say anything. "Eli, what else would keep you in the house?"

"What about Ilsa? She's already peeved at Tony and Lyle."

"No, she isn't." He stared at her until she rethought her position. "Okay, perhaps… but—"

"I'm not…. I'm not ready to completely undo our family."

"This is about Bennett."

"No—"

"Yes, it is!" A couple of heads turned toward their table, and Casey lowered her voice. "What did Alec say when you told him you didn't want to move out?"

Eli signaled to the waiter for the bill but didn't say anything.

He finally looked into her eyes. "We haven't talked about it yet." Casey was clearly confused, and he told her about that morning and how he'd pretended not to hear Alec.

Casey smiled, shaking her head. "Smooth move, Casanova."

He laughed. "What was I supposed to say? At first I was so stunned I couldn't speak... and I sort of just let the silence stretch out, and then he was gone."

"It's obviously on his mind. It'll come up again."

"I know."

"What will you say?"

"No idea."

They paid their check, left the restaurant, and hugged.

"Good luck with your woman," he said.

Casey grinned. "Thanks, but I don't know if I can exactly call her mine, sweetie."

They smiled sadly at each other and parted ways.

Chapter 11

FOR the next day or so, Eli was able to avoid discussing moving out easily enough, because Alec didn't bring it up again. He seemed preoccupied by something, so Eli had time to think. Wednesday afternoon, following two clients and one intense study session for his signing certification, he returned to a seemingly empty house. Alec had planned to go directly from the university to meet up with the Kestrels for training that evening, and from the silence that greeted him, Eli guessed Ilsa was either working late or with Casey somewhere.

He slung his messenger bag off his shoulder and onto the floor, heading for the kitchen in search of food, but paused at the stairs, hearing movement above him.

"Hello?" He heard a muffled response, but he couldn't make it out. Eli eyed the stairs and considered the possible consequences of attempting them alone. "Fuck it." He started climbing.

The last time he'd done this alone was to check on Alec's injuries after a fight with skinheads outside a local club. That night he'd struggled up two flights of stairs, fearing the entire time what he'd find in Alec's attic room. He thought this time would be easier for several reasons: his goal was only the second floor, to discover who their mystery guest was; and this time he wasn't motivated by the terror of losing someone.

"Hello?"

"In here!" Ilsa said, stepping out of Tony and Lyle's former room and greeting him on the second landing. She had a tape measure in one hand and a pencil behind her ear. "What the hell are you doing climbing those stairs on your own?"

He finally reached her and sighed. "Why the bloody hell are you skulking about up here?"

She smiled at him, took his arm and led him back into the room. "I was taking measurements." She spread her arms and spun around in the center of the room. "I'm thinking about making this my bedroom. It's so much bigger. Big enough to—" she crossed to the windows facing the front of the house, "—have a little reading area here by the windows." He shook his head, following her movements as she dashed around. "Or maybe some tall bookshelves here." Ilsa put her hands on her hips, scrunching her lovely face in concentration. "I'm wondering about the color," she said, looking around. "I'm thinking something a little less neutral? Maybe a faux treatment." She looked at Eli and smiled broadly. "What do you think?"

Her enthusiasm had infected him, and he grinned at her. "I think it will look spectacular."

She flashed a satisfied smile at him before her eyes began to wander over the room, apparently imagining what it might look like soon.

"My momma and daddy had a really nice bedroom," she said, her hand absently stroking the wall as she looked around. "She used to read to me and my sister there before bedtime." Ilsa smiled wistfully at him. "I remember climbing into their bed was like trying to climb a mountain. It seemed so tall." She laughed to herself.

Eli watched her. "You miss them, don't you?"

Ilsa's face clouded, and her voice became hard. "Their decision, not mine." She ran her hand roughly through her tangle of dark brown curls.

"When did you speak to them last?"

"I talked to Sissy a couple of months ago. She'd like to visit, but she's afraid of what Momma and Daddy will say." Ilsa made some notations in the pad she held. "She's become more involved with the church, and it might 'look bad'." She turned to stare at the windows again, waggling the eraser end of her pencil at them. "I was thinking of getting some input from Lyle. He has great taste."

Sensing the discussion of family was over, Eli jumped on board. "What kind of reading area were you thinking of? A leather wingback, or maybe a chaise?"

Ilsa considered for a moment. "I think Casey would like a chaise. She's on her feet so much at the hospital, she'd probably appreciate being able to stretch out, right?" She looked to Eli and seemed taken aback by his expression. "What?"

"I... I just didn't realize you were taking Casey into account."

She turned fully around to face him. "Why wouldn't I?"

"I wasn't sure where... uh, you two were..." he said, waving his hand in an unfocused gesture, "in all this."

Ilsa stared at him for a few moments. "What do you mean, 'in all this'?"

"I've been wondering how serious you two were getting, that's all."

Ilsa flinched and began furiously scribbling on her notepad. She focused intently on it, writing measurements and ideas for the room. "I... I'm not sure." She didn't look at Eli as she spoke. She only shrugged and made more notations. "I just thought of her... thought maybe she'd appreciate a chaise by the window." He stared at her, smiling, but she wouldn't look at him again. "Doesn't mean anything," she mumbled, dropping the pad, turning her back to him, and pulling out her tape measure for the largest wall.

"It's okay if you're falling for her, Ilsa," he said very softly, and suddenly he felt the urge to hug her, comfort her.

She turned suddenly to face him. Her expression was unreadable, but before she could speak, the phone rang.

"I'll get it," she said, rushing past him and down the stairs. He sighed and walked over to pick up the notepad she'd dropped. He read the list of colors she was considering, all of them rich, deep, and luxurious. He looked up, trying to imagine those colors and treatments on the walls surrounding him. He could hear Ilsa speaking with someone, and he smiled. She apparently had hopes for an opulent love den for her—and Casey.

He continued to explore the notepad as he waited for Ilsa to return. He found magazine clippings secreted away within its pages. There were stunning examples of bedrooms with rich, dark wood furniture, modern artwork, and lush bedding and linens. He heard her say goodbye.

"You know what you need, Ilsa?" he asked, expecting her to return soon. He held up one of the clippings to compare the burgundy comforter on the bed in the picture to the current wall color. "You need some fabric pieces... uh... *swatches*?" He turned to see her standing in the doorway. "Wait... those are watches, right?" Eli's expression puckered as he tried to make his brain work. "I'm getting something wrong, aren't I? Anyway, you need something more than pages ripped from—" He stopped when he saw her face. "What's the matter?" Ilsa didn't say anything, but he saw a small piece of paper in her hand. "What's that?"

"Why didn't you tell me?"

"Huh? Tell you wh—"

"That you and Alec were planning to move out?"

He blinked at her, unable to speak, and the devastated look on her face wasn't making it any easier to collect his thoughts.

"Ilsa... I... we're not plan—"

She held up the paper in her hand and crossed the room to him, holding it under his nose. "This is a message about apartments in Tony and Lyle's building," she accused. "It's from Chase Mackens, some Realtor." Eli couldn't read the note with it held so close to his face, so he took it from her. "He said the units are coming ready sooner than expected," she continued, "and he's urging interested buyers to act now." He stared at it for a couple of moments. *That's what it says, all right.* He looked at her, saw the hurt in her eyes.

"Ilsa...."

"You can't tell me Alec would do this without running it by you first."

"He mentioned something about it Monday morning, but we haven't discussed anything."

She took a deep, slightly shuddering breath and smiled weakly. "Well, whatever you want to do," she said lightly, whirling around and heading for the stairs. "I'm going to get dinner going."

Eli stood there, holding the note tightly. He was torn between being furious with Alec and thinking of a way to put Ilsa's mind at ease. He turned off the light as he left the room without once considering what it was he wanted.

Chapter 12

"YEAH?"

Alec squinted at the pair of brown eyes peering at him through the narrowly opened door. "Uh, hi, I'm Alec Sumner. I called the other day about—"

The door slammed in his face, startling and disappointing him until he heard the security chain being removed. The door swung wide, revealing a thin, shirtless, young man securing a pair of freshly pressed black trousers, followed by his belt. His hair was so blond it appeared nearly white and was so short it stood up rigidly in an oddly hip military cut. He also sported a matching neat, blond goatee.

"Come in, mate," he said, stepping back from the door. "I'm just gettin' fixed for work."

Alec stepped in and closed the door behind him. The young man struggled into an undershirt, shouting a muffled, "Mum! Where is it?"

"Comin', dear." A short, round woman came rushing from what looked like the kitchen, holding a crisp white dress shirt in front of her. "Here it is. Here it is," she said handing it to her son. He took it and slipped it on hurriedly as she spotted Alec standing in the entryway. "And who are you, then?" she asked, looking him up and down, wrinkling her nose at his tousled hair, grass-stained T-shirt, shorts, and the pair of black soccer cleats slung over his shoulder. From her scrutiny, Alec was glad he'd stopped outside to knock the grass free of the shoes. "Just come from a match, have you?"

"Uh, yes, ma'am, I'm Alec Sum—"

"He's here to ask me about Mickey, Mum. Leave him be."

"You don't talk to your mother like that, Lincoln," she snapped as she rushed back out of the room.

"In here," Lincoln said, pointing to Alec's left. Alec followed him out of the hall and into another room where they sat down. "Sorry about her. She's in for the week. She's afraid I'm lonely here without Mickey." He lowered his voice. "I've nearly got the screamin' ab-dabs she won't want to leave," he said with a smile and a wink. Lincoln grabbed a highly polished black shoe from next to his chair. "Mum, did you pick up the laces I asked for?"

"Yes, yes, here they are." His mother dashed in, deposited the laces, and dashed back out again. Her son opened the package and began lacing up a shoe.

"So Michael's gone?" Alec asked.

"Huh? Oh yeah. Sorry. He's moved back to Liverpool, back in with his parents, sorry to say." He began looking around his chair for something. Alec discovered another black shoe by his seat and passed it to him. "Oh, cheers."

"Any idea when he'll be back?"

Lincoln paused in his lacing and looked at Alec. "He ain't comin' back, mate." His face fell, and he went back to fixing his shoe.

"Can you tell me what happened? Why'd he freak out at the party?"

Lincoln sighed, finished tying his shoe, and then looked around to make sure his mother was still in the kitchen. "At first I thought it was because he'd come back to work too soon after, that all those tossers— no offense—all that noise, and stress of the job had set him off."

"Too soon after what?"

Lincoln lowered his voice. "After...." He stopped and didn't seem able to continue.

"Look, I realize something happened, something traumatic, but I came here because I'd like to help if I can."

Lincoln nodded. "When I got him home, got him all tucked in bed and all... you have to understand, he hadn't said a word all the way here, not a peep."

"Then... you got him tucked in and what?"

"He told me he saw him."

"Who? Saw who?" Alec moved forward onto the edge of his chair.

"The wanker who hurt him."

"He was bashed? That can do a lot of damage, and not just

physically. My boy—"

"No, he wasn't bashed. He was forced...."

Alec's eyes went wide. "He was raped?"

"Shush now! Mum's in there."

"Sorry."

"She's worried about me enough bein' in London!" he hissed. Lincoln stood and grabbed a container of deodorant from the mantel, rolling it under each arm before buttoning his shirt. "Mum? Tie?"

She ran in again with his tie. "I'll have your vest done straight away." She turned to go but stopped and whirled back around. "Would you like some tea or somethin'?" she asked Alec. "I've got the kettle on. I'm afraid there's not much else to offer. The boys don't know how to shop properly."

"No, Mum. He's only here to check on Mickey. He's the bloke who helped us at the party."

"Oh, I see. That *was* a shame. Mickey and my boy grew up together back home and then this one decides he wants to move to the big, flashy city and leaves his mate all alone."

"Mum...."

"Mickey finally makes it here and less than a year later, he's been mugged and suffered a breakdown."

"Mum...."

"Now he's home where he belongs, but you can't tell this one nothin'. Big cities are dangerous, but you know that, don't you? You're American, yeah?"

Alec nodded.

"I thought so." She moved to the arm of her son's chair and sat. "You probably have shootings and such all the time, don't ya?" she asked, wide-eyed.

"Mum, vest!"

Lincoln's mother squeaked, smacked her son on the bottom, hopped up, and rushed from the room to check on her ironing.

Alec waited a few seconds and then looked up at Lincoln. "Mugged?"

"He's not out to the family. He couldn't very well tell them what really happened, now could he?"

"What really happened?"

Lincoln sat and told Alec that after Michael moved in with him, he had quickly started going out every night, feeling free to be himself for the first time. They went clubbing and partying every weekend when they were off or sometimes right after a job. One might Michael met someone he described as "the most beautiful man he'd ever seen" and disappeared with him.

Lincoln looked at the floor. "I probably should have kept a closer eye on him." He looked up sharply at Alec. "He didn't come home all night, and the next mornin' over breakfast, I saw bruises on his neck and arms. I asked about them, but all he'd say was things got a bit rough."

"You thought there was more to it?"

"Only after he started havin' trouble fallin' asleep, stopped goin' out, and then started wakin' up screamin'."

"Did he see someone, a therapist?"

Lincoln shook his head. "After a while he seemed fine, like his old self. The nightmares stopped, and we even went out a couple of times. I thought he was comin' out of it—until the party, that is."

"So you don't know this guy's name or what he looks like?" Alec asked, his thoughts racing back to all the unfamiliar faces he'd seen at the party.

Lincoln shook his head. "All he ever said was 'he was beautiful'. Won't say no more about him." He looked at Alec sadly. "Doesn't exactly narrow things down, does it?"

"Your friend needs to see someone, talk to someone." Alec stood and fished a business card out of his wallet. It made his blood run cold to think of that kid surrounded by people who didn't even know who he truly was while he had this horrible, painful secret inside him. "If you're still in touch with him, try to get through to him. I'll help if I can, if he'll let me."

Lincoln took the card, looked at it, and pocketed it. "Thanks, mate." He smiled. "I'd like to have him back, it's true."

"Vest." Lincoln's mother stood by, holding his red vest up for her son to take.

"Thank you, Mum." He kissed her on the cheek. "I'll bring a nice dinner home for us, okay? I shouldn't be too late."

His mother followed Alec and Lincoln to the door. "Are you some kind of doctor?" she asked Alec. "You know Lincoln has a lovely *single* sister."

"Mum!"

Alec chuckled nervously.

"Or if you're... uh... Lincoln isn't seeing anyone."

Alec laughed out loud, and Lincoln, struck dumb, stared at his mother as if she'd suddenly grown antlers.

"I appreciate that, ma'am, but I *am* seeing someone."

"Just for that," Lincoln said, shaking his finger at her, "I'm not bringin' you puddin'."

"Then you won't be gettin' back in, will ya?"

They laughed, and he kissed her on the cheek again before she closed and locked the door after them. He and Alec walked out. When they reached the sidewalk, there was a car filled with men dressed similarly to Lincoln waiting at the curb. He waved to Alec before climbing in. As they drove away, Alec could swear he heard one of the men shout, "Who's the lovely?"

Chapter 13

ALEC tried to enter the house as quietly as possible. He wasn't very graceful about it, however, because his muscles were beginning to stiffen from his exertions during training with his team. He shed his jacket and hung it on the hall tree before heading for the stairs. His foot was on the third step when he heard Ilsa shout from the kitchen, "Dinner will be ready soon."

"Erm, I just need to wash up, thanks." He took another step and paused. "Is Eli home?"

After a moment of silence, he heard, "I'm here." There was nothing further, and he heard something odd in Eli's tone, but he shook it off and dashed up the rest of the stairs to shower and change.

When he came back down, freshly scrubbed and starving, Eli and Ilsa were already seated in the dining room.

"Hello," Alec said brightly, leaning in to kiss Eli before taking his seat next to him and giving his thigh an affectionate squeeze. No one else said anything as he opened his napkin and fanned it over his lap. "This smells wonderful, Ilsa." He lifted the lid on a large dish in the center of the table, but the continued silence gave him pause.

With Tony and Lyle gone, he knew things might be quieter, but *this* was strange and uncomfortable. He took a good long look at their faces. Eli's eyes were fixed on his plate, and Ilsa looked as if she'd been crying.

A shudder ran through Alec. "What's happened?"

Eli didn't say anything. He just reached into his pocket and pulled out a slip of paper, sliding it along the table toward him. Alec picked it up and read it.

"Oh, he called back. Great!"

Ilsa bristled and left the table, taking her dinner with her. Alec watched her, perplexed.

"How could you go forward with this without discussing it with me?" Eli asked.

"Eli—"

"You have to understand this is coming out of nowhere. You only just mentioned it Monday and—"

"You heard me?" he asked, his eyes narrowing. Eli didn't speak. "Why didn't you say anything?"

"I needed time to think."

Alec stared into his boyfriend's eyes, but he heard Lyle's voice in his head bringing up Bennett. He felt chilled and removed his hands from the table, resting them in his lap where Eli wouldn't see them if they started to shake. He tried to smile but failed.

Ilsa left the kitchen and headed for the stairs. Alec jumped up and caught her before she got too far. "Ilsa, I didn't mean to upset you. I just—"

"I asked you to move in here to help Eli get over—" her eyes darted to Eli, then back to Alec—"not to undo my family."

"Ilsa, that's not fair."

"No, no it's not, but I'm not going to pretend I'm happy to lose him too."

"You're not losing him. You'll never lose him."

She wasn't listening. Her eyes roamed over the walls and rooms of the house. Alec followed her gaze, puzzled at first but then taking in the photographs, Tony's early artwork, a pillow Lyle had helped Ilsa embroider for the sofa—Alec grinned slightly, remembering the string of profanity that had been involved—a vase Bennett had given her for her first birthday in the house, the hall table where everyone's mail was still piling up. Alec followed her eyes to Eli's bedroom door, and then the two of them looked at each other. Her heated gaze drilled into him as she said, "First Bennett, Tony, Lyle, and now Eli and *you*."

Alec cringed at the emphasis she placed on that 'you,' and feared she was wishing he'd never moved in.

"We haven't gone anywhere, Ilsa. You're being—"

"If you say irrational, I'll punch you."

"We are not your pets!" Alec's outburst silenced both of them. He had surprised himself. "I know you love them," he continued more calmly, "but you also want them to be happy, right? No matter where that is?"

She took one step back down toward him. "And if Eli is happy here?"

Alec didn't say anything. *What if Eli is happier here... here with all his memories of Bennett?* No, this had gotten too heated too fast. It didn't make sense. They were pulling too hard in opposite directions out of... fear? She was being ridiculous. They all were. *He won't look at me when we make love.*

"Y-you could move into Tony and Lyle's old room," Ilsa added hopefully. "I was going to take it, but it's big enough for the two of you, and we were just up there earlier." She glanced at Eli as he approached them. "It wouldn't be that tough for you to manage, right?"

Eli held up a hand to silence her and turned to face Alec. "I'm not ready."

"Why?" Alec asked.

"I don't see the need."

"Eli, your room is too small for us to share, and mine... well, it may be large enough, but it's on the top floor and too difficult for you to reach every day." Alec paused, looking at Ilsa. "And taking the other bedroom isn't going to work, either. It's still an unnecessary flight of stairs." He paused again, but Eli didn't appear to have anything to add. Alec reached out for him, gripping his shoulders. "I want to wake up next to you and not have to rush elsewhere to get dressed and ready for the day." He ran his fingers through Eli's hair and rested his palm against his face. "I want us to *really* live together... as a couple. Can't you understand that?"

"I hear you, Alec, but the situation we have isn't all that different from a couple living at different flats and—"

Alec sighed, closed his eyes, and began massaging the bridge of his nose.

"Please don't do that," Eli said.

Alec looked at him and took a deep breath. "Just tell me one thing." *Don't ask, don't ask, don't ask.*

"What?"

"Tell me that your reluctance isn't because of... Bennett." Ilsa looked sharply at Eli as Alec continued. "This is the home you shared with him. Tell me that's not why you won't consider it."

Eli glanced between them. "Why would you think that?"

"I can't think of any other reason, and you're not offering me one."

"Here's one," Eli said, his face darkening and his eyes going cold. "I'm happy here. I'm not ready to move." He stepped around Alec and headed for his bedroom. Ilsa and Alec watched him go and then looked at each other. She smiled sadly and headed upstairs. When Alec heard her door close, he followed Eli into the room. Alec found him staring at his shelf of photos, but Eli quickly turned to face him when he walked in. They stood looking at each other in silence, and then Alec turned, grabbed his jacket, and walked out of the house.

Chapter 14

ALEC blinked a couple of times at Mirabell. He opened his mouth to speak, but no words came out, so he blinked some more. She stood in her doorway in a simple, plush, beige, terrycloth bathrobe and matching slippers. His eyes began to water from a strong, acrid odor emanating from her hair, which appeared to be filled with thick, gelatinous hair color. A cigarette hung from her lips.

"Should you be smoking while coloring your hair?"

She turned and headed back down her hallway. "Come to rescue me from my fags, have you?"

Alec entered the apartment, closing and locking the door behind him. "I just—"

"How long?"

"Huh?" Alec rushed down the long, dark hall in her wake.

"How long do you need to stay?"

He frowned, stopping in his tracks and watching her disappear into her kitchen. "Mira, I'm not some struggling, penniless college student. I don't *need* to stay with you."

"Then what is it you 'need'?" He didn't know quite how to answer that. She peered at him around the corner. "Coming?" That shook him from his thoughts, and he joined her in the kitchen. It was cluttered, and his eyes roamed over dishes piled on the table, the counter next to the sink, and on the stove.

"This is a new look for you," he said hesitantly.

"You like?" she asked, spreading her arms and modeling her outfit, "I got it from the Grand Hyatt in New York last night." She winked. "Didn't cost a thing."

"No, Mira, I meant this…." Alec gestured toward the disorder surrounding them.

"Oh." She finished her cigarette and snuffed it out in one of a number of strategically placed ashtrays. "Just got back, love. Haven't had time to clean the place, I'm afraid."

Alec gingerly lifted a plate on a stack to his left and peered beneath. "So it was like this when you left?"

She looked at him sharply. "New York was a sudden trip. An emergency."

"A fashion emergency?"

She ignored him, looking at the surrounding chaos. "I was only gone two days," she said, shoving a few items out of the way. "It's not like vermin have begun to gather."

Alec began collecting dishes and clearing the kitchen table just as a bell sounded on the counter near Mirabell. She quickly turned on the faucet, grabbed the spray nozzle, and wet her hair. She turned back to Alec as she worked up a lather in her hair. "Don't bother with that, babe. I have a boy come in to clean."

Alec paused, his hands filled with cups and saucers. "A boy?"

Mirabell smiled as her hair began to resemble a cotton ball. "Yes. A boy. What of it? He's a struggling model at the moment. Needs a few extra quid."

Alec grinned and carried the dishes over to her. He put them on the counter and leaned against it, standing next to her as she continued to work the coloring out of her hair. They stood silently for several minutes as Alec tried to find an explanation for why he'd come to Mirabell's.

"Mira, I—"

"Hang on, have to rinse." She turned the water back on and shed her robe in one swift move. She was topless, but wearing a pair of lacey black panties and black silk stockings. Alec blushed brightly as she leaned over the sink to rinse her hair. "Pass me that, will you?" Mirabell reached out toward Alec, flailing her fingers without lifting her head from the sink.

Alec looked around, spotted an apparently clean towel on the back of a chair, and handed it to her. Mirabell squeezed the water from her hair and carefully wrapped the towel around it, tucking the end tightly under at the nape of her neck. She lit up another cigarette and turned to face Alec, who quickly leaned over, grabbed her robe from the floor, and handed it to her, while averting his eyes.

"Aww, are my boobies frightening you, dear?" She took the robe and slipped it on. "Here," she said, gesturing toward the table, "sit." They sat. "You want a drink?"

"No, but you probably do."

"Thanks. I'll have bourbon."

Alec grinned, got up, and poured her a bourdon from a bottle he found in the cabinet. "Here you are, my dear."

"Thanks." Mirabell gulped the drink, winced, and looked into Alec's eyes. "So, what have they done to you now?"

He shook his head. "What makes you th—"

"Save it. You're obviously upset, and since you're here instead of snuggling and talking with your man about it, I conclude he's the problem." Alec didn't say anything as she took a long drag off her cigarette, her eyes narrowing either from the smoke or in examining his expression. "Out with it," she commanded.

"I want to move out."

"And?"

"Eli doesn't."

"So?" They stared: Mirabell at him and Alec at everything else in the room but her. She tapped her cigarette on an ashtray and waited. After several more moments, she leaned forward and asked, "How is it a psychologist with your skill and insight is unable to make his life run more smoothly?"

"It doesn't work like that, Mira. Looking at something from the outside is very different from navigating my own relationships. That's... that's—"

"I shall give you the benefit of my years—"

"You're only four years older than me."

She held up a hand. "A lot can happen in four years. Now... tonight, for instance, I have a date. Met him at some club two weeks ago. Decent dancer. Lovely to look at. Adequate fashion sense... smart Buddy Holly glasses. Oh, and his name *is* Buddy!" She laughed. "He doesn't smoke, but I can probably get him to—"

"You want him to start—"

"I don't have the energy or inclination to defend myself. Therefore he'll have to start." Apparently it all seemed very simple to her. "What I'm getting at, love, is you need to do what's best for you. If you want to move out, move the fuck out."

"What's best for me is Eli."

She shook her head violently, but the towel held. "You don't know that." Alec began to squirm under her certainty. "Why do you think he doesn't want to leave that house?" He didn't say anything. "Alec? You must have some idea, dear."

"It's the home he shared with Bennett," he whispered.

Mirabell stood and tore the towel off her head. "You shouldn't go through life living to make someone else happy." She ran her fingers through her reinvigorated bright red hair. "Get yours first."

"What if it's Eli who makes me happy? His feelings—"

"What about *your* feelings? Who takes care of those?" She snuffed out her cigarette. "Trust me. Only you can do that, Alec." She walked out of the kitchen, shedding her robe again as she headed for her bedroom. He followed her, first stepping over the robe but then stopping, picking it up, and carrying it with him. He tossed it in a chair just inside the bedroom door while Mirabell grabbed a black lace pushup bra from her bed, stood in front of a full-length mirror, and struggled into it. She admired her petite form for a moment, smiling at how full her breasts looked in the new bra before caressing them.

"Uh, would the three of you like to be alone?"

Her eyes caught his in the mirror, and she grinned wickedly at him. "Pass me that little black Isabel Lu out of the closet, will you?"

Alec went to the closet and, faced with an abundance of colors, fabrics, tops, and bottoms, lamented that not all gay men knew fashion. He glanced pleadingly at her.

"Sorry, it's actually on the back of the door. Price tag still on."

He found it: a tiny, silk, strapless, dress that cost…. "You're shitting me!"

She took it from him with only a slight roll of her eyes, snipped off the tag with a miniscule pair of scissors that she produced apparently out of thin air, and slid the dress on. "Zip me?" Alec stepped behind her and drew the zipper closed. He stood there behind his friend as she continued to examine herself from all angles. "Product," she said, holding out her hand. This he could handle.

"What are you going for?" he asked, quickly scanning her dressing table and its contents.

"I don't wish my hair to move for at least twelve hours."

He snatched up a spray can. "Shine or no?"

"Shine."

He put the can back down and grabbed another. "Here you are."

She took it from him and sprayed a good bit into her hand where it expanded, nice and foamy. She worked it into her hair, straightening, shaping, and twirling around her finger as she went. When Mirabell was satisfied, her flaming red hair shone like curly copper ribbons and would likely survive a hurricane, provided it occurred within the next twelve hours.

She dropped into the stool in front of her dressing table. Shoving a shoebox aside, Alec sat on the bed to watch her apply her makeup. He might have been concerned for the dress, but she had flawless skin—despite the smoking—so she only put on mascara, eyeliner, and scary red lipstick. She stared at herself long enough for Alec to ask, "What else?"

"I'm torn on the beauty mark." She turned to look at him. "Yay or nay?"

He picked up the shoebox and sat it in his lap, absently drumming his fingers on it. "Uh… well, did you have one when you met?"

She thought for a moment. "Not sure." She frowned, but Alec could offer no help in this department. She sighed. "I'll take a chance. Go without." She turned all the way around on the stool to face him. "Don't want it rubbing off against the pillow when he flips my arse over tonight."

"Mira!"

"Oh, please. You can be such a prude sometimes." She reached out to him, wriggling her fingers, and he realized this was Mirabell for "Hand me my pretty, new shoes, please."

She took the box and grinned seductively at him, but didn't open it. "Guess."

"What?"

"Guess what color they are."

He looked her over, taking in the hair, her pale, perfect skin, the black stockings, and the sexy black dress. "Black and red?"

She frowned. "You're no fun!" She whipped the lid off the box— Alec followed its chaotic arch through the air before it hit the bathroom floor behind her—and pulled out a low shiny, black boot with a two-inch, flame-red heel. She slid them on quickly and stood, smoothing her dress, to look in the mirror again.

He rose and stood behind her, placing his hands on her shoulders. "You look fantastic, Mira." She smiled at him, and he leaned down to kiss her cheek. She smelled faintly of cigarettes and surprisingly of spring rain. He had no idea how she managed that.

She patted his hand and turned to face him. "Get your own flat, Alec," she said softly. "You moved into his life, into his world. You need to make one of your own, just for you. If he wants to be part of it, you can make room for him."

"Mira—"

She walked away from him suddenly but stopped in the center of the room. She crossed one arm over her chest and tapped her chin with her index finger as she scanned the room. "What?" he asked.

She looked at him. "Handbag?"

He spotted it hanging on the back of the closet door where her dress had been and passed it to her.

"Cheers," she said absently, searching through its contents rapidly. Satisfied, she snapped it shut. "As you pointed out earlier, you are no penniless, homeless college student. You have the cash to buy your own place, and a nice one, at that." Alec nodded. "Decorate to your taste. Fix it just the way you like. If he wants to be with you, he will." She draped the strap over her shoulder.

It's all so simple for you, isn't it? His chest tightened at the thought of being without Eli. "No jacket, Mira?"

She leveled her gaze at him. "How long have I been doing this? If I wear a jacket, he may not feel compelled to wrap me up in his." She rolled her eyes, and Alec followed her out of the room and her apartment.

Chapter 15

COMING home to a quiet, mostly dark house, Alec knocked on Eli's bedroom door. "Eli, we need to talk." There was no sound from within the room, and he feared Eli had already gone to bed for the evening. He sighed, resting one palm against the door, and whispered, "I'll see you tomorrow."

Beginning to feel more of his soccer workout, he slowly made his way up the stairs to his room. With every few steps, he practiced what he would say to Eli tomorrow about his moving out—his reasons, his hopes, and his desires. He opened his door and flicked on the light.

"Holy shit!" he gasped, stumbling backward into the doorframe. "Eli! What the fuck?"

Eli chuckled. "Sorry I startled you." He sat in the chair closest to the door but got up and quickly crossed to Alec. "I had gone to bed, but I couldn't sleep, so when I heard Ilsa turning in for the night, I snuck up here to wait for you instead."

Alec's racing heart began to slow, recapturing a more steady rhythm. "Y-you… didn't have to. I don't like the idea of you coming up here on your own like that."

"I was careful." He stepped closer. "I took my time." Eli pressed his hand to Alec's heart. "You were gone so long." He kissed Alec lightly and tucked a stray lock of hair behind his ear, "I began to worry."

"I was at Mira's—talking."

"About—"

"About several things." He reluctantly moved away from Eli. His proximity was making it difficult to think clearly.

Eli didn't follow. He remained by the door as Alec sat on the bed and removed his shoes.

"Did it help?" he asked, and Alec looked up at him questioningly. Eli leaned on his cane and hugged himself with the other arm. "The talking, I mean?"

Alec dropped one shoe. "Yeah, I think it did." He smiled, remembering his friend's advice. "Mira has a way of cutting straight to the heart of things." He dropped the other shoe. "I don't agree with her view on everything," he said, "but she made some good points." He looked Eli up and down as he stood there, just out of reach. He could get it all out now or.... "Coming to bed?"

"You *want* me to?"

Puzzled, Alec paused in removing his T-shirt. "Of course I do." He smiled and pulled the shirt off over his head.

Eli grinned broadly, quickly shedding his shirt and sweatpants and revealing nothing but a firm, ripped body—a slight body, lightly dusted with dark hair and marked by those oh-so-familiar scars, the scars that inevitably led back to Bennett.

"You know, I wasn't snooping or anything, but I noticed your football togs in the floor from earlier." Staring at Eli, Alec's mouth had gone dry, and he was having trouble thinking. "Alec?"

"Huh? Oh, yes… football."

Eli took a couple of steps closer. "They were fairly grimy for someone just *watching* training." Alec didn't say anything. He only licked his bottom lip and nodded. Eli smiled and came within touching distance. Alec's hands automatically shot out, taking hold of Eli's hips and pulling him closer, within the circle of his legs.

Eli was already half-erect, but as Alec kneaded his bottom and pressed his face against his chest, suckling each nipple, Eli quickly responded, and his rigid cock was soon bumping Alec's chest. Alec moved to take Eli in his mouth, but Eli stopped him, grabbing his hair roughly and pulling his head back. "You *played* today, didn't you?"

They searched each others' eyes for several moments, and then Alec grinned. "Yeah, I did. What of it?"

Eli's expression softened. "You must be exhausted," he whispered, gently stroking Alec's face. He tossed his cane against the wall by the headboard, and steadying himself with Alec's help, he carefully got on his knees, pushing Alec's legs farther apart. Alec shivered as Eli's hands slowly traveled up his thighs. *I know what you're doing.* Eli's hands stopped when they reached his belt, undoing it. *I know what you're trying to do, and I don't care.*

Eli paused before unzipping his jeans, cupping Alec through the material and squeezing a delicious gasp out of him. Each held the other's gaze as Eli opened the jeans, and Alec lifted himself off the bed a bit to shimmy them off to his ankles. Alec grinned drunkenly when Eli's fingers closed around him, freeing his stiff cock from his shorts.

"How eager it is," Eli said when it sprang into view. He playfully licked the slit, capturing drops of pre-come dangling there right before sucking the head into his mouth. Alec groaned, dizzy as so much heat and blood rushed to his lower region. A tremor ran through his body, and Eli pulled back, placed one hand against Alec's torso, and pushed, encouraging him to relax and lie flat on his back, which he did.

He would rather be watching Eli, but he found himself staring at his ceiling and getting lost in the feel of Eli's lips and tongue sending blissful shivers through him. His eyes fell shut, and a smile spread across his face as Eli relaxed his throat, taking all of him in. Alec's brain wouldn't allow any negative thoughts or concerns about tomorrow and the conversation they would have to have. There was simply no room for them. All his gray cells were occupied with the baser needs and instincts of their owner. Eli sped up, and Alec began to moan and grunt, his hands gripping the bed as he fought back the urge to grab Eli by the hair and fuck his mouth. His abdomen rippled and flexed; his balls drew up tight; and, with a shout, he came, spilling into Eli's mouth and down his throat.

While his head cleared, he had a vague sense of Eli stripping him completely, and when he opened his eyes again, Eli was standing over him, smiling and sporting an impressive erection that made Alec's insides start to flutter all over again. He watched as Eli reached into the bedside table and removed a small tube of lube.

"Roll over, love," he whispered, and Alec did. The position that worked best for Eli was taking Alec from behind while lying on their sides. They'd found that when on his knees behind him, or with Alec missionary, the muscles in Eli's leg fatigued too quickly, and standing and topping was out of the question—or, at least, all this had been the case. Alec knew Eli's increased workouts were part of an attempt by him to gain more strength and stamina in his leg to remedy the situation. Alec had to admit to himself that he wouldn't mind Eli taking full control once in a while—fucking him hard and fast.

In the meantime, he rolled on the bed so that he was on his left side and facing the wall. The light dimmed, casting most of the room in shadow, and a moment later he felt the bed dip as Eli climbed in, scooted over, and snuggled close behind him. The sensation of Eli's cockhead bumping him just at the curve of his ass knocked all coherent thought from his head, which was good. His mind had begun to ratchet up again—the tickle of an idea at the back of his mind that Eli's attentions tonight were his boyfriend's way of reassuring himself that all was well between them, that the argument about moving out was over, that it was settled.

Eli's fingers, cold with lube, pressed against the cleft of Alec's behind, and he wordlessly bent his right leg, bringing it forward to give Eli better access. He turned his face into his arm and moaned as Eli massaged him, starting just behind his balls and drawing his finger upward and deep to brush against his opening. He closed his eyes as he pushed back against Eli's hand. He felt Eli's other hand grip his shoulder, steadying him, and then Eli's finger pressed into him, past the tight ring of muscle. Smiling, Alec's breathing stuttered. Eli finger-fucked him slowly, kissing his neck as he added another finger and began to curl them inside him.

"Eli, please... *nguh!*" Alec moaned as Eli added a third finger and increased the pressure, rubbing Alec in the right spot. Just as Alec began to writhe and pant, the fingers left him. A moment later, he felt his cheeks being spread, and he involuntarily tensed in anticipation as Eli pressed himself into him gradually. Alec bit down on his arm, trying to breathe through it and relax. It felt so good to be filled like this, to have Eli inside him. He heard the change in Eli's breathing, felt it on the back of his neck, and smiled. When Eli's hips met Alec's, they sighed together, holding still for a moment. And then, just for fun, Alec worked his inner muscles, causing Eli to gasp and shudder.

"Alec!"

He chuckled to himself until Eli gripped his hipbone, pulled back, almost falling free of him, and then drove forward into Alec hard and deep, thereby knocking the chuckle right off his lips.

Eli gripped Alec's hip and lightly bit into his shoulder as he fucked him, and soon Alec was panting, "Yes," and biting his own bicep, twisting his covers in his fist. "Don't st-stop—*uh!*"

Eli's thrusts became harder, more frantic as Alec pushed back to meet them. At each thrust the glorious tension in Alec climbed until lights flashed behind his eyes, and he shouted surely loud enough to wake Ilsa. Eli followed him over the edge, gasping and panting in his ear. They lay together, sweaty and shaking, as Eli placed tiny, gentle kisses on Alec's neck and across his shoulder. It tickled, and the occasional nibble sent shocks along Alec's skin.

He stirred about an hour later, and simply out of habit, reached in front of him for Eli. But the bed was cold on his left. Then what they'd done came rushing back to him, where his last conscious sensation had been Eli slipping out of him. He turned over gently and smiled when he discovered Eli sleeping peacefully beside him. His hair: a chaotic mop, as usual. His face: angelic and untroubled, for a change. Alec lost track of how long he watched Eli's chest rise and fall. He thought he could easily have watched all night.

He suddenly wrapped Eli up tightly in his arms and began stroking his hair. He didn't want to go anywhere without him, but he knew Mirabell's advice had been right.

"Alec," Eli mumbled, pushing against his chest. "I can't breathe." Alec loosened his grip, and Eli looked at him, confused and sleepy. "Are you all right?"

"Sorry. Yeah, I'm fine. It's just...."

"What?"

He kissed Eli deeply and stroked his thigh. "I wish we could be like this always... you know, not just when we're making up."

Eli frowned. "It isn't like this just when we're making up."

"Oh yeah? After Tony and Lyle's party? Remember? You'd gotten upset about Dray." Eli didn't say anything. "And then at the gym, in the shower, after you got upset about Dray." Alec smiled wistfully. "I was ready to fuck you through that shower wall," he said, laughing and nuzzling into Eli's neck.

"And tonight? No Dray *tonight*." Eli's fingers strayed into Alec's hair, carrying chills to the nape of his neck.

"True, but we did argue about moving out."

"We're not going to do that again, are we?" Eli asked, looking pointedly at him. "We're okay, right? I'm not ready to move out."

"We're okay, Eli. I'm not going to ask you to move out again."

Eli pulled Alec into a kiss, and reached between them to stroke him back to life. "You're welcome to fuck me now, if you're up to it." He kissed Alec's neck and nipped playfully at his collarbone.

"I don't know." Alec thrust into Eli's fist. "Am I up to it?"

"It feels like a definite possibility."

Alec laughed and rolled Eli onto his back and then positioned himself between Eli's legs. He pressed his palm playfully against Eli's cock, trying to make it lie flat against the man's abdomen, but it wasn't having it. Alec grinned as he popped open the lube and slicked up his fingers. He hovered over Eli, smiling as he ran his palm over Eli's chest and nipples. He kissed Eli, pushing his tongue into Eli's mouth just as Alec pushed his fingers into him. Their tongues danced against each other as Alec's curling, active fingers soon had Eli whimpering and squirming beneath him.

When Eli was ready, Alec quickly shifted position, rising up on his knees and pulling Eli forward until his bottom was resting in Alec's lap, one leg on either side of him. Eli lifted his bottom a bit, and Alec slid gently into him. They made love slowly but to exhaustion, and as Alec drifted off—Eli's steady breathing tickling his neck—he succeeded in keeping his fears about tomorrow at bay. *Tonight is good. Right now is enough.*

Chapter 16

THE buzzing came again—the buzzing and the knocking. In his sleep, Eli furrowed his brow and changed position in the bed, rolling away from the sound. He ignored the slipping sheet and the cooler air kissing his bottom. Sometime later the buzzing came again—the buzzing and the knocking. This time he raised his head, and through blurry eyes saw, on the other side of the bed, a cell phone dancing across the nightstand. He thought that was funny and smiled. *A dancing mobile.*

He slowly came a bit more awake and stretched, groaning as his aching muscles made themselves known. "Jesus, Alec." He reached out across the bed and realized two things: he was on Alec's side of it, and he was alone. His head flopped back down on the pillow. He smiled. It smelled like Alec. He hugged the pillow and began to drift off again. Then he heard the shower, the sound floating in around him as if from across the world.

He sat up, contemplating joining Alec in the shower, but before he could get out of bed and execute his plan, the buzzing and the knocking came again. He rolled over and grabbed the phone, flipping it open.

"Hello?"

"Mr. Sumner, so glad I caught you. This is Chase, and I wanted to change the order of properties I'm showing you today, if you don't mind." Eli heard the rustling of papers. "Since you obviously favor Prescott Towers, if you would please meet me at—"

"I'm sorry. This isn't Mr. Sumner," Eli managed. "Um, he's—"

"Oh, I was sure I had the correct number—"

"Yes, yes, this is his phone. I'm just not him," Eli laughed. "But about those prop—"

"Could you please take a message for him? I'm in a bit of a rush and want to make sure we meet at the right—"

"That's just it, I'm afraid. He's no longer looking to view any—"

"Eli?"

He turned to see Alec standing just outside the bathroom door, a towel around his waist while he dried his hair with another one.

"Oh, here he is. Just a moment."

Eli smiled and held out the phone to Alec, who rushed over to take it but then turned his back and walked back across the room to stand in front of the windows.

He grabbed his cane, got out of the bed, and padded over to the bathroom, passing Alec on the way and dodging a poorly aimed smack to his bottom. He was laughing as he closed the bathroom door, but he heard Alec say, "I'll be there by nine. Thank you."

Once again Eli found himself standing on the other side of a bathroom door, experiencing a rush of dread. He tried to shake it off and went to relieve himself. Afterward he stepped in the shower, rushing through to get back to Alec as soon as possible. He stepped out of the shower and toweled off quickly, exiting the bathroom to find Alec on the bed, tying his shoes.

"Hey, that was fast," Alec said, standing and tucking in his shirt.

Eli nodded and vigorously rubbed his hair with a towel. "You're dressed and ready."

"Yep."

"For what?"

"Why… are you wanting to spend more time in bed?" Alec asked with a wink.

"Always," Eli said with a chuckle, "but I have a client today."

"Lynette?"

"No, I'm tagging along to a job interview." Eli slipped back into his sweatpants from the previous night and located his T-shirt. "If he gets the job, the company will provide an interpreter."

"Sounds great." Alec went to his dresser and brushed through his hair a few times, massaging in some product to tame the waves. "Best of luck to the two of you."

"Thanks." Eli finished pulling on his shirt and waited for Alec to say more, but after checking his reflection in the mirror, Alec turned to face him, saying nothing. "Where are you off to?"

Alec sighed and stared at him for a couple of moments, long enough for the dread inside Eli to expand, clutching at his heart and lungs. "I'm meeting Mr. Mackens to look over some properties."

Eli blinked at him. "What?"

"I'm meeting him at Tony and Lyle's in thirty minutes."

Eli felt as though ice water was pouring over him. "I thought we settled this last night."

Alec held up a hand to forestall any outrage. "Eli, I admit I shouldn't have moved forward before getting a definite answer from you, and I'm sorry for that." Alec walked over to him. "But I meant what I said last night. I won't ask you to move out again."

"Then why the appointment—"

"There's no reason I can't look for myself."

Breathe, Eli. Breathe. "But you…. Alec, you live… here," he said softly, though his heart was racing.

"It's time I got my own place."

"I don't see—"

"Each time I've relocated, I've moved into a group situation like this. It was easier to acclimate to a new city that way, surrounding myself with the natives, so to speak."

"I get that, but I—"

"And I was always running from a failed relationship, running from our home, their home. The success of my book means I've got the money now." Alec smiled wistfully. "And I want a home of my own this time. Now is as good a time as any." Eli's mouth was working, but he couldn't manage to comment. Alec glanced at his watch. "I need to get going. If you're ready, I'll help you downstairs." Alec reached for him.

Eli looked at his outstretched hand, but he didn't move toward it. He could feel the anger building in him, and he couldn't contain it. Even though he knew it was fueled by fear, he couldn't name the fear, so he looked into Alec's eyes and simply said, "I can make it on my own."

Alec frowned. "Don't be that way."

"What way? Last night was amazing! Bloody fucking amazing!" He advanced on Alec angrily. "And you knew then, didn't you? You knew that you were moving out!" Alec nodded. "Why?" Eli turned from him and dropped onto the bed. "We're here together, happy. Why—?" He stopped and stared at Alec. "We are… you *are* happy, right?"

Alec went to him, dropped to his knees, and took Eli's hands in his. "Eli, I'm happy with you. There is no one else I want to be with."

"But—"

"No, it's a fact. Just because I'm moving out doesn't mean I'm ending us. And I hope to God it's not a deal-breaker for you." Alec stroked Eli's face. "Please tell me you understand that." Alec kissed him, and Eli tried to stay strong, pulling away from him. *Yes, I'll stay strong by pouting.* But Alec held his face fast, kissing him again, and he swooned, his heart beating faster and aching at the same time. He found himself leaning into Alec, gripping the sleeves of his shirt, and moaning.

He could feel his throat tighten around the sob fighting to escape. *Why do I want to cry?*

"Please, don't go," he managed after their lips parted.

Alec embraced him, whispering in his ear, "I'll find a place, and when I get it just the way I want, I'll have you over. I'll make you dinner. And we can christen it together." They kissed again, and Eli managed to grin. Alec got to his feet but paused in the doorway, turning to look at Eli as he remained sitting on the bed. "You sure you don't want to go down with me?"

"I'm good. You go on. I'll see you later."

"You're okay?"

Eli nodded. Alec turned, headed down the stairs, and out of the house. Eli stared at the empty doorway a bit longer. He knew he was being silly. He had said himself that their current living situation wasn't any different than the two of them living in separate flats. Now that was going to happen. Feeling a familiar fear twist his gut, he rolled himself back into the bed and wrapped his arms around Alec's pillow, burying his face in it and breathing in his scent.

Chapter 17

ELI went about his day a bit on edge. He didn't want Alec to move out, and he kept telling himself it was entirely possible Alec wouldn't find anything he liked. That's when another voice in his head would shout, *Bollocks!* and he'd want to hit something. What Alec had proposed made perfect sense—a place of their own, no stairs, and properly sharing a bedroom—but Eli didn't feel ready, nor was he ready to examine the reasons why. Work saved him. He was able to put all his concentration on his client, and wonder of wonders, the man got the job. He was so thrilled he took Eli out for a pint.

Afterward he walked around London, window-shopping at first, and then he went into a bookstore and grabbed the latest copy of *British Deaf News*. He passed a small display of Alec's book, the one that had made him a good amount of money, the one that had prompted Ilsa to seek Alec out when she'd read about it online. Eli picked up a copy and stared at Alec's photo on the jacket, tracing the outline of his face.

"I guess, in a way, this brought us together," he said out loud. Suddenly remembering where he was, he quickly replaced the book, fearing people had heard.

As he waited in line to pay for his magazine, he grinned, recalling how he had successfully and secretly read the book. It was difficult to accomplish without Alec finding out because they spent so much time together, but it had been a good read, not dry and clinical as he'd feared when he'd first sneaked it into the house. The book didn't pull any punches or offer miracles. It urged people to walk through their heartache. It honored those feelings and urged the reader to face them. It assured them they were stronger than they thought.

The book postulated that the loss of a loved one did not have the power to destroy you, as many people thought. Yes, it turned your life upside down. Yes, it hurt like hell. But these conditions were temporary, unless you clung to the pain—which was about as useful as a life vest filled with lead. Eli had squirmed a bit upon reaching that passage. *I wallowed. I'm a wallower.* Alec's book didn't suggest you suffer your loss and then just shake it off—only that you remind yourself that it *will* get easier, that the empty, dull ache at your core will end. It will change. You will keep breathing, getting up in the morning, working, even laughing at some point—usually unexpectedly.

When he was done, Eli could see why it was so popular. Grief was universal, and the book offered hope. Who didn't need that? His smile faded somewhat, however, as he realized that though he'd read and enjoyed it, he hadn't really allowed the book to sink in or to touch him. How could it? There was more to his loss than anyone else knew.

Still, he was happy with Alec and moving on, wasn't he? *Aren't I?*

After paying for his purchase, he stepped back out onto the street and, not eager to return home just yet, he decided to sit in a nearby park and read for a while. He stopped to buy a sandwich and water and spent the next two hours eating, reading, and watching the goings-on around him. A breeze stirred the pages of the magazine, his hair, and the trees. He could smell the promise of rain on the wind, even though it was a fairly sunny day. There were children running around in no particular order or with any discernible purpose. Eli smiled to himself. *That must be where 'willy-nilly' comes from.* There was a pick-up football game on a distant field and a healthy collection of joggers running by.

Eventually he glanced up to see parents trying to corral their children; runners were becoming fewer and far between; and there were more footballers lying in the grass panting and holding their sides than taking the ball in for a goal. He sighed and gathered the remnants of his lunch, tossing it in a trash bin. He'd have to go home at some point. It might as well be now. He decided he'd have to get used to going back to the house and Alec not being there.

AS HE slid his key in the door, Eli was startled by an explosion of raucous laughter coming from inside.

"Hello?" he shouted as he entered the house.

A chorus of "Eli!" greeted him. He slowly walked into the living room and, looking into the dining room, saw a crowd of people around the table. There were the familiar—Alec, Casey, Lyle, and Tony—and the not so well-known—Shana and Lori, two of Ilsa's ex-lovers, and two men, one of whom looked familiar. They were all smiling at him.

"Uh, heya," he managed as he advanced slowly into the room. Alec hopped up and greeted him with a kiss. It ended too quickly, but Eli smiled at him. "What's going on?"

"We're planning Ilsa's birthday party," Casey said. "She's at work and won't be home for a while."

"I didn't hear about this."

"It was a bit impromptu," a handsome black man said. He had a kind face and was a bit older, maybe in his late thirties. He was tall and slender with a bit of a swimmer's build, his skin a beautiful caramel brown. His eyes were coal-black, but not cold or lifeless. In fact, they seemed to twinkle like the night sky, and Eli found himself smiling unconsciously. The man stood and extended his hand. "I don't know if you remember me. I'm Keith—"

"Albee?" Eli asked in almost a whisper. "DS Albee?"

"Yes, but it's Detective Inspector now." He beamed at Eli, apparently pleased he'd been remembered.

"Congratulations."

"Thank you." Keith's eyes narrowed. "How are you, Eli?"

Eli felt his face flush, and he looked quickly from Alec to Ilsa. "I'm fine," he mumbled. "Ilsa told me you were very helpful when… you know."

"Uh, yes." Keith cleared his throat and, glancing at the man seated near him said, "This is my partner, Bishop."

A slightly younger man with light brown hair and large hazel eyes stood, his eyes flicking to Eli's cane before he reached out and shook his hand. "Nice to meet you."

Eli smiled and nodded. "Are you in law enforcement as well?"

Bishop shook his head. "I'm a solicitor. Haven't had much experience with dangerous criminals, but it's not beyond the realm of possibility, I guess."

"At least he's not defending the blighters, getting them off," Keith added with a laugh.

Several of the others joined in.

"Good to see you, little man," Shana said, all five-eleven of her leaning in the kitchen doorway, nursing a drink. Her long blonde hair was pulled back in a ponytail, and she watched Eli through amused, yet predatory eyes.

"Shana," Eli said coolly before squeezing Alec's hand and moving a bit closer to him.

Her partner, Lori, reached out and took Shana's hand to remind her that she was sitting nearby and could see Shana openly fantasizing about Eli.

"Keep it in your pants, sweetie," she said with a toss of her short, silky black hair. Despite her diminutive stature, Eli got the sense that she was practiced at keeping Shana in check. "Good to see you again, Eli," Lori said. "It's been a long time."

He nodded and smiled at Lori, but then his eyes went warily to Shana, who was still watching him. To this day, the woman unnerved him. At a party years ago, when she was still with Ilsa, Shana had gotten drunk and cornered him in the kitchen. She seemed to regard Eli as some adorable toy or pet, and she'd grabbed him and kissed him, giving his package a possessive squeeze. Eli shuddered just thinking about it. Bennett had walked in and shut her down, rather forcefully, if he remembered correctly. She and Ilsa had split shortly thereafter, probably more to do with her drinking than with her kink for him.

"Well, now that you're here, Eli, I think I'll take my leave," Tony said as he slid out of his chair and over to the bar, where he mixed himself a drink. "Call if you need me." And with that he headed through the kitchen and out onto the deck.

Eli took a seat, and Alec sat next to him, resting his hand on Eli's thigh. "So what have you all decided?" he asked, giving Alec a smile and covering his hand with his own.

Casey, Keith, Lori, and Lyle launched into a detailed description of the music, food, gifts, and decorations they had planned for the party. Eli smiled at their enthusiasm and chuckled at the bemused expressions on Alec and Bishop's faces as they tried and failed to keep up while the four others ran down the list of preparations. Shana had apparently lost interest and wandered out onto the deck to join Tony. Eli was feeling better about his day, almost hopeful.

When the ideas petered out and the discussion wound down, Casey hurriedly showed Keith, Shana, and their respective partners out. Ilsa would be home soon. Eli took Alec by the hand, and they went into the kitchen. He backed Alec up against the island and kissed him.

"It seems you've had a busy day."

"Yep," Alec said, grinning. "The party should be spectacular." He glanced back into the dining room. "And it was nice meeting others who knew you before I did."

Eli followed his gaze. "You mean Keith?"

Alec nodded. "And Shana and Lori." Eli frowned. "They each used to date Ilsa?"

"At one time or another," Eli said with a chuckle.

Smiling slightly, Alec shook his head in disbelief, and then his expression became guarded.

"Keith… he was there that night… right?"

Eli frowned and nodded. "I only have a vague memory of him before I was loaded into the ambulance." Alec's arms encircled him and tightened, and Eli felt revived. "The next time I saw him was in the hospital, six weeks later." He rested his head against Alec's shoulder, reveling in the feel of him, the scent of him, and closed his eyes. They stood like that for several minutes.

Eli opened his eyes. "I'm sorry about this morning," he said softly.

"It's okay."

It was his turn to tighten his grip on Alec. This comfort felt too good for either of them to end it, but Mirabell had no such qualms.

"Are we ready?" she said, bursting into the kitchen from the deck, with Tony on her heels, laughing.

"This she-devil is wicked!" he said. "Wherever did you find her, and why haven't we met before now?" He slid up to Lyle, who was entering from the dining room, and kissed him automatically. Lyle's hands were filled with folders, papers, and notes of party data, but he shifted them quickly enough to accommodate Tony.

Eli gripped Alec's bottom and whispered, "How about you come to my room for a proper apology?"

"I'd love to... b-but we're all headed back to my new place to take some measurements and make decorating decisions."

He pulled back from Alec abruptly. "You already have it?"

"Yeah," Alec said, smiling nervously. "It's several floors below Tony and Lyle, but it has a similar layout. And it's early enough in the construction for me to customize it to my liking. It's beautiful."

"Not yet, it's not," Mirabell said. "It needs a makeover." She sighed. "I love makeovers." She looked pointedly at Alec and then at Eli. "Let's go, shall we?" She walked by them and out of the kitchen.

"I don't think she likes me," Eli said.

"What's not to like?" Alec squeezed Eli's hand. "Come with us."

"Um, I'm... I'm afraid I'm in for the night." He gave Alec a quick kiss.

"There'll be pizza."

Eli smiled and patted Alec's chest. "I'll see it another time. I promise."

Alec watched him closely, and Eli tried to keep his expression pleasant.

"I'll be back soon," Alec said, pulling him in for a deeper kiss. "I promise."

Chapter 18

ALEC parked his car, switched off the engine, and sighed as he rested his head against the headrest. He looked up at the house, noting the dark sky and bright moon above it. He hadn't meant to be so long at his new place, but the moment he'd unlocked the door, Mirabell and Lyle had rushed in with tape measures, notepads, camera, and swatches flying. Tony had continued up to his apartment and ordered pizza, giving Lyle a call on his cell when it arrived.

They had eaten, discussed, laughed, and argued for hours. Alec found it odd that he had no recollection of asking Mirabell or Lyle to decorate his new place, but he did remember expressing interest in their opinion. Maybe that was all they needed to attack the project so enthusiastically. Tony seemed quite taken with Mirabell, like he'd discovered a younger, more colorful, but equally cynical sister. He and Lyle watched as the two of them discussed art, music, films, and the idiots involved in it all.

Sometime around midnight Alec had glanced at his watch and been reminded of a very warm, firm, welcoming body waiting at home for him. He swore out loud and hustled Mirabell out the door, dropping her off before heading home.

"Come to a full stop next time, ya git!" she'd shouted as he'd driven away, honking his goodbye.

Now here he was sitting outside the house and looking at it with dread. He wanted to rush in and find Eli, tell him about the apartment and his plans for it, share with him how his hand was shaking when he signed the contract, but he wasn't sure how his enthusiasm would be met. He sighed, unbuckled his seatbelt, and climbed out of the car, immediately spotting Ilsa walking up the street.

"Ilsa?"

She glanced at him but kept walking. "Alec."

"Where's your car?" he asked, catching up to her.

"Died on Wardour," she said, not looking at him. "Couldn't get it started again. Towed away. Took the bus."

Alec smiled to himself. "Not very talkative tonight, I see."

"I'm just tired." They headed up the walk side by side, and she glanced at him out of the corner of her eye. "Where are you coming from so late?"

"My new place."

She stopped and looked at him directly. "Already?" He nodded. "You and Eli are leaving already?"

"No... uh, Eli isn't moving out. Just me."

"But...."

"But what?"

She immediately resumed her path to the house with Alec on her heels.

"Nothing," she said, shaking her head and unlocking the door. They both noticed the silence upon entering. Ilsa went to the hall table and dumped her keys in the dish there, but Alec noticed the pale light flickering in the living room.

"Looks like there's been some movie watching, huh?"

Ilsa turned, following his gaze, and then turned back to going through her mail.

"Guess so," she said. He noticed the chill in her voice, but he ignored it.

"I promised Eli I'd be home sooner," he whispered as he quietly entered the living room. He didn't say anything more, but when Ilsa finished, she turned to see where he was and found him standing by the sofa in the darkened room. When they caught each other's eye, he waved her forward silently. She walked in and stood next to him, looking down at two sleeping figures, their faces bathed in the glow from the television.

"Why do I keep coming home to this?" Ilsa asked softly.

Eli and Casey were huddled together, their arms around each other. Ilsa and Alec smiled and then turned simultaneously to look at the wreckage of stress-eating strewn over the coffee table. But as they took in the empty beer bottles, remnants of popcorn, chips, and day-old lasagna, the smiles fell from their faces, and they looked at each other.

"I guess we're pretty hard on them, huh?" Ilsa asked, leaning closer to the pair. She rose back up and whispered to Alec, "Casey looks like she's been crying."

Alec nodded. He leaned over and carefully removed the empty pint of cookie-dough ice cream from Eli's lap, taking care that the two spoons in it didn't rattle. "I think Casey was expecting you home sooner too."

"Yeah, I had something to do," Ilsa said, "and afterward is when my car decided to truly torpedo my evening." She walked around the sofa to take hold of Casey. "Sugar? Casey, wake up."

Casey stirred and then groaned. "I feel horrible," she said as Ilsa's face came into focus. "Where were you?" she whined.

"I had something to do after work, babe," she said as she carefully disentangled her girlfriend from her best friend.

"You mean *someone* to do," Casey said, getting unsteadily to her feet. Ilsa froze, stunned, but shook it off and steered Casey toward the stairs. Alec looked at his sleeping boyfriend and then at Ilsa and Casey. He rushed over and took hold of Casey, swinging her up into his arms. He nodded at Ilsa to lead the way. She smiled gratefully and sprinted up the stairs ahead of them.

They reached her bedroom at the end of the hall, and Alec carried Casey in and put her on the bed.

"My hero," Ilsa whispered as he passed her in the doorway. "Thanks."

"You're welcome." He headed down the hall on his way back to Eli, but he stopped and turned back. "Ilsa?"

She had almost closed her door but stuck her head back out. "Yes?"

"I know it's none of my business, but what *were* you doing tonight?"

She quickly glanced back over her shoulder at Casey and walked out into the hall to join him. "I went to a meeting."

"Meeting?"

"AA."

"Oh, I see." He looked at his feet. "I didn't know you still went to those."

"I go whenever I need to. They're always there to help."

"I didn't mean to upset you with this moving out thing."

"I'm okay, Alec. I know when I need help… I know when to ask for it." They stood in silence for a few moments, until she sighed and leaned back against the wall. "I've been… I've been thinking about my family a lot lately, missing them." She folded her arms across her chest and rubbed her tired eyes. "Especially my little sis."

Alec leaned next to her. "When did you see her last?"

"Right before moving to London. My parents had written me off, but Sissy was struggling."

"How so?"

"You know my father is a Baptist minister. So were his father and grandfather. I grew up surrounded, embraced in faith. Sissy is studying now to join Dad in it, but she loves me. She loves me just as I am."

"And that's a struggle?"

"It is when you've grown up being told one thing and suddenly you discover someone you love is… 'on the express train to hell'." Alec grinned, and Ilsa returned it. "Dad is Southern Baptist. He can be colorful."

"Did you have much of a struggle… with…?"

Ilsa shook her head. "Not much. As I said, I grew up surrounded in the faith, and a big part of those teachings is 'God is love' and that He doesn't make mistakes." She looked Alec in the eyes. "I am not a mistake. Who I love doesn't hurt anyone else, and I am who I'm supposed to be." She sighed. "Unfortunately my parents didn't focus on those messages."

Not knowing what else to say, Alec said, "I'm sorry, Ilsa."

"No, Alec, I'm sorry." She reached out and touched his arm. "I shouldn't have come down on you the way I did Wednesday. I just panicked, felt like another family was unraveling in front of me." She laughed and spread her arms wide. "I suddenly saw myself rattling around this big old place alone."

"Forget it, Ilsa. We'll never leave you alone." He wrapped her up in his arms. "You're stuck with us."

She hugged him tightly. "You'd better get back to Eli. He's liable to have a stiff neck if you don't put him to bed properly."

"I'll see you in the morning."

Alec headed down the hall, but Ilsa called to him before he got too far. "Did you mean what you said about Bennett? About Eli not wanting to leave here because of him?"

He looked at her standing in her doorway for a few moments, not exactly sure what to say.

"It's just a fear, Ilsa."

She glanced over her shoulder at Casey and smiled. "I guess we all have those, eh?"

He nodded and went back downstairs into the living room, but the television was switched off, and Eli wasn't on the sofa. Alec quickly cleaned up the bulk of the mess on the coffee table, taking the empty containers, bowls, and bottles into the kitchen. The rest would have to wait.

He went to Eli's bedroom and found the door wide open. The bedside lamp was askew but on, casting a soft glow over the prone figure lying face down on the bed. He smiled to himself as he approached. Eli had almost succeeded in getting undressed. His T-shirt hung loosely from his left arm. He'd managed to take off one shoe and almost an entire sock, and the waist of his jeans was around his thighs.

Alec sat on the foot of the bed, carefully removing Eli's right shoe and sock and then his left sock before setting the shoes neatly, side by side, under the bed with the socks shoved in them. Then he gently rolled Eli over, pulled the shirt free, and finished pulling off his jeans. He tossed the clothes in the chair at the foot of the bed and undressed himself before climbing in bed and shoving Eli over to his favorite side, rolling him under the covers as he went.

He slid up behind Eli, embracing him and sighing into his hair. Eli mumbled something as he took Alec's hand and held it against his abdomen.

"Hmm?" Alec asked.

"You're late."

Alec grinned as Eli's breathing quickly became even again.

Chapter 19

ELI felt lousy the next morning, but Alec joined him in the shower, and he soon felt fabulous. Over the next few weeks, he simply watched, smiled, and nodded as Alec, Lyle, and Mirabell rushed in and out discussing décor for the new flat. Eli had even gone over to have a look at the place during the repainting, and he was surprised by the amount of space. Alec seemed so happy and excited, so Eli kept his unfocused trepidation in check, but it remained just under the surface, humming and ever-present.

Aside from the painting, Alec was making a couple of other adjustments to the property: darker hardwood floors and a spacious, glassed-in shower with slate tile and a bench. Alec caught Eli eyeing the bench and smiling to himself as the workman installed it.

"What are you thinking about, Mr. Burke?"

"Oh, um… nothing," Eli said. "That's just… that's a fairly deep bench."

"It's a steam shower." Alec grinned at him and pointed to the rain showerhead in the ceiling. "I might like to linger in comfort."

"Fair enough," Eli said with a chuckle. A soft thrill ran through Eli as Alec grabbed him and kissed him, but then he went rigid in Alec's arms, pulling back and glancing nervously at the workmen. But nary an eyebrow had been raised. He looked at Alec, who smiled.

"Many of them are… uh, *family*."

Eli looked sideways at one of the workmen: a large, muscular, blond brute in overalls who winked at Eli, causing him to blush violently.

The routine at the house was essentially unchanged: Ilsa, Alec, and Eli going in and out for work; Tony and Lyle coming by for décor discussions or surreptitious party planning; Casey visiting for some quality Ilsa-time; and now and then—a dash of Mirabell.

As the day of the move drew closer, Eli became restless and agitated, seemingly unable to settle. He noticed and appreciated Alec giving him extra attention, extra affection, and extra time, but it didn't fully dispel his unease. No matter how often Alec stuck to his side when he was home—gazing at him, touching him, talking, laughing, and making love to him—it didn't erase the fact that he was moving out, and in the pit of Eli's stomach it felt like they were moving apart in much more than a physical sense.

"Dray's not going to help, is he?" he asked one night, staring at his ceiling.

"Hmm?" Alec asked sleepily, stroking Eli's hair and nuzzling his neck. They'd made love, and with the way Alec's thigh was restlessly rubbing between Eli's legs, Eli would soon be ready for another round.

"Friday. Is Dray helping you move on Friday?"

Alec raised his head and looked at him. "You're joking."

Eli laughed. "Just curious."

Alec began viciously tickling Eli. "Don't play that with me."

They wrestled around, Eli trying to tame Alec's wicked hands, failing miserably, and finally shrieking.

"Shush!" Alec said. "You'll wake the house."

"S-sorry," Eli said, covering his mouth but unable to stop laughing. He threw his leg around Alec's waist, allowing them to grind deliciously against each other. "If I'm making too much noise, you know how to silence me."

Alec grinned and kissed him, his hands exploring. Eli closed his eyes and concentrated on the feel of Alec's lips on his, tongue against his, hands sliding over his skin. He didn't cringe away anymore when his scars were caressed. He smiled at that realization and wondered if Alec had noticed.

"I was going to hire some guys to help me move," Alec was saying as he kissed and nibbled at Eli's collarbone. "But a couple of my teammates offered to help in exchange for pizza and beer." He sucked Eli's earlobe into his mouth, causing him to gasp and quiver beneath Alec. "But in answer to your question…" Alec said, pausing and looking him in the eye, "which I know had some honesty in it." Eli smiled and looked away. "Dray will not be attending the move."

"Good to know."

"Lincoln might show up, though."

"Lincoln?" he asked as he gripped Alec by the hair and held Alec's mouth against his left nipple.

"Mmmm...." Alec's tongue swirled busily. "He's keeping in touch with his friend Mickey for me... the waiter who froze up at the party."

"You n-never told me—*oh yeah*—why he f-froze—or c-can't you say?"

Alec paused, thinking. "Suffice it to say, he's been... through something and is living in a neighborhood surrounded by people who don't know he's gay." A chill ran through Eli, his playful, sexy energy immediately evaporating. He wondered if Alec sensed it.

He had.

"No, no, babe," Alec said, quickly cupping his face, "he wasn't bashed." Eli grinned uneasily, relaxing again into the feel of Alec on top of him. He was warm, safe, and turned on, so he showed Alec just how good he felt by making sure Alec felt spectacular.

THE night before the move, Alec was delighted to discover a surprise dinner waiting for him. He noted Ilsa had become strangely accepting of the move and had prepared a meal to wish him well. He remembered being welcomed into the house nearly a year before with her home-cooking, and apparently she wanted to send him off the same way, knowing it would be a very long time before he had any more.

As he took his seat, he also noticed that the dishes in front of him were virtually the same items the two of them had ordered when he first came by her restaurant to inquire about renting the attic room. He and Ilsa shared a private smile as Alec recalled how she'd tested her waitstaff by having them practice at serving them.

After a slightly inebriated Tony chased a giggling Lyle out to their car so they could get home and likely tear each other's clothes off, Casey and Ilsa retired to the deck with their coffee and pie while Alec and Eli started on the dishes. But the two of them didn't seem to have much to say to each other beyond working out who would wash and who would dry. As they worked their way through the last few dishes, the uneasy silence reached its most uncomfortable.

"Eli, would you have dinner with me?" Alec asked.

"Just did." Without looking at Alec, he took a plate from him and quickly dried it, placing it on a stack of others to his right.

Alec sighed and turned to look at him. "I know you're worried about this move, but I've been working very hard to show you it's not the end of us." He stepped closer to Eli, invading his space. "Tell me what you're afraid of, please."

Eli looked directly into his eyes. "I'm not afraid—"

Alec closed his eyes and shook his head. "Don't tell me you're not. I can feel it pouring off you." He suddenly grabbed Eli's waist, pulling him closer. "I don't know what else I can do to reassure you." Eli didn't pull away, but Alec could see the inner struggle on his face and wondered what had him so torn. "Talk to me, babe," he whispered, but Eli only smiled weakly. Alec sighed. "Okay, come to my place for dinner, a romantic dinner—just the two of us."

Eli blinked at him, mulling the invitation over and then smiling. "Hmmm... I don't know. Will you be cooking?"

"Haven't really worked all that out yet." Alec leaned in and kissed Eli's neck. "I just want to get you alone and at my mercy."

Eli chuckled and wrapped his arms around Alec, holding him tight against the length of his body.

"So I'll be able to make as much noise as I want?"

"Oh yeah," Alec said, nodding and smiling and gripping Eli's bottom roughly.

"Will you two get a room?" Ilsa asked as she and Casey entered from the deck.

ELI watched Alec wave goodbye—or rather "see ya"—from the driver's seat of the small moving van that contained his chest of drawers and work desk. His bed belonged to Ilsa and had only been lent to him while he lived there, so it remained behind.

Eli waited until the van had disappeared around the corner and then walked back into the house to find Ilsa and perhaps another slice of pie with ice cream. He stopped short, surprised to see her sitting on the stairs watching him. "What?"

"You're going to follow him, aren't you?" she asked softly.

"Ilsa—"

"No, it's okay." She stood up and came down the stairs to meet him. "You love him—don't bother denying it. I know you do." She reached out and straightened his collar. "Just like I know he loves you." She brushed back an unruly lock of hair off his forehead. "I just wish you would say it to each other."

He grinned. "What makes you think we haven't?"

Ilsa smiled. "There's too much fear swirling around each of you, sugar. Alec's afraid you still love Bennett, *maybe* even thinking of him at the most inopportune moments—"

"What?"

"—and you're afraid Alec will find someone better, someone whole and healthier, and cut you loose." She winked. "That fear wouldn't be there if you had said the L-word."

Eli rolled his eyes, suddenly stepped around her, and headed for the kitchen.

"Trust me, Ilsa, 'the L-word' does not end the fear." He paused before entering the kitchen and looked at her. "You, of all people, should know that." Ilsa stopped in her tracks, her mouth open in silent retort, but he simply smiled at her teasingly before disappearing into the kitchen. After a couple of moments, he looked back into the hall at her standing there. "Join me in some pie?" he asked with a grin. Ilsa smiled back and quickly went after him.

EXHAUSTED from moving and trying to get his apartment perfect—or, more accurately, irresistible to Eli—in time for their date next Friday, Alec didn't see him Saturday, but he did give Eli a call.

"What are you wearing?" Alec asked.

He heard Eli chuckle softly. "Most people say hello first."

"Hello, Eli. What are you wearing?"

"Just my sweatpants." He could hear the grin on Eli's lips as he spoke.

"Which ones?"

"The navy."

"I like those. They're practically new, very soft, supple."

"Yeah. They feel good against my skin. And you?"

"Just out of the shower. I'm lying on the bed, wearing a towel."

Eli didn't have a comment about that, but Alec hoped he had painted a vivid enough picture for his boyfriend. He could hear Eli breathing, and then Eli said, "Why don't you pull back that towel a bit and reach underneath?"

"Okay. What am I looking for?"

Eli laughed. "I think you'll know it when you find it."

Staring at the ceiling of his new bedroom, Alec did as he was asked. He took himself in hand and began stroking slowly. "Oh, yes, now I remember."

"You git! It's hardly been two days."

Alec just laughed. "Do something for me?"

"Yes?"

"Touch yourself through those sweats. Press your palm down on yourself."

"Done and d-done. And what is your hand doing, Alec?"

"Uh... g-guess."

"I think you're ahead of me."

"Slide your hand past the waist of those newish blue sweats for me," Alec directed, closing his eyes, stroking himself a bit faster, and imagining his fingers caressing Eli's treasure trail. He'd often thought it shaped like a diamond or sometimes a Christmas tree. He heard Eli's breathing change and knew he was following his directions well. "That's my hand on you. I'm right there, whispering in your ear and touching you." Alec smiled, hearing Eli's breathing catch again.

"Fuck... I've got to get out of these," Eli announced right before Alec heard a lot of frantic movement on the other end of the line, and then a sigh.

"You settled again?"

"Yeah."

"So am I right in assuming you're nude?"

"Utterly starkers."

"Lovely."

Eli's laughter tickled Alec's ear. "Where's that towel?"

"Wide open, babe."

"Bend those knees for me."

"Am I going to need lube?"

"Of some kind, yes… and for both hands."

"Ooh." Alec rummaged in his nightstand drawer without even looking and picked up his tube of lube. "Ready, but you have to match me," he said.

"Fair enough—wait, wait."

"What?"

"Go to speaker."

"Good idea." Alec pushed the button on his phone and then hung up the receiver.

Next they both applied a tiny bit of lube to their cocks—not much was needed with the pre-come already weeping from them—and began stroking slowly. Their breathing became slightly harsher, then each man slicked up the fingers of his other hand and reached around to spread himself and brush a finger against his opening, toying with it, teasing it.

"Yes," Alec sighed. "Like that. Now p-pushing in."

"God, I wish you were here," Eli sighed. "I suspect we're much more graceful about this when we're together."

Alec laughed, imagining the contorted position Eli was speaking from—much like his: knees drawn up, one hand on his cock and the other working at his ass. "I miss you too," he whispered, but Eli didn't say anything. "Eli?"

"*Deeper….*"

Alec's cock twitched, and he pushed in deeper. They didn't speak again, simply lay in the dark, working themselves into a froth, eyes closed, breathing erratic, and listening only to the soft moans, gasps, and whispered names coming from their speakers.

DRIVING to Middlesex on Sunday to support Alec, the group had to endure Tony complaining about the early hour for the entire short trip.

"Much too early to be playing football!" he spouted periodically.

The match was to begin at noon, so he was soundly ignored. Eli sat forward on his seat, eager to see Alec, and Ilsa kept glancing over and smiling at him. Casey wasn't able to attend because of work, but she sent her love and good wishes. Arriving a bit late, they were still able to find an excellent spot on the bleachers, because the match was a friendly competition and didn't count in the rankings. Only the die-hard supporters were there.

The match was exciting, hotly contested with a lot of steals and passing. But Alec didn't come out until late. Announced as "our resident Yank and newest teammate, Alec Sumner," there was a bit of booing, much to Eli's fury. He actually looked around for the offenders. Alec had looked spectacular in his red shirt, white shorts, and black socks—noticeably cleaner than his teammates, a proper player—and Eli felt pride swell in his chest and the stirrings of arousal in his gut as he watched his boyfriend trot out onto the field.

They watched and cheered as Alec and his teammates took the ball up the field, then they groaned collectively when the goal was denied. That scenario repeated itself three more times but, by some miracle, Alec's team came away victorious by one goal. They were thrilled, as were their supporters. Their next stop was a local pub for celebratory drinks and good-natured arguments about the match.

Ilsa begged off. "I want to be home when Casey gets off."

"Aren't you always?" Tony asked wickedly, and she tried to swat him as the rest of them laughed.

"I'll see they all get home safely, Ilsa," Lyle said. "Drink up, Alec." He dangled Alec's car keys in front of his face. "I've got you covered."

Shocked, Alec quickly checked his jacket pockets. "How did you get—?"

"I gave them to him," Eli said with a grin before signaling the bartender for two pints.

"Coming, Tony?" Ilsa asked. "You've been whining all day. I figured you'd appreciate a ride home." But Tony was staring around the pub at all the sweaty, fit men as they talked loudly, drank, laughed, hugged, and slapped each other on the back—and the bum.

"Uh…."

"Tony, are you coming?"

"Quite nearly," he mumbled, unable to tear his eyes away. Lyle pinched his ass, and Tony yelped, then turned a bright red. "Sorry," he said as he moved to Lyle's side with a guilty grin. "I'd better head home, yeah?"

"Yeah. I'll see you later," Lyle said, looking into Tony's eyes, gently cupping his face, stroking his eyebrow with his thumb, and kissing him goodbye. "Get some rest. You're going to need it." Tony was smiling from ear to ear as Ilsa pulled him out of the pub by the collar—but now it was Lyle he couldn't take his eyes off of.

"Who's this, Yank?"

"Oh, uh… this is my boyfriend, Eli… Eli Burke," Alec said to the tall, brutishly handsome man who had sidled up to him. His head was covered in tight, blond curls. "Eli, this is Conley."

The man grabbed and shook Eli's hand, in fact, his entire arm forcefully. "Just Conley?"

"Just Conley, mate." He hadn't released Eli's hand yet, and his green eyes sparkled as he grinned at him.

"Conley, you can let his hand go, now," Alec said.

"Oh, sorry." He laughed. "I wasn't comin' on to ya."

"Yes, you were," Alec said.

Conley smiled again. "Yeah, I was." He laughed and winked at Eli. "But no worries, right? I'm here with my current."

Alec seemed surprised. "Is this the guy you told us about?"

"Yep," Conley said, looking around the room. "Although I don't see him at the moment." He turned back to them and shrugged. "So what do you do, Eli?"

"I interpret for the deaf."

"Awesome!"

"Oh?"

"Yeah. I dated a deaf guy a couple of years back." Conley's eyes glazed over. "He was dreamy."

"Did you learn the language?" Alec asked.

"I learned to fingerspell."

"I still can't get it."

"You're doing fine," Eli said, rubbing Alec's back gently.

"Eli knows BSL *and* ASL," Alec said proudly, and Eli grinned.

"Ooh, a bloke with a big brain."

"Two blokes with big brains," Dray said as he strolled up to them carrying two pints.

"There you are, love," Conley said. Kissing Dray, he grabbed one of the beers with one hand and Dray's ass with the other.

Eli and Alec were rendered momentarily speechless.

"Two pints," the bartender announced, setting the drinks on the bar in front of them. Dray and Conley watched them as Eli and Alec remained frozen in place.

"Your drinks?" Conley asked, looking pointedly at the bar behind them.

Alec snapped out of it first. "Oh, sorry," he said, turning to the bartender. "How much?"

"They're paid for, mate," he said, nodding toward Dray.

Eli hadn't taken his eyes off Dray. "What the fuck are you doing here?" he asked.

"I'm thinking about joining their social club," Dray said with an easy smile, punctuating it with a long, lingering kiss for Conley. "I should support my favorite Kestrel, yeah?" Dray asked, looking pointedly at Alec as he nibbled Conley's ear.

"Yeah," Conley said breathlessly, turning to Alec and Eli. "He came to see my first match about a week ago and decided to… uh, lend a hand."

"A week ago?" Eli asked, turning to Alec.

"I didn't see him," Alec said, lifting his hands in surrender.

"Is there a problem?" Conley asked, looking into each of their faces. In Alec's he saw confusion, in Dray's: amusement, and in Eli's: rage.

Alec looked around the room for Lyle. "I think we'll be heading out," he said as he caught Lyle's eye. He appeared to be discussing a recipe with one of the wives, but he acknowledged Alec.

"Oh, no need to go," Dray said amicably. "Conley and I will just go snog in the corner. How's that?"

Alec glanced at Eli, then back at Dray. "We're heading out. Have a good night."

Dray smiled as he watched them leave.

Eli was very quiet on the ride home. He was afraid to speak, of what he might say to Alec. He knew Dray being there wasn't something Alec did.

"Not in a talkative mood, I see," Alec said from the back seat.

"I'm not angry with you," Eli said, turning around in his seat to look at him. "It was a great day, and I'm trying to focus on that, and not...." He turned away, looking out the window.

"On how much you loathe Dray?" Eli smiled, but Alec couldn't see it. "I wish you'd tell me the whole story," Alec mumbled.

Eli whirled on him. "What? *You* know the story!"

"Uh, guys," Lyle said, "I'd really rather not be in such close proximity to you during this discussion."

Alec shook his head and sighed. "I'm not stupid, Eli, and I know you pretty well, I think."

"Meaning what?"

"Meaning I think your hatred of Dray is out of proportion to what he's done."

"I could get out and walk?" Lyle offered.

"He tried and failed with Bennett," Alec continued. "He's tried and failed with me. His continued attempts are more pathetic than anything else. Certainly not threatening." Alec took a deep, thoughtful breath. "I'd actually be interested in learning what makes him tick."

Eli turned away from Alec and focused on the road ahead. "Great! That's all we need: a case study of Dray Jenkins." He didn't say another word.

Chapter 20

ALEC welcomed the lusty hunger in Eli's eyes as he advanced, gently pushing Alec backward until he dropped onto the bench. With no cane in the shower, he held Eli's hand to steady him as he came closer. All the kissing, hot water, rubbing, soaping, and rinsing had them both achingly hard. Eli carefully straddled his lap on the deep bench, their cocks brushing against each other briefly as Eli positioned himself. This, more than relaxing during a steam, was more what Alec had in mind when he'd ordered the custom job.

His tongue slid past Eli's lips as his hands slid over Eli's skin, reveling in the firm muscle beneath. Eli was slight but much more powerful than he appeared, and Alec squeezed and massaged the lean muscle in Eli's thighs and licked the center of his chest where the water had darkened the hair there, creating an apparent arrow pointing straight to Eli's cock. Alec smiled as it bumped and brushed against his abdomen. Suddenly Eli's fingers tangled painfully in his hair, jerking his head back so Eli could smile wickedly down at him—his blue eyes flashing—as Alec gripped Eli's ass and guided him onto his cock.

"Sir?"

"Mr. Sumner?"

"Huh?" Alec blinked several times at the students standing in his doorway watching him curiously. "Uh... yes, what can I do for you?" he asked.

"We have a couple of questions about this paper you've assigned."

"Oh, yes, yes. Please come in." Alec shook his head to clear it, remembered he had papers in his hands, if not what they were for, and donned his glasses as the three students filed in hurriedly. His reading glasses helped him better examine what the students were presenting, but more importantly, they allowed him to hide behind his professor face, a face he had not been wearing seconds earlier. He shuddered to think what expression he'd had as he imagined fucking Eli in his new shower.

Their disagreement—*yes, that's what it was*—on the way back from the match had cooled any hopes of intimacy for the evening, and Alec had simply returned to his place, alone and confused. He hadn't seen Eli for days, and it was wearing on him. During the following week, their time on the phone before bed wasn't nearly enough, and he was already tired of pretending. Alec wanted to *feel* Eli, smell him, hear him, taste him, fuck him, but more than anything, hold him. He felt a distance growing between them and didn't know how to close it. *I don't regret moving out. I don't.* He laughed to himself. *I'm afraid of the distance, but I'm afraid of needing him, of missing him so much. Mental note: seek therapy.*

He suspected this first week apart had been an anomaly. Surely it wouldn't normally be this difficult to arrange some time together. With Eli's sign language certification and Alec's course work and perfectionist snit over the new apartment, they had not enjoyed each other's company for nearly seven days. Nevertheless, he was pleased he had worked out his dinner plans, and the apartment would be ready in time for their date tomorrow.

He couldn't deny that in the back of his mind he was hoping Eli would be so impressed with the place and the evening Alec had planned, he'd want to move right in. But Alec also kept telling himself that probably wouldn't happen. His head was beginning to hurt swinging between his dreams and his reality.

"Sir?"

"S-sorry, Dody," Alec said, refocusing on his notes. "Which point are you concerned about?" The sooner he could get his hands on Eli, the better. That contact settled him, settled his mind and his fears.

Once the questions were answered and the students had filed back out, Alec was alone for exactly three minutes before another knock sounded at his office door.

"Come in."

"Cheers!"

"Lincoln?" Alec stood up and shook the young man's hand. "What are you doing here?"

"Sorry I missed your move."

"No problem. We had plenty of help. How are you?"

"I'm good, thanks." He took the seat Alec offered. "I tracked you down from that card you left me. Wanted to let you know Mickey might be comin' back to London."

"That's wonderful."

"Yeah, he's clawin' the paint off the walls back home." Lincoln chuckled nervously, but then he grew quiet—quiet and fidgety. He wouldn't meet Alec's eye.

"Aren't you happy about his return?"

"He… he still doesn't talk about what happened."

"That takes time, I'm afraid, but I think returning to London is a good start. He needs to be somewhere he can be himself."

Lincoln nodded thoughtfully. "I know." He sighed. "I just hate that he was just beginnin' here, beginnin' to be himself, and then *that* happened."

"He was raped, Lincoln. You can say it."

Lincoln finally faced Alec directly. "What if I can't help him or… say the wrong thing?"

"Just be his friend. Be ready to listen when he's ready to talk."

Lincoln stood awkwardly, hovering in the doorway as if he might bolt at any second. His unease and fear were apparent. "I don't know if I'm what he needs." Lincoln hugged himself. "I don't know if I'm good enough. I don't want to mess him up more."

"Lincoln, I'm here for you both. You know that, right?"

Lincoln nodded. "He remembers you, ya know. He's grateful."

"I'm glad I could help.

"And… and Mum says hi." Alec grinned broadly. "She wants to know if you're still seeing someone."

"Uh… yeah. Yes I am, actually. Same guy."

"Good on you, but she'll be disappointed. She'd like to see me with a doctor."

"Forgive me, but I got the impression you had feelings for Mickey."

Lincoln turned several shades of pink in quick succession, and Alec grinned.

"Oh, well… he and I… we just grew up together. That's all."

Alec leaned forward. "I have two very good friends who have known each other since they were kids, and they're a couple now." Lincoln grinned weakly, never turning fully toward Alec. "I'll send you an invitation to a surprise party we're having for a friend, and you can meet them. Okay?"

"That would be great."

"Hopefully Mickey will be your 'plus one'."

"Fingers crossed," Lincoln said, absently tracing Alec's name on the glass in his office door.

Alec got up and went to him. "Caring for someone who's been traumatized obviously isn't simple," he said, gently placing his hand on Lincoln's shoulder. "You second-guess yourself. You're terrified of making a mistake, maybe making things worse." Lincoln looked up into Alec's face. "But it's important to remember that it takes time. There will be setbacks, but trust in your love for the man, and he'll come to trust in it too."

Lincoln finally smiled and seemed to relax. He thanked Alec, and they shook hands before he left the office. Alec went back to his desk, reflecting on what he'd just told the young man, and his gaze settled on a recently framed picture of him and Eli.

Back in January all the housemates and Casey had attended a small benefit for Gay's the Word. The gay and lesbian bookshop had survived some heavy threats since opening in 1979, not the least of which was the ever-present financial struggle that all independent bookstores had to deal with. Lyle had been passionate about helping out because the store had been a safe, welcoming place for him when he first arrived in London. Tony had donated a painting for auction, and Ilsa had provided the refreshments.

The artist, as always, had been snapping pictures, and this one had caught Alec's eye. In it he was embracing a laughing Eli from behind as they stood by a shelf of books. Alec remembered clearly that he'd been watching Eli during the event as he meandered throughout the store, strolling up and down the narrow aisles, stopping to chat with someone, or pausing to look at a book.

Alec had slowly made his way over to him, coming up behind him as he stood, engrossed in the back cover of a novel. He had embraced Eli suddenly, startling him and sending him into a fit of laughter. Just then, Tony had appeared and shouted at them to look his way, then snapped the picture. So here they were, forever frozen together in a moment of joy and intimacy.

Alec sighed, tracing Eli's image with his finger. "And he'll come to trust in it too."

Chapter 21

"WHICH one?"

Ilsa sat on Eli's bed flipping through a magazine. "Which what?—Oooh!" she said, a recipe catching her eye. "That looks tasty." She carefully tore the page from the magazine and laid it on the bed next to her.

"Tie... Ilsa, which tie?"

She looked up to see Eli holding a dark gray tie and a navy tie. As he took turns holding each just under his chin for comparison, she saw a lot going on in his eyes: he was eager, excited, nervous, and afraid, but she also saw hope there. All of that couldn't possibly hinge on which tie he chose.

"Have you chosen a jacket yet?" she asked. He indicated the navy jacket hanging on the back of the bedroom door. "Then definitely the gun-metal gray one. It's lovely." Her eyes returned immediately to the magazine.

"And it's the one *you* bought me," he said. Ilsa smiled to herself as he quickly flipped up his collar, moved to the mirror hanging inside his closet door, and began tying his tie. "I don't know. Maybe I should go with the white shirt," he said, glancing at her in the mirror, "or maybe the light gray one."

"Nope. The blue shirt sets off your eyes." She met his gaze in the mirror. "And we all know how much Alec *loves* your eyes."

"YOU don't think my hair is too short?"

Enjoying a cigarette on the balcony, Mirabell glanced into Alec's bedroom, where he was running his fingers through his newly trimmed hair. "It's not too short, love. There's still plenty for him to grab hold of."

She was dressed head-to-toe in sunshine yellow: hair ribbon in her shocking red hair, a simple, sleeveless shell dress, stockings, and shoes. She resembled a petite—or organic—banana enjoying the night air from Alec's bedroom balcony. He tugged on his hair, trying to get it to lie right as he looked in the mirror. Mirabell watched him fuss for a few moments.

"Perhaps if you concentrate hard enough it will grow back before he gets here," she said, taking another disinterested puff from her cigarette.

"Mr. Sumner?" someone shouted from the kitchen.

"Yeah?"

"Dinner's ready."

Struggling into his shirt and nearly walking into a wall, Alec rushed into the kitchen. "Thank you, Jacob."

"You're sure you don't want me to stay and serve?"

"No, no, I can handle that. Thanks."

"Okay. The chicken is out of the oven, here," Jacob said, indicating a pan on the top of the stove. "I've covered it to keep it moist until it's served." Alec nodded. "Now the rice should be turned off and drained in exactly"—he glanced at the clock—"eight minutes. Got that?" Alec nodded again, and Jacob sighed heavily. Alec was sure the man didn't believe he could handle it. "The vegetables are grilled and wrapped in foil under the lid with the chicken."

"Got it, Jacob. Thank you so much for your help."

"Hang on, I haven't explained the sauce yet."

"Yes, you have. It's just there," Alec said pointing to the small white container sitting in the center of the stove top. "You told me earlier that it goes in the microwave for ten seconds on high before pouring it over the chicken."

Jacob smiled, suspiciously impressed. "Very good." He gathered his things and headed for the door. "Best of luck with everything."

"Thank you." Alec walked him to the door, and once Jacob had gone, he returned to the kitchen and stood staring at the rice on the stove. He periodically checked the clock above the sink. "Mira!"

"Yes?"

"Could you grab two white candles from this drawer on my left?"

Mirabell strolled into the kitchen at a pace that made Alec want to scream.

"Where?" she asked. He hit the drawer with his knee and then removed the rice from the burner and took it to the sink to drain. "Why go to all this trouble?" She found the candles and stood there holding one in each hand, her cigarette hanging from her lips as she spoke. "You're acting like you've never tasted each other's candy, like it's a first date." She turned and headed back into the living room.

"It's our first date since I moved out. It's special, or at least I want it to be."

She didn't respond, and he poked his head out of the kitchen. He watched her place the candles in their holders on the table he'd set earlier, then light them. He was thankful she wasn't using her cigarette.

"Things have been a bit strained, and we've both been busy—classes, clients, certification, students, and even some friends are conspiring against us, it seems."

She flicked her lighter closed. "Expecting him to spend the night, huh?" she asked smiling wickedly.

"Hoping. It'll be his first time staying over."

"Well, as long as you've remembered the lube, you're golden, my dear."

"Thanks, Mira."

The dinner was all set, candles lit, Alec clean and pressed, and *yes*, he had remembered the lube.

"Your silence tells me our conversation is at an end, and I'd better get my arse outta here before your *luvah* arrives."

Alec laughed out loud and helped her into a jacket so deep purple that he could almost taste the grape.

ILSA waved to Eli as the taxi pulled away and then went back into the house and closed the door. She leaned against it and listened to the silence around her. Casey was working all night at the hospital. Everyone else had moved out. And Eli was probably gone for the night on his date with Alec. There was no one to cook for, no one to talk to, no one to fight with; it was unnatural and uncomfortable. *Too much empty space now.*

She ticked it off in her head: *attic room with bath, two bedrooms and a bath on the floor below that, bedroom with bath on the main floor, big kitchen, dining room, living room, large backyard, and a deck. All that and just me.* She still had Eli, but she didn't honestly expect him to stay much longer, not with Alec in a brand new apartment. He'd more than likely follow his heart.

She sighed and headed for the kitchen, the place where she usually found solutions to problems. She flicked on the kitchen light and retrieved her recipe scrapbook from the island drawer. Pulling up a stool and using a hair tie from her pocket to hold her hair back, she laid the book open and began slowly flipping through the pages in search of something new to cook.

There were recipe clippings from magazines pasted to blank sheets of paper, quickly jotted notes, ingredient lists, and playful recipe titles scribbled in the margins. Ilsa remembered the recipe she'd discovered while Eli was getting dressed and fished it out of her pocket. She smoothed it out on a page and dug out some glue from the island drawer to secure it into place.

There was a colorful array of fingerprints on every page, left there from any number of sauces, greases, flours, eggs, icings, cheeses, and cake batters she'd had on her hands over the years. She paused in her search and listened, but there was only the ticking of the clock and the hum of the icebox.

None of her recipes were catching her eye. She folded her arms over the book and rested her head on her hands. She could nap right here and no one would be the wiser. Why? *Because no one else is here.* Her insides felt hollow—nope, there was a quiver of fear alive and well inside. She glanced up at the phone and considered calling her sister, but she thought better of it. She didn't want to risk her mother answering.

Ilsa had walked away from her own family because they wouldn't accept her as she was. After meeting and befriending Bennett, her alternative clan grew quickly to embrace Eli, Tony, and Lyle. But then they'd lost Bennett—and effectively Eli. Lyle dealt with it by taking care of everyone else, Tony by painting relentlessly, and Ilsa by working extra hours and bedding every woman, and occasional man, she could get her hands on.

Then Alec came into their lives and things shifted again. When the light came back into Eli's eyes, she'd been hopeful—hopeful that despite the loss of Bennett, her family could move on and be happy together. Now she'd lost Tony and Lyle just as they found each other. Alec had moved out, and Eli was close behind. Maybe she could ask Casey to move in. *Come live with me so I won't be lonely.* Would she do that? It's not very romantic. *Are we ready for that?*

The phone rang, startling her. She stood, leaned over, grabbed the receiver, and put her head right back on top of her recipe book.

"Hello?"

"Hey, babe."

"Casey? I thought you were working all night. Where are you?"

"I'm on a break. I was just thinking of you and thought I'd ring you up."

Ilsa smiled. "I'm glad you called." She laughed nervously, ashamed. "I was starting to feel sorry for myself."

"Why, sweetie?"

"The house is empty, and I guess I was feeling a bit forgotten."

The silence on the other end worried her, but then Casey finally spoke.

"You are unforgettable, Ilsa."

Ilsa lifted her head and smiled. *Yeah, we're ready for that.*

Chapter 22

ELI tried to calm his heart as he waited for Alec to open the door. He felt ridiculous being this nervous about a dinner date, but he couldn't settle himself. He'd abandoned the idea of a tie and changed his clothes several times before choosing a simple blue jumper and dark jeans. Then he had to decide what to bring: flowers, wine, dessert? He knew he should bring something other than himself and his needs—or his fears.

The door opened and there was Alec, looking fantastic and chasing all previous concerns from his head.

"Come in," Alec said, stepping back to allow him to pass. The first thing he noticed as he brushed past his boyfriend was Alec's familiar and much-missed scent. Then the aroma of dinner overtook him, and he grinned, opening his mouth to comment on it, but suddenly he found himself silenced by Alec's kiss and dizzied by a full-body embrace.

"God, I've missed this, missed you like this," Alec groaned against Eli's ear as his lips made their way to his neck.

Eli nearly dropped the bottle of Chardonnay he'd brought, but he tightened his grip on the bottle's neck just as his knees threatened to give way under Alec's onslaught. "I... I brought wine," he gasped out between kisses.

"Uh-huh." Alec kissed him deeply again, their tongues sliding over each other, and Eli gave up, throwing his arms around Alec's neck. He bumped him softly on the back of his head with the bottle and the handle of his cane as he returned the kiss enthusiastically.

"Oh, sorry."

Alec drew back. "No problem," he said, taking the bottle from Eli and setting it on the bar by the door. Then he got back to manhandling him. Alec backed him up against the bar and began rubbing him through his jeans.

Eli grunted and gripped Alec by the back of his head. "Hey," he said, pausing and searching Alec's face, "you've cut your hair!"

Alec smiled. "Just a bit. More of a trim, really." They looked into each other's eyes, Eli reaching up to comb his fingers through Alec's hair and brushing a lock off his forehead.

"It looks good," Eli said softly.

Alec smiled and inclined his head slightly to the left. Eli followed the movement and was clearly delighted by the spectacle staged in front of the large windows that looked out over London. The room had been arranged to make space for the table. It was set beautifully with two simple, armless chairs, a burgundy tablecloth, and two white candles, glowing as they stood sentry over a collection of simple, elegant china. Eli slipped free of Alec and slowly made his way across the room, unable to tear the smile from his face.

"Have a seat, and I'll be right with you," Alec said. Eli sat, gazing at the table and then out the window. He unfolded his napkin and spread it on his lap. Somewhere in the room, soft music began to play, and then Alec was there, bearing plates filled with the most wonderfully aromatic meal Eli could remember. And that was saying something, considering he lived with a chef.

Alec set the plates down in their proper places. "Just a sec," he said, disappearing again. Eli looked over his meal, eager to have a taste. He glanced at the bar in time to see Alec work the cork of the wine loose with a muted *pop*, then Alec dimmed the lights, grabbed the bottle, and joined him at the table.

Eli watched him pour them each a glass of wine. "You went to a lot of trouble," he said.

"You're worth it."

Eli grinned and sipped his wine, and Alec did the same, gazing at him over his glass. But when they put their glasses down, an uncomfortable silence fell. And as it stretched out between them, Eli began to fidget, his eyes searching for something to light on other than Alec's handsome, yet equally befuddled face. This unfamiliar awkwardness was so different from their passionate greeting.

It had only been a week. A man didn't forget how to talk to his lover in seven days, and he and Alec always had plenty to talk about. *Plenty to fight about lately.* Maybe that was it. Maybe the things they had to talk about, needed to talk about, were too difficult and likely to ruin a carefully planned and potentially lovely evening together. The candles were no longer romantically warming their intimate space, but instead casting disturbing, chaotic shadows between them.

"Let's dig in, shall we?" Alec said finally.

Eli sighed happily and began to eat. It was delicious, which gave them something safe to discuss. "Did you make all this yourself?"

Alec laughed. "No. Jacob did, from Catering Jake? He did Tony and Lyle's party."

Eli nodded. "The chicken's so tender and moist." *Okay, that's too safe.* "Is that the only help you had for all this?"

"Nope. Mirabell was here."

"I thought I saw some tiny, yellow legs climbing into a car as I pulled up."

Alec chuckled. "Yep, that was her. She trimmed my hair for me, helped me pick out what to wear, and... oh, she lit these," he said, indicating the candles.

"I nearly drove Ilsa nuts getting ready tonight."

"How is she, by the way?"

"Better, I think. Although lately she seems... I don't know... lonely?"

"Even with Casey?"

Eli shook his head as he quickly finished off another bite of the chicken. "I think she's afraid of Casey, afraid to be in love. In fact, we had a short discussion about love and fear the other day."

"I can understand that."

"Really?" he asked, pausing to look closely at Alec. "To be in love is to be afraid?"

"Ultimately what people fear isn't love, it's the possibility of pain that comes from the vulnerability." They stared silently at one another for a moment. "You were afraid of me moving out." He began to protest, but Alec raised his hand to quiet him. "I understand it, Eli. You were nervous about what the change would do to us, to us as a couple."

"You have to admit there were some dodgy moments just now."

"I don't consider a lull in the conversation a disaster."

They both laughed. "What about you?" Eli asked.

"What about me?"

"Why the sudden urge to move? It can't just be about me avoiding the stairs."

Alec appeared caught off guard with that question. He drained his glass and poured a bit more wine into it, offering the same to Eli, who declined.

"What did Ilsa tell you?"

"She said you were afraid I was still hung up on Bennett, that maybe—because I don't always look at—maybe I was even thinking of him when we were—"

"I *never* said that."

"Once I thought it through, I didn't think you had, but her sauces are not the only things our friend embellishes. She can also extrapolate like nobody's business." Alec didn't know what to say to that. "It must have shown on your face at some point," Eli finished softly.

Alec nodded, and Eli reached for the wine bottle, filling his glass halfway. He stared at the wine, swirling it around in his glass, smiling as it caught the light from the candles. Then he took a sip and looked at Alec. "Do you remember the night we made love for the first time?"

"Of course."

"You found me crying in your shower." Alec nodded. "Why did you think I was crying?"

Alec thought about it, trying to remember what had been going through his mind as he comforted Eli. "I figured you were... it was very emotional. I was the first man you'd been with since his death." Alec sighed and shifted nervously in his seat. "I thought you were missing him."

Eli shook his head. "That was the night I stopped thinking of Bennett as my lover, and I was torn between mourning and joy." He reached out and brushed Alec's fingers with his own but cast his gaze down.

"Eli, look at me," Alec said. "Please look—"

"And you need to understand something about why it's difficult for me to look at you when we're making love." Eli's gaze came back up to meet Alec's, his eyes fiercely blue. "I am *not* thinking of Bennett or imagining you're him."

Alec nodded and watched his boyfriend struggle to articulate what he was feeling.

"It has a lot to do with that vulnerability you mentioned before," Eli continued. "You know my scars aren't too much of an issue for me anymore, but the way you *look* at me... at times... it's like you can see straight to my core, and maybe there are things about me I don't want you to see." Alec tried to cut in, but he headed him off. "The idea that someday—or some night—you might look at me and see that I'm not the man you want or need, not the man you think I am... Alec, that terrifies me."

"Why would I ever think that?"

"I just don't want to be looking at you when you realize it." The silence began to stretch between them again, so Alec changed the subject.

"After dinner, I'll give you a tour of the place," he said. "You saw some of it in transition, but now that it's complete, I'm really happy with it."

"I'd like that," Eli whispered, then more forcefully, "I'm especially interested in seeing that shower." He didn't know what he'd said wrong, but even in the candlelight, he could see Alec's gray eyes go wide and dilate drastically.

"I REALLY like the cabinets. Simple, functional, but the frosted glass fronts give them a little punch."

"You sound like Lyle," Alec said, smiling. "It's funny, but after it was completed, I was standing here in the middle of this room, looking around, and suddenly realized how much it reminded me of Ilsa's kitchen."

"I wasn't going to say anything," Eli said, grinning crookedly. He ran his fingers over the black granite on the island and noticed Alec following his fingers with his eyes. "It's much more modern, though."

"This was the lower, middle-end option. Decent surfaces, but, for example, the island is smaller than in Tony and Lyle's kitchen, and there's less counter space."

Drawing his fingers slowly over the cool brushed nickel of the faucet and smiling as Alec watched intently, Eli said, "Well, those two are more the big, dinner-party types, what with the artistic community and antique hounds to entertain."

"True, true." Alec nodded. "I can think of only a few people I'd like to have over."

They looked at each other and smiled. "What else do you have to show me?"

"Uh... okay, you've seen the living room—the table is normally in here, of course, so you'd have to imagine that." Eli nodded. "The kitchen—I guess that leaves the bedroom."

Eli smiled and glanced at the entry to the living room, waiting for Alec to lead the way. He did, but Eli could see he was nervous about something. They crossed back through the living room, heading for a darkened hallway. Just beyond the bar was a closet. On their left, Alec opened a door to a small room.

"This will be the guest room and office," he said, flicking on the light briefly. Eli spotted the old chest of drawers and work desk from Alec's room at Ilsa's. Alec turned off the light and they walked a bit farther, pausing at another door. "This is the guest bathroom." Eli stepped forward and scanned the tasteful, simple interior. "Mira wanted to paint it orange and green, but I shut her down."

"Thank goodness for that," Eli said.

"Yeah, you'd think her place would look like a carnival," Alec said, "but it's really rather sedate."

They continued to the end of the hall, and Alec opened the door to his master bedroom. Eli's insides fluttered a bit in anticipation, and it wasn't because of the décor. A few lights were already on, casting a warm glow around the room. It was large with an impressive bed and dark, modern furniture. Eli stepped deeper into the room, trying to take it all in. He turned slowly and smiled at Alec.

"What do you think?"

"Alec, it's... it's beautiful." Eli reached out and stroked the comforter on the bed, surreptitiously pressing down to gauge the firmness of the mattress.

Alec stepped up behind him. "Can't think of anything you'd change?"

"Me? It's not my—" Eli felt Alec hesitantly touch his shoulder.

"I've missed you." Alec slowly slid his arm around Eli's waist and hugged him back against his body. He pressed his lips to Eli's ear. "I know it's only been a week, but it's been tough not having you at hand."

Before he could stop himself, Eli said, "You're the one who moved out."

He felt Alec immediately tense, but he couldn't take it back, so he closed his eyes and breathed deeply, waiting for Alec to say something. *Please say something. Forgive me. Pretend you didn't hear.* Eli could feel Alec's arousal pressing against his bottom, and his gut quivered with need. He quickly covered Alec's hand with his own, holding it against his abdomen in silent apology, and after a few seconds, he felt the tension leave Alec's body. They both sighed.

"It *could* be our bedroom," Alec whispered in his ear. "We could easily move the bed against the wall, the way you like it."

Eli smiled at the suggestion and the warmth of Alec's breath against his skin. But as he struggled to remain lucid, Alec's hands slid beneath his jumper, caressing his back, slipping around to his chest, and sending his thoughts spinning. With his lips and teeth, Alec worked on Eli's neck, one hand teasing his nipples, the other pressing backward, holding him in place as Alec rubbed himself against Eli's bottom.

Eli gasped. *God, I missed this.* His head spun. He could hear and feel the blood pounding in his ears, which was strange because he was convinced most of it resided farther south at the moment.

"I... I can't think like this. I... c-can't—"

"You can think after," Alec growled as he withdrew his busy hands, grabbed Eli's cane, tossing it on the bed, and removed his pullover in one fluid effort. Suddenly Eli was bare-chested, spun around to face Alec, and being backed toward the bed, hair wild, eyes wide, and panting. They fell together, Alec on top, his lips taking Eli's, a thumb insistently brushing over a nipple, and the other hand unbuckling Eli's belt.

"How… how m-many hands do you have?"

Alec laughed, pausing to look in Eli's eyes. "I want to taste you," he moaned, shifting on the bed again, moving them farther up toward the headboard. Eli heard his cane fall to the floor with a thud. That's fine, he thought as he lay his head back on the pillow and stared at the ceiling. *I'm not going anywhere.* He felt Alec's breath on his cock just before it was engulfed by his warm, wet mouth.

Chapter 23

OPENING his eyes was the last thing he did. First Eli stretched, arching his back against the mattress, feeling the tension and release vibrate from one end of his body to the other. Good God, but he felt fantastic—exhausted and fantastic. He slowly became aware of his perfect place between the sheets, sliding his legs and arms across them, welcoming the luxurious feel of them against his skin, relishing the weight of the comforter on top of him. His arm brushed over the cooler, left side of the bed, and he knew Alec wasn't next to him, but still he didn't open his eyes.

He simply rolled over and buried his face in Alec's pillow, embracing it and breathing in his scent. He pressed his satisfied penis into the mattress, hardly believing it was stiffening again as he recalled Alec's lips around it. He remembered the feel of Alec filling him, stretching him. He flexed his inner muscles, felt that ache, and smiled.

Next he allowed his ears to reach out. He didn't hear the shower running, but he heard noises from the next room, or maybe the kitchen, faint and distant. And then the aroma of coffee reached him. His eyes came open then and found the room dim, muted light sneaking through the drawn curtains. Eli rolled over again and looked at the curtains. They'd been open to the night sky when Alec had taken him, the French doors slightly open, allowing a breeze to blow in from the balcony, across the bed and their naked, sweaty bodies.

He smiled and laughed a bit as he remembered how loud he'd been when he came, and how loud he'd been during the twenty minutes before that. Had they heard him on the street below? Had they figured out what he was doing or what was being done to him? Later, after a nap, they'd made love again, less hurried but just as passionate and the ending just as happy. Now he could smell a proper fry-up—or Alec's version of one—and he realized he was starving. He sat up in bed and looked around the room. He could get used to this.

"Coffee?" Alec asked, appearing in the doorway wearing a T-shirt, pajama bottoms, and slippers, and bearing a mug with steam rising out of it.

Eli nodded. "Yes, please," he croaked, then cleared his throat. Alec sat on the edge of the bed and passed the mug to him. Eli took a sip and sighed. Then, self-consciously, his hand went to his hair, which was, as he suspected, truly fucked. He smiled. *Just like me.*

"How'd you sleep?" Alec asked, reaching out and stroking his bare arm.

"Don't remember sleeping." Eli leaned forward and kissed Alec. "I just passed out. How about yourself?"

"Much the same. You wore me out, Mr. Burke."

"Sorry," Eli said, taking another sip and giving Alec a wicked smile. He was not sorry.

"No need to apologize. That kind of exhaustion I'll always welcome."

They kissed again, this time lingering and unwieldy, Eli rising up on his knees and almost spilling the coffee. They broke apart, laughing.

"Here," Alec said, laughing and reaching for the mug, "let me take that. Hungry?"

"Very. Where are my clothes?" Eli looked around the room.

Alec was already at the door. "They're in the chair, there, but I thought we might lounge around some, watching movies, eating, drinking—making love?" Eli smiled. "You'll find some sweats and T-shirts in that dresser, there, and your cane is—" Alec pointed to the nightstand on Eli's side of the bed.

"Thanks. I'll just pop in the loo and join you at the table." Alec nodded and disappeared. Eli slid out of bed, grabbed his walking stick, and approached the bathroom door, the bulk of which was frosted glass. He slid aside the pocket door and stepped over the threshold into an elegant space. As he remembered from his previous visit, there was no tub, just that grand shower. But he did take note of the evenly spaced hand rails set in the shower's tiled wall. *Those weren't there before.* To his right were dual sinks with oval mirrors above them framed in dark wood, possibly mahogany.

The room had a subtle masculine feel to it. The color scheme reminded him of a forest with its pale green tiles, warm brown walls, and dark wood trim. The vanity resembled a piece of furniture more than something you'd normally find in a bathroom. Eli ran his fingers over the surface, smiling appreciatively.

There was a small closet to his left, right before the shower, that he suspected held towels, and at the back of the room, beyond the shower, was another door. Eli went over and opened it, finally discovering the toilet. When he was done relieving himself, he stopped at one of the sinks to wash his hands and face. Curious, he opened the central medicine cabinet and found a toothbrush still in its package.

He fingered it thoughtfully, then glanced down at a silver cup on the vanity that held what was obviously Alec's toothbrush. He closed the cabinet door and went back into the bedroom. He went to the dresser and fished out a pair of sweatpants and a T-shirt. Both were a bit big on him, but he tightened the drawstring on the pants sufficiently. He was about to search for his socks and shoes when he stumbled across a pair of leather slippers tucked neatly under the bed on his side.

He picked them up and examined them—they were his size. Not exactly a subtle invitation. Eli struggled between being annoyed or being thrilled that he was welcome.

"Eli, the food's getting cold!" Alec called from the kitchen, so Eli put the slippers on and went to join his boyfriend.

The table was still in the living room by the windows, but the tablecloth was gone, revealing the glass beneath. Alec poured orange juice as Eli approached, and instead of candles, there was now a glass vase with a few roses in it. Eli took his seat, smiled at Alec, and began to eat. The food was delicious and still sufficiently hot. He cocked an eyebrow at Alec, wordlessly asking a question as he ate.

Alec grinned shyly. "Breakfast I can do."

"I'd say so."

They continued in silence for a while, both desperately needing sustenance. Then Alec spotted Eli's footwear through the table top.

"Oh... you, uh..." Alec said, wiping his mouth and quickly sipping some juice, "you found those, I see."

"Yes, and how odd that they're in my size. And how very strange that there's an extra, brand new toothbrush in your cupboard and hand grips in your shower."

Alec grinned shyly. "Well, yes… I wanted you to have everything you'd need when you're here."

"*When* I'm here?"

"Eli, I'm not going to lie to you." Alec sighed. "I would love for you to move in, to live here with me, but I know that has to be your decision. I'm not pushing."

"Just making it damn near irresistible."

"I'm not apologizing for that," Alec said, smiling. Eli returned it, watching fondly as Alec unconsciously raked his hand through his hair to get it off his face. He was suddenly reminded how frightful his hair must look. *Haircut, next thing on my list.*

When they finished their meal, they carried the dishes to the kitchen, and Eli began filling the sink with hot water, adding a squirt of liquid soap.

"I have a dishwasher," Alec said.

"It's just a few things. I'll help."

As the suds grew in the sink, Eli added the dishes, and Alec stepped up behind him, close behind him, encircling him with his arms and reaching around to shut off the water. Alec's hands covered Eli's in the hot, soapy water. Together they grabbed a sponge and slowly began washing a plate. Alec nibbled Eli's earlobe, causing him to shiver, grin, and lay his head back against Alec's shoulder.

He felt so at home in those arms. "What movie would you like to watch?"

"Movie?" Alec asked.

"You said we'd be lounging and watching movies." Eli stopped washing and turned within Alec's arms to face him. "You don't have a game today?"

"Uh… there's a friendly scrimmage this afternoon, but I'm not going." Alec's lips found Eli's neck again. "I'd rather stay in with you."

"Good to know," Eli said as he gripped the back of Alec's head with his sudsy hands and brought their mouths and tongues together. He raised his leg, wrapping it around Alec a bit to bring him forward, pressing them more tightly against each other as Alec's hands, still hot from the water, slid past the waist of Eli's sweatpants and cupped his bottom, squeezing and pulling a moan from him. Alec's grip and the rim of the sink held Eli safely in place as his cane leaned unattended in the corner where the oven met the counter.

"You know, the other day," Alec panted, as Eli kissed him between his words, "I was daydreaming at my desk."

Eli grinned against Alec's lips. "Tell me," he whispered.

"I had you in the shower, and we—"

A knock at the door cut him off, and both he and Eli groaned out loud. They smiled and rested their heads against each other, waiting, hoping, that whoever it was would move on. But when the knock came again, followed closely by the doorbell, they sighed and released each other.

"I'll meet you in the shower," Eli said, grabbing his cane and following close behind Alec to the door. He kept walking as Alec paused in front of the door, tamping down his arousal before opening it.

Eli was nearly to the bedroom when he heard Alec say, "Dray?"

ALEC'S stomach dropped when he saw Dray's bright smile, and he almost groaned out loud. *Not now!* From the corner of his eye, he could see Eli had frozen and turned back around.

"Hey, Alec," Dray said, gliding through the door, carrying two coffees. "Conley had to go to the field early, and I thought maybe I could give you a ride to the scrimmage."

Bracing himself, Alec glanced at Eli, but his boyfriend was simply standing there watching them from the hall. "D-Dray, I'm not going to the scrimmage."

"Really? Conley said he'd call you for me. I was working late last night, or I would have done it myself." Alec saw a brief puzzled look pass over Dray's face when he spotted the table for two by the windows, but the man recovered quickly and smiled brightly. "Coffee?" He held one of the cups out to Alec.

Before Alec could respond, Eli did. "We've already had our coffee," he said, stepping from the shadow of the hallway.

Dray's eyes widened. Obviously he hadn't expected to see him. "Erby! How are you, love?"

"I'm great, Dray," Eli said, slowly advancing. "Fucking fantastic! Bloody brilliant! Now what the f—?"

"Eli—"

"No, Alec! Enough!" He pulled his eyes away from Alec and looked directly at Dray again. "You are to stay the fuck away from Alec. Do you hear me?"

Dray sipped his coffee and grinned. "Now, Eli, don't get so worked—"

"Up? Don't get so worked up?!" Eli took several steps closer to them, and Alec moved to intercept his boyfriend. He knew Eli had a temper, but he'd never seen anything like this. The shift in him from how he was mere moments before was staggering. "You pulled the same shit with Bennett!"

"Eli," Alec said, taking hold of his shoulders and holding him in place and away from Dray, "I'm not interested in Dray." He gently shook Eli, forcing him to meet his gaze. "I've told you that several times."

"It's true, Erby. He's told me more than once he's not interested."

Alec ignored Dray. "Why don't you believe me, babe?" he asked, gazing into Eli's eyes and stroking his face. He could feel the tension in Eli, a low hum of fury running through him, and he still didn't understand it, not completely.

With him blocking Eli's view of Dray, his boyfriend softened. "I'm... I'm sorry. He just... he has this... this way of—"

Alec kissed Eli deeply. "Trust me," he whispered. "Trust that I love you."

Eli smiled, closed his eyes, and melted against Alec. "You love me?"

"Absolutely," Alec said, kissing him again.

"I don't think you've ever said that before."

Dray sighed more loudly than necessary. "Well, I'll take my leave. Sorry I interrupted your lovely—whatever this is." He turned to leave. "Don't be too hard on him, Alec. He's just insecure. He's afraid you won't be able to resist me because he couldn't."

Alec felt Eli go rigid within his arms and pull away.

"What?" he asked, finally turning to face Dray as his words sank in. "What did you say?" Alec watched Dray grin pleasantly—*no, wickedly*—at Eli, then his hazel eyes widened in shock.

"*You* didn't tell him! He doesn't know, does he?" Dray asked, and then he burst out laughing. Alec glanced between the two of them. Eli looked like he was going to be ill and was backing away from them.

Alec laughed weakly at Dray. "What are you talking about?" He turned to his boyfriend. "Eli?" But Eli wouldn't look at him, so he turned back to Dray. And for the first time since he'd moved to London, Alec felt like he was invisible, because Dray was glaring happily at Eli, ignoring him, and obviously delighted by whatever had just happened.

"Good Lord, Erby, if I'd known Alec didn't know, I would have said something sooner." Dray's eyes grew even wider as comprehension dawned. "That's it! All this time I thought you were worried about him succumbing to my charms, formidable though they are, but you were afraid he'd learn of our little encounter." He began laughing again. "You didn't want him to know you'd cheated on Bennett—with me!"

"No!" Alec spoke up. "He told me... he told me he knew what you were up to, that you were using him just to get close to Bennett. He saw right through you, Dray."

Dray smiled sadly at Alec and nodded in Eli's direction. Alec turned toward his boyfriend and found Eli had gone ghostly white. He was backing away and shaking his head, his eyes cast down.

"Eli," he said, stepping toward him. Eli held up a hand to stop him where he was. "Eli, you said you told Dray 'No'."

Dray chuckled. "Well, he didn't say 'thank you', but he didn't say 'no', either."

"Dray!" Alec roared, rounding on him.

"*Leaving now*." The door closed, and Alec rushed forward to lock it. When he turned back, Eli had disappeared into the bedroom. Alec ran back into the room. The first thing he noticed was Eli's clothes were no longer in the chair by the bed.

"Eli?" he called, heading straight for the bathroom. He tried the door, but it was locked. "Eli, please talk to me." Alec listened at the door. He heard movement and then a phone ringing. He heard Eli answer it but couldn't really make out the conversation. He waited for several minutes, and then the door opened. Eli stood before him, fully dressed and talking into his cell.

"Tell Casey I'll be right there." He hung up. He wouldn't look at Alec.

"Eli—"

"I just found two messages from Casey," Eli said, moving swiftly around him. "I'd turned my mobile off... last... n-night. She's been trying to reach me for two hours." He continued walking, out of the bedroom, heading for the apartment door. The way Eli refused to look at him had Alec panicked, so he rushed by him and blocked his way.

"Eli, talk to me. Look at me."

He didn't look at him.

"That was the hospital just now." Eli stepped around him. "I'm on my way there."

"Please, let someone else handle—"

"Some tourists were injured in a car accident—Americans. The boy is deaf and the parents are in surgery."

"We need to talk. Let me drive you."

"No!" Alec cringed at the volume of his voice, and Eli continued more quietly. "I've called a taxi already. Should be downstairs any minute." He reached for the doorknob, but Alec grabbed his shoulders and spun him around, pushing him back against the door.

"Tell me," Alec pleaded, gently gripping Eli's chin and raising his face to look at him. "Tell me, and I'll believe you."

"Dray and I fucked," Eli said matter-of-factly, his eyes filling with tears. Alec tried to keep his expression from changing, but he failed. "I cheated on Bennett. I broke his heart." Alec's hands fell away, and Eli turned his back to him and opened the door. "And four months later, I lost him." Eli left the apartment, shutting the door behind him.

Alec stood frozen in place.

Chapter 24

"ELI. It's good to see you."

"Oh, uh… hi, Jason. Casey around?"

The nurse nodded. "She told us she called you. End of the hall. On your left." Eli turned away from the nurses' station. "Eli?"

He turned back. "Yeah?"

"You okay?"

Eli thought about it and lied. "Yeah, I'm fine, thanks." He turned and continued up the hallway.

On the way over in the taxi, he'd struggled to get himself under control, tried to shut down all the emotions Alec had freed in him, had set loose so many months ago. Part of him longed for the quiet, self-imposed numbness he'd known after Bennett but before Alec. He felt his throat tightening, but he shook it off, swallowing the tears before they could begin spilling out of him again.

Alec knew now, and Eli had seen what he'd feared most on his face: disappointment. He stopped walking and supported himself against the wall for a moment, trying to rid himself of the image of Bennett and the similar expression he'd had when Eli confessed what he'd done with Dray. It was different, of course. Alec was disappointed, surprised, and probably hurt that he'd lied to him, but Bennett had been devastated. Eli shuddered at the memory.

He pushed himself away from the wall and walked on, remembering that he was needed and that work, being able to help someone else, would blessedly occupy his thoughts for a while. As he neared the last room on the left, he heard the shouting, the crying, the unintelligible wailing, and above that, he heard Casey's frantic voice trying desperately to sound calm. He knocked on the door.

"Come in!"

Eli pushed open the door and saw his friend and two other nurses trying to get a small tow-headed boy to settle down in bed. Wearing a hospital gown and about to lose a sock, the boy cowered in the far corner of the room. He had big, brown, frightened eyes and was signing frantically. One of the nurses held a small notepad and pencil. She kept holding it out to him, encouraging him to write, but the boy was too worked up to notice.

A hospital being a frightening place at the best of times, Eli could imagine how terrified the boy must be: probably in pain from his injuries, wondering where his parents were, surrounded by silent strangers trying to control him, hold him down, and stick him with needles. Eli balanced his cane against the wall and clapped his hands together loudly several times. Everyone froze and looked at him, the boy lagging a few beats behind but following the nurses' gazes.

"Eli!" Casey said rushing to his side. "Thank God you're here." She grabbed him by the arm, pulling him forward. "I'm so sorry I had to call you, but the interpreter on call isn't answering his mobile."

The boy watched this exchange, clearly wondering about this new threat. Eli smiled at him before turning to the others and saying, "Can everyone else leave the room, please?" Casey nodded to her coworkers and they headed for the door. "Casey, please stay."

She stopped and closed the door after the others, rejoining Eli. He faced the boy, who watched him warily. Eli went closer, making sure to keep the bed between them. The boy pressed himself as deep into the corner as he could go, all the while watching Eli's cane curiously.

Hello, Eli signed. *My name E-L-I. You?*

The boy's eyes widened, but he stepped forward slowly. *B-R-A-D. Where Mom and Dad?*

"Where are his parents?" Eli asked Casey, never taking his eyes off Brad.

She seemed startled but answered, "Uh, they're recovering from surgery."

"Are they going to make it?"

"It looks good, yes."

Eli turned back to Brad and signed that his parents were hurt in the same accident he'd been in, but that the doctors had helped them, and they were sleeping right now.

I want see.

"Can he visit them?"

"Once they're awake, yes," Casey said. "Oh, and after his stitches are done." She pointed to her head, then looked at Brad. "That's what we've been trying to accomplish. That wound needs to be cleaned and closed."

Eli winced when he noticed the cut on the boy's head. He explained to Brad that once his injury was fixed, he could see his parents. Brad reached up and gently touched the wound on his head as if he'd forgotten about it. He cringed and began to cry softly.

I want Mom. I want Mom. I want Mom.

Soon.

Without thinking Eli sat on the bed and, looking at Brad, held a hand out to the boy, inviting him to climb aboard. Brad hesitated, staring at Eli's outstretched hand. Then he looked into Eli's eyes and slowly came forward, reaching out, taking his hand, and allowing Eli to pull him up into the bed. Eli reached down and straightened the sock that Brad was about to lose, pulling it firmly back into place. Brad looked at him through tear-filled eyes and sniffled a bit.

"I'll... I'll get the doctor," Casey said and left the room.

Brad and Eli sat together for a few moments, the boy nervously wiggling his feet and periodically glancing at the door. He never released Eli's hand.

Okay? Eli asked.

Brad tightened his grip. He looked at Eli's cane resting against the mattress, and Eli passed it to him. Brad ran his fingers over the dark wood as Eli watched, smiling. The boy took a closer look at the brass collar joining the handle and shaft together. He squinted, trying to make out the scrolled lettering. He looked up at Eli questioningly.

It's me: E-L-I-A-S—he hesitated before continuing with the middle name he hated—*R-O-S-C-O-E—B-U-R-K-E. Understand? E-R-B.*

Brad beamed up at him, and Eli smiled back, but slowly Brad's smile faded, and he frowned looking at Eli's leg. *It hurts?*

Sometimes. A little.

You sad? Brad asked, searching Eli's face. Apparently the boy saw something else there.

Eli smiled nervously, but the doctor rescued him as he came sweeping into the room.

"Brad Woods?"

The boy immediately shrank down next to Eli, grabbing his hand with both hands now as if he feared the doctor was there to spirit him away.

"Yes, this is Brad," Eli answered.

"And you are?"

"His interpreter. Eli Burke." The doctor looked perplexed and paused in donning his surgical gloves. "Brad is deaf... um, Doctor...?"

"Cooper, Dr. Cooper."

"If you'll tell me what you plan to do, I'll explain it to Brad," Eli said, pausing as Dr. Cooper huffed, clearly exasperated. "And together you and I can keep him calm."

Eli stared at Cooper pointedly, making it clear that they would be doing things his way despite the doctor's busy schedule. Just then Casey entered the room carrying a suture kit, but stood by, awaiting the outcome of the stalemate.

Eli smiled at her before turning back to Cooper and continuing. "I'm sure you understand Brad's very frightened in this strange place and missing his parents."

"They're in recovery, Doctor," Casey added.

"I see. I see." The doctor nodded, trying unsuccessfully to gain Brad's trust with a phony grin that, when translated by frightened child eyes, could only be described as menacing. "I need to clean the wound, disinfect it, and sew it shut." He finished putting on his gloves, and then he and Casey looked expectantly at Eli, who tapped Brad on the shoulder.

I need my hand.

Brad released it reluctantly, and Eli quickly explained what the doctor needed to do. Brad's eyes widened even farther. He and Eli stared at each other for a few seconds.

You stay.

I stay, Eli promised.

Chapter 25

"WE'RE here because of that call, right?"

Mirabell glanced at Buddy and smiled, preferring the look of him to anxiously watching the lift numbers blink as they climbed through Alec's building. She closed the tiny distance between them and held her arms out to be picked up, which Buddy did, allowing her to kiss him. He was delicious, and not for the first time did she feel that nervous twinge in her gut warning her.

She pulled back and looked through his glasses to the warm brown eyes beyond. "I expected a call from Alec. Not this soon, but definitely a call." Buddy put her back on her feet. "I was ready for rave reviews about his date, but—"

"That's not what you got."

It wasn't. On their way to the club, she'd answered an aborted call from Alec. Something along the lines of "I give up" was all she could make out before being disconnected. She definitely hadn't liked the sound of that. The lift stopped on Alec's floor. "*Ding*," Mirabell mimicked as she stepped off, Buddy following with a smile. His legs were even longer than Alec's, so he had no trouble keeping up with her rapid gait.

They reached Alec's door and she knocked. There was no answer, so she knocked again.

"Come in!" a voice shouted from within.

She glanced at Buddy, and he stepped forward, gently pushing the door open.

"Who the fuck are you?!" Alec shouted from the sofa.

Mirabell quickly stepped around her protector and glared at Alec. "He's Buddy. He's with me. Who the fuck are you?!"

Alec's eyes widened. "Oh, Mira," he said, reaching out to her, "Mira, I'm sorry."

Both Buddy and Mirabell took a quick scan of the immediate vicinity, then he looked down at her just as she looked up at him. "Pissed!" they declared in unison. Buddy closed the door, and Mira strolled to Alec's side, standing just out of his reach.

"How much have you had to drink?"

"Not a lot."

She looked around and noted two wine bottles on the coffee table. One had a tiny bit left in it, and the other had a broken, but still secure cork.

She swung Alec's legs off the sofa and took a seat. "But, love, this *is* a lot when you're not a tosspot like me." Buddy stepped forward and collected both bottles, carrying them into the kitchen. "Are we going to keep drinking?" she asked Alec.

Alec shook his head. "I don't think so. I'm not feeling so good."

"Tell Mirabell what happened," she said as she helped him sit up.

With a fond smile of remembrance, he told her all about the evening he'd had with Eli, and then with a frown he told her about Dray and about Eli's confession. Mirabell nodded slowly.

"I see." They stared at each other for a few moments. "Do you love him?"

"Of course I do!"

"So what was this 'I give up' bollocks on the phone?"

She could see Alec trying to remember, trying to understand what she was talking about.

"I... I remember thinking that...."

"But you don't remember dialing my number and saying it into the phone."

He shook his head, then his eyes rolled back in it. "I'm dizzy."

Mirabell could smell coffee brewing from the kitchen. She smiled, realizing, not for the last time, that Buddy was a dream. "Alec, why were you thinking of giving up on Eli?"

"I suck!"

"I've heard that about you."

He sat forward on the sofa so quickly that she almost lost him to the floor, but she steadied him. "No, no. You don't understand. I'm a lousy psychologist."

"Since when?"

He looked into her eyes, and she could see the tears in his. "I didn't see it. I didn't see the guilt... or, or how deep it went. Don't you understand? I thought he was lingering at the house, clinging to Bennett because he didn't love me as much."

"But... you were wrong?"

Alec nodded rapidly, then swooned. "Oh... uh, I'm not feel—" He leaped to his unsteady feet and rushed past Mirabell to the guest bathroom. She watched him go, then Buddy entered the living room, his arms full.

"What's all that?"

He looked innocently down at the tray he was carrying. "Just coffee and croissant for us and bottled water for—" Buddy looked around. "Is he—?"

She nodded as they both waited until the retching paused.

"So no club tonight?" she asked.

Buddy set the tray on the coffee table. "I thought we might have this and watch a movie or something. I didn't think you'd want to leave your friend unattended."

Mirabell smiled, kicked off her shoes, and stood on Alec's sofa. "Come here, love." Buddy walked over to her, and she kissed him long and deep, stroking his hair. His long arms went around her tiny frame, and she felt him shiver. When they parted, and before she could stop herself, she said, "I love y—" Buddy grinned, but she looked horrified, hopping quickly down from the sofa. "Uh, can you come help me get him into bed?"

Buddy grabbed the bottled water and followed her obediently to the guest bathroom. They found Alec on his knees in front of the toilet, his face resting on the cool porcelain seat.

"Alec, hon?" she said, sweeping a lock of his hair off his face. "Buddy's going to put you to bed." Buddy stepped around Mira and grabbed Alec under the arms, lifting him effortlessly. Mirabell flushed the toilet and left the room, turning left. Buddy, with Alec, followed. They got him in bed, Mira stripping off his pants and shoes and rolling him under the comforter.

Alec came around a bit. "This is Eli's side of the bed," he said. "I can smell him."

"I know, love."

Alec looked Mirabell up and down. "You don't look like a kaleidoscope today."

Buddy chuckled behind her, and she grinned at him against her will. Turning back to Alec, she said, "Don't I?"

"No, you look like a—where's James?" Alec asked, chuckling quietly to himself.

Buddy bent over to her ear. "James?" he asked softly. Mirabell smiled and glanced down at her outfit.

He was right. She was apparently going through a monochromatic phase: shoes, stockings, dress, sweater, handbag, and hair clip—all peachy. One would be surprised to reach out and stroke her and not find her fuzzy.

"I'll explain later, dear."

"I should call him," Alec said suddenly, his face growing terribly serious.

Mirabell removed the phone from its cradle before Alec could, passing it deftly to Buddy. "Not yet, Alec. Sleep for a bit first. You don't want to make a call you can't take back." She watched him relent and relax against the pillow once again. "Remember: drunk dialing can be fatal." She pulled the comforter up to his neck, tucking him in properly. "Alec, you said you were wrong about Eli not loving you as much as Bennett. What did you mean?"

"He's hanging on to the past because he doesn't think he deserves a future." Alec fought to keep his eyes open. "He cheated on Bennett, then he lost him." Alec yawned, and Mirabell and Buddy smiled warmly at him, much like parents would smile at their child as they put him to bed. "I think Bennett forgave him, but... Eli... he...." Alec fell asleep.

"Can't forgive himself," Buddy whispered, and Mirabell nodded. They left the room, leaving a lamp on in the corner and the water on the nightstand.

Chapter 26

ELI'S hand shook as he tried to fit his key into the lock. The horrid end to his night with Alec, followed by hours at the hospital at Brad's side, had left him exhausted and rattled. He stopped, took a deep breath to steady himself, and then the key slid in perfectly. He unlocked the front door and slipped quietly into the house. A pale, white light emanated from the kitchen at the end of the long entry hall, but there was no sound of movement, and he hoped Ilsa had gone to bed.

He leaned back against the door and closed his eyes, just wanting to crawl into bed. He headed toward his bedroom door, but before he reached it, he heard Ilsa on the next landing above him.

"I knew you'd be spending the night at Alec's, but I had no idea you'd be so late in coming home today."

He could hear the smile in her voice, and he so wanted to match her tone so she wouldn't worry, but he couldn't bring himself to, so he simply said, "Ilsa... I need to talk to you." He continued into his bedroom. Seconds later she was standing in his doorway.

"Sugar, what's wrong?" He sat on his bed, toeing off his shoes. "You look awful." She came over and sat next to him. "Didn't the date go well?"

"It was spectacular," Eli sighed. "But I left Alec's this morning."

"Where have you been?"

He told Ilsa about Casey's call for help and how he'd sat with Brad until his concerned grandparents had shown up, cooing over the boy and looking in on their daughter and son-in-law.

"You're a prince, sugar," she said, smiling. "Sorry Casey's call ruined your date, though."

He looked into her eyes and grinned weakly. "It wasn't Casey who ruined the date."

"Huh?"

"Dray came by this morning and—"

"Son of a bitch!" Ilsa rocketed off the bed, but Eli raised his hand to calm her. She fell silent, pacing back and forth a few times, watching him, and then she gradually settled back down on the bed. "Sorry, what happened?"

"Me… I happened." Ilsa just stared at him. "I exploded and tore into Dray. You know I promised Alec I'd keep that in check." He looked at her, and she nodded. "But last night… it was so amazing, and then there Dray was this morning with coffee and schemes—and I just lost it."

"Understandable."

Eli hesitated. He wasn't sure how he'd continue, but he knew he had to. "Alec told me he loved me."

"Eli, that's wonderful."

He closed his eyes, remembering. "It was, Ilsa. It was," he whispered.

"Then Casey called?"

His eyes popped open, and he swallowed nervously. "N-no…."

"Eli?"

"Dray told Alec that… years ago… I slept with him."

"You're joking?" She was off the bed again before Eli could stop her. "Dray accused you of cheating on Bennett—with *him*?" She paced around the room looking as though she wanted to break something, and if Dray's neck had been handy at that moment, he might not have gotten out alive. "How dare he!"

He watched her pacing angrily back and forth in front of him, so filled with righteous indignation. Eli didn't know where he found the strength to continue.

"Ilsa—"

She stopped in the middle of the room and glared at him. "What you and Bennett had was—"

"It's true," he whispered.

They stared at each other in silence for a good thirty seconds.

"What do you mean 'it's true'?"

"I cheated on Bennett." Ilsa's mouth worked without producing anything more than a strangled squeak. Eli nodded. "Dray shagged me—shagged me rotten… in the gents' at Rocko's."

"I… I don't know what to say."

She didn't move any closer to him, just stood there, hugging herself and letting her gaze wander around the room. Eli waited, but when nothing more seemed forthcoming from her, he continued getting undressed, tugging his jumper off over his head.

"Alec and I are done, and I'm going to bed."

The note of finality in his voice jarred Ilsa into speaking. "Are you certain? That doesn't sound like Alec."

He pulled the covers back before shedding his jeans. "It's been a very long day." He fell in the bed and tugged the covers up to his neck.

"Eli, did Alec actually end it?"

"Good night." He rolled over to face the wall. "Turn the light out when you leave, please."

"Oh no!" She yanked the covers off him. "You don't drop something like that on me and think you're going to just roll over and go to sleep!"

"What do you want me to say?!" Eli shouted, bringing Ilsa up short. He struggled off the bed and glared at her. "It's quite simple. I cheated on Bennett! I dragged Dray Jenkins into the loo! I let him press my face against that cold tile and fuck me!" Eli gasped, his eyes clamping shut.

"That… that doesn't sound like you."

"I was drunk. I was angry. I was selfish. I… I… Bennett…." He choked up, tears coming to his eyes so quickly that Ilsa instinctively stepped forward to embrace him as she'd done so many times before, but she stopped herself. "I… hurt him. I h-hurt him so badly and… and then he was gone."

Then she did try to wrap him up in her arms, but he didn't want comfort and shoved her away. "You can't make this better," he said, holding up a hand to keep her back, his eyes flashing angrily. "Not with a hug or freshly baked bread or chocolate." She looked affronted, and the strength went out of him. He dropped back onto his bed, staring at the floor. "I did this."

He felt her eyes on him for more than a minute, then she took a tentative step forward. "Bennett…," she began in a whisper. "He loved you, Eli." She came a bit closer. "He knew, and he forgave you—" He looked at her sharply. "No, Eli. I saw the two of you together before we lost him, and he must have forgiven you." She sat next to him, reached out, and lifted his face to hers. The depth of his guilt and grief was etched on his face. "Why didn't you ever tell me?"

He pulled away. "I was ashamed. We—Bennett and I—we'd had a fight. He was working all the time, and I was just angry." A few tears had spilled onto his cheeks, and he roughly wiped them away. "I just wanted him to spend more time with me." A bark of bitter laughter escaped him. "More time," he mumbled, shaking his head.

Suddenly he gripped Ilsa's hand tightly. "I didn't storm out planning for that to happen. I just wanted to go out dancing, just a couple of hours… the two of us dancing like we used to. But he had an important project to complete and refused. The next morning… I knew I had to tell him." He looked at Ilsa with haunted eyes. "I couldn't *not* tell him."

"And he forgave you, right?" Eli nodded and shrugged. "Sugar, I remember those months before we lost him. You two couldn't keep your hands off each other. You were closer than ever." His gaze returned to the floor, and she reached out, taking his chin and lifting it again. "He forgave you. He loved you." His tears came heavier now, and he couldn't stop them. This time he let her hold him—briefly. "You need to talk to Alec."

"I can't face him." Eli shook his head.

"Do you love him?" He nodded. "Then face him. Fight for him."

"I don't suppose he's called?"

Ilsa shook her head, and then she quickly added, "But maybe he just needs time to digest things."

Eli rolled himself back into bed, once again facing the wall. "Yeah, he needs time to digest that I lied to him. He needs time to decide if he wants to waste his time on some bloke who cheated on his lover, some git who's too fucked up to—"

"To what?" Ilsa whispered.

Eli rolled over to look at her. "To love him the way he should be, the way he deserves to be." He turned away from her again, and she left his room, turning out the light and closing the door.

Chapter 27

THE phone was ringing. Right. Inside. His. Skull. Alec blindly reached out for it, knocking it off its cradle and onto the floor. He felt like it was trying to escape him, but with a sudden, rapid, painful, concerted effort, he captured and answered it while hanging halfway off the side of the bed.

"Uh...."

"Alec?"

"Mm."

"It's Mira, love." She fell silent, waiting. "How are you today?"

"You should have smothered me with my pillow last night."

She laughed. "Couldn't, love. Your man would never forgive me."

"Mira—"

"If you tell me you don't love him, I'll leave you be."

"I can't say that."

"I know. Fix it, Alec. Get up, drink plenty of water, shower, make yourself bloody beautiful, and go collect him."

The line went dead, and Alec struggled to place it back in its cradle before rolling onto his back and staring at the ceiling. *Collect him? Would it be that simple? Not a chance.* He threw the comforter back and forced himself to sit up.

"Oh my God!" he said, clutching his head.

Alec took several deep, cleansing breaths, grabbed the bottled water, and struggled to open it as he stumbled to the bathroom.

TWO hours later, he was parking in front of Ilsa's house. His headache was on the wane, thankfully, and he had mentally prepared himself for battle—yet again he'd have to try and convince Eli he wanted to be with him. As he approached the house, he thought about what he'd told Lincoln: *Trust in your love for the man, and he'll come to trust in it too.*

He was about to unlock the door and simply walk in, but thought better of it. After all, he didn't live here anymore, even if he still had a key. It felt wrong just to walk in, so he knocked and waited. He glanced around his old neighborhood, spotting Mr. and Mrs. Brandt, the next-door neighbors, working in their front yard together.

"Ah, Mr. Sumner," Mr. Brandt shouted, his wife smiling and waving also.

"Hi, sir. Ma'am. How are you today?" Alec rang the doorbell, shifting nervously from foot to foot.

"Fine, fine," Mr. Brandt said. "How are you liking your new flat?"

"Oh, it's fantastic. Just what I was hoping for."

"If you're looking for Ms. LaCoste, she left earlier," Mrs. Brandt said.

"Oh, uh... actually I was hoping to speak to Eli... uh, Mr. Burke."

"Sorry, we haven't seen him today."

Alec nodded and reached out to knock a bit louder, but then Casey opened the door.

"Whuh?" she asked as she leaned against the doorframe, her eyes barely open.

"Casey," Alec said, stepping up eagerly. "I need to see Eli."

Without a word she stepped back, allowing the door to swing wide and revealing the simple oversized nightshirt and socks she wore.

"Knock yourself out. Ilsa's doing early prep for the lunch crowd at Peaches."

Alec entered the house, shutting the door behind him as Casey shuffled away, heading for the stairs and mumbling something about "nutters next door and yard work." He watched her go, then went to Eli's bedroom door.

He knocked gently. "Eli? Eli, can we talk?" There was no answer. He hesitated a moment, took a deep breath, and opened the door a crack. "Eli?" The room was dark and silent. Alec swung the door wide and flicked on the light. The bed was empty but had obviously been slept in. He turned and glanced back at the stairs before stepping into the room and softly closing the door behind him.

Part of him felt terribly naughty being in Eli's room while he was out, but a bigger, stronger part of Alec had missed the room and the time they'd spent together in it. He went to the shelves on the wall just outside the bathroom and looked over the photos there. The first time he'd ever been in the room was to help Ilsa pour Eli into bed, and while she undressed her friend, Alec had distracted himself by looking over these photos.

As he looked at them now, he noticed there was only one of Bennett: he sat on the beach, smiling up at the camera, looking perfect, and Alec was positive Eli was on the other side of the lens. There were no longer photos of Eli and Bennett together. That's all there had been that first time. Now the other photos were of Eli and Alec at various activities: cooking dinner, working in the backyard, slow-dancing at a party—Alec smiled at that one. He'd had to hold Eli tight to his body to compensate for his weaker leg. There was even a copy of the photo Alec had on his desk at the university.

He sighed. *Here I am jumping through hoops again, not only trying to convince you I love you, but now I have to convince you that you deserve to be loved.* He turned and looked at the bed, imagining Eli sleeping there. As he walked toward it, he paused to turn off the light, and then he crawled onto the bed and buried his face in Eli's pillow.

"God, Eli, I'm tired," he said.

"ALEC was here?" Eli asked, walking into the living room and carrying the note he'd found. Ilsa and Casey were curled up on the sofa about to watch a movie.

Ilsa turned to Casey in surprise. "Was he?"

"Yep. This morning after you left for work, he showed up looking for Eli," Casey said.

"What's that?" Ilsa asked.

Eli glanced at the note in his hand. "Just... he left me a note saying he wanted to talk."

"You going over there?"

He shook his head. "I'm knackered." He joined them on the sofa.

"I had two clients today, stopped by to check on my certification, and then went to see about Brad."

"Did you?" Casey asked. "That's so sweet. How is he?"

"Good," Eli said, digging a handful of popcorn out of the bowl on the coffee table. "His mum is up and about, and they'll be staying with her parents until his father is well enough to travel." Ilsa watched Eli fold up the note from Alec and stuff it in his pocket. "What are *we* watching?" he asked. "It's not lesbian porn, is it?"

Ilsa smiled and reached over to squeeze his knee. "Maybe," she said with a wink.

Casey leaned forward to look at Eli around Ilsa as the movie began. "Aren't you going to call him, Eli?"

"I might call him tomorrow."

"Might?" Ilsa asked.

Eli sighed. "I'm still trying to work out what to say to him."

"That's easy," Ilsa said as Casey listened and smiled knowingly, munching happily on a fistful of popcorn. "I. Love. You. Alec. Ta-da!" Eli shook his head, but he couldn't help smiling.

About forty-five minutes into the movie and thirty minutes into Casey and Ilsa snogging, Eli excused himself, going to his room to call Alec. When he'd first returned home and entered his room, he felt there was something off. It took him several minutes to realize his bed was made and that it hadn't been when he left that morning. He thought maybe Ilsa had made it, but she'd never done that before. Right after Bennett's death, Lyle had taken to making Eli's bed—when he wasn't in it, of course, which was rare in those days. When Eli had spotted the note, he had understood it had been Alec who made the bed, and he had immediately felt a hollow ache in his gut.

"I want to—I *need* to see you, Eli."

"Alec, let's just take—"

"No."

"No?"

"We don't need time, Eli. I *know* what I want—"

"*I* need time." After several moments of silence, Eli said, "Alec?"

"Take all the time you need." Alec hung up.

Eli couldn't deny the fear that gripped him in that moment.

Chapter 28

"AS MUCH as I've wanted some time alone with you, Alec, I've never actually given you my number."

"I got it from Conley, Dray. Please, come in." Alec stepped back from the doorway to allow Dray to saunter into the apartment. He carried a bottle of wine and wore a torso-hugging cream shirt and loose linen pants of the same shade. The outfit set off his rich, dark skin perfectly, and he knew it.

"Where can I put this?" Dray asked, holding up the bottle.

"Meet me on the sofa there. I'll grab a couple of glasses and corkscrew."

Dray smiled that electric smile of his and walked over to the sofa, which was now against the massive windows on the far wall. They could sit, drink, and look out over London. It was a beautiful night.

"The place looks different from the other morning."

"Ah, yes." Alec walked over, set the glasses on the coffee table, and dropped down several feet away from Dray. "I had the table set up here for the view the other night." He began working on the cork but paused for a moment. "It was more romantic."

"I understand." Dray looked at him with phony sadness in his eyes. "Sorry about you and Eli, mate."

Alec smiled. "No you're not, Dray." He popped the cork with a flourish and filled Dray's glass.

"True," he said, laughing as he picked up his glass of wine.

Alec picked up his and faced him. "To getting to know you better," he said. Dray nodded, and they tapped their glasses before taking a couple of long sips.

Dray put his glass back down and scooted closer to Alec. "I'm all for that." He put his hand on Alec's thigh. Alec looked at it resting there, squeezing insistently. He met Dray's gaze over the rim of his glass and took another long sip as Dray watched him, smiling.

"I just have a couple of questions for you."

Dray looked at Alec lips hungrily. "My, but you're fit," he whispered, inching even closer.

"Dray? Questions?"

"Can't those wait?" His hand slid higher on Alec's thigh.

"No, they can't." Alec grabbed Dray's hand to still it. Their eyes locked, and Dray relented.

"Fine, then… ask." He settled back on the sofa and retrieved his glass, smiling as he sipped.

"Will you tell me what happened between you and Eli?"

Dray watched him for several heartbeats. "What *exactly* do you want to know?"

"I want to know how… *it* happened," Alec said evenly.

Dray stared at him again, taking a deep breath before beginning.

"Back then most of us hung out at Rocko's." Alec looked confused, and Dray shook his head. "It's closed down since." He sighed. "Anyway, I was there one night, dancing, having a glorious time, and in walks Eli. I perk up because I think Bennett's right on his tail, as always. But no. He's nowhere to be seen.

"So I keep dancing but watching, and Eli proceeds to get pissed. Just sits at the bar drinking. After about an hour, he turns toward the dance floor and spots me, right? He walks out there, sweet as you please, and he starts dancing with me." Dray pauses and smiles at Alec. "It was wicked sexy, I have to admit."

Alec didn't say anything, but he could feel a tightness in his chest. He could imagine Eli and how he must have looked, how Dray must have looked—probably shirtless, all that shining dark muscle looming before Eli's slight frame, the two of them sweating and grinding against each other. "We danced for another… oh, thirty minutes or so."

"And then?"

Dray held his glass out to be refilled, and Alec obliged.

"You have to understand, Alec," Dray said, taking a sip, "I was baffled, but…."

Alec sighed. "You danced for thirty minutes and then what?"

"He kissed me. He slid his hands all up my front and pulled me down into a kiss. And this was not some friendly kiss; this was a 'come fuck me' snog."

"So, naturally, you…." Alec's voice was strained.

"You sure you want to hear—"

"Tell me!"

"We went into the gents', found an empty stall, and went at it."

"And not once did you ask about Bennett? Where he was? You ignored the fact that Eli was obviously drunk, not himself."

Dray grinned wickedly and drained his glass. "No, Alec," he said, glaring at him. "I locked the door, turned him to the wall, yanked his kit down, grabbed his cock, and fucked him." Dray scooted close to Alec again. "I ask you, what healthy, young Englishman wouldn't? The only time Bennett crossed my mind was me wondering how soon I'd have a crack at him once he found out Eli had cheated. He's the one I wanted. Any more questions?" Dray's hand landed on Alec's thigh again.

"Why do you continue to pursue me when you know I'm in love with Eli?"

"You love him?" Dray appeared amused by the concept.

"Yes, Dray." Alec blinked at him a couple of times. "You were standing right there when I told him the other morning."

Dray sighed and allowed his eyes to roam over the room. "Sorry, I wasn't really listening."

"You did the same with Bennett."

Dray ignored the statement. "If you loved Eli, you wouldn't be here with me, would you?" He came so close to Alec that, any closer, and he would have been in Alec's lap. Alec scooted back a bit, but Dray grabbed him suddenly, pulling him into a kiss. His tongue fought to get past Alec's lips, his arms encircling him so tightly that Alec thought he might not be able to break free. He squirmed and turned his head, breaking the kiss, but Dray's mouth simply found his neck.

"Dray!" he shouted, trying to push him off. "Dray! I asked you over to get some answers, to understand your motivations. Not to fuck you!"

Dray pulled back but didn't release him completely. "I do the fucking, my friend." He moved in to kiss him again, but Alec grimaced and turned away, and Dray froze. "Hang on." He released Alec and sat back on the sofa, nearly to the other end. "My *motivations*?" he repeated quietly. "What does that mean?"

It took a few moments for Alec to right himself and catch his breath. "It means… you've demonstrated a pattern. You pursued Bennett while he was with Eli, and you're doing the same with me. Why?"

Dray blinked at him. "Am I to understand that you invited me up to your flat to… *analyze* me?!" Alec didn't say anything, and Dray chuckled, looking away. He grabbed his wine glass and grimaced when he saw it was empty. Then glaring at Alec, he said, "Let me ask *you* something, *doctor*. What is this hold Burke seems to have over you? Wait… no… *you*, I get. You've got some kind of wounded-bird kink, but his hold over Bennett made absolutely no sense to me."

"You mean it made no sense that Bennett would choose Eli over you?"

"Bloody well right!" Dray spread his arms wide. "Look at me! Even after he found out about Eli cheating, he forgave him! But he came after me quick enough."

"What?"

Dray grinned crookedly. "He. Came. After. Me." Alec smiled then, openly amused, but Dray, massaging his temple, missed it. "Ask that artistic tosspot, Tony. He was there. Saw the whole thing."

Alec stared at Dray for a few moments, his mind working quickly. "I see."

"What?" Dray's head came up sharply, his eyes narrowing. "What do you see?"

Alec smiled. Dray frowned.

"Bennett was the first one to turn you down, wasn't he?" Dray said nothing, just stared at him. "You're not attracted to me at all. This is payback for Eli ruining your record."

"Doc, before you pulled this analyzing shite, I would have fucked you blue!" Dray got up and headed for the door with Alec on his heels. "And understand this, Eli didn't ruin my record. Those bloody skinheads did! If Bennett hadn't died, I would've had him!" Dray yanked open the door. "I always get what I want!"

The door slammed hard enough to rattle the glasses in the bar.

"No, Dray," Alec said softly. "Not always."

He stared at the door for a few moments and then warred with himself about calling Eli. Feeling certain they were free of Dray now, he eyed the phone. He wanted to tell Eli, but he had asked for time, and Alec was determined to give it to him. He turned and headed for the kitchen, but before he reached it, the phone rang.

Chapter 29

THE insistent pounding on the door pulled Ilsa from the sofa. After cutting Eli's hair, she'd left him sitting on the deck, watching the sun sink in the sky and listening to the birds.

More pounding. "I'm coming, goddamn it!" She opened the door and was unceremoniously shoved aside by Lyle, of all people.

"Where's Eli?" he asked. Tony entered right behind him, but at a much slower pace. He looked decidedly apologetic, a totally new look for him.

"L-Lyle? What's got your panties in a knot?"

"Um... knickers in a twist, actually," Tony offered.

Lyle whirled on him. "Shush!" He turned back to Ilsa. "Where is he?" He continued deeper into the house, stopping at Eli's door and swinging it open. He flicked on the light. The room was empty. Lyle then headed for the kitchen, but Ilsa caught up to him and blocked his path.

"Hold it!" She wasn't sure she wanted such an uncharacteristically agitated Lyle near Eli right now. "He's out on the deck." She placed a hand on Lyle's chest. "He doesn't need any more grief. He's still upset about what happened with Dray and Alec."

Lyle froze, the intensity draining from his eyes. "He knows?" Ilsa saw Tony peek around Lyle in interest. He looked strangely relieved.

"Knows what?" Ilsa asked.

Lyle sighed, gathering his thoughts. "We're sitting at dinner tonight, looking over the wine list, when this one," he said, jerking his thumb back over his shoulder at Tony, "mentions he'd like to try the wine Dray had the other night." Ilsa looked from Lyle to Tony and back again. "So I ask, 'Where did you see Dray?' And he says, 'When I ran back in to get my mobile the other night. Met him in the lift. He was on his way up to Alec's with the wine and a big smile'." She could tell Lyle's story was done from the "What the fuck do you think about that?" expression on his face.

She removed her restraining hand from Lyle. "So? Dray's been known to pop in, and he's been after Alec since he met him at the Blast last year."

Tony shook his head and stepped around Lyle, taking the lead. "He said Alec had invited him over—*called* him and *invited* him."

"You see?!" Lyle said. "This was days ago and this one only brings it up because of the wine Dray had... as if that's the most significant portion of the encounter!" Lyle glared at the back of Tony's head. "Honestly!"

"You look surprised, Ilsa," Tony said, ignoring Lyle. "But you said Eli knew."

"Eli...." She stopped herself, shook her head. "Dray showed up at Alec's the other morning. There was an argument...." She couldn't go on. It had been torture for Eli to admit his infidelity to her, and she didn't think he'd want Lyle and Tony to know.

"We're done."

All three reacted as if they'd been slapped at the sound of Eli's voice. He stood behind them in the doorway leading to the deck—for how long, they didn't know. His hair had been practically shorn. Ilsa had protested at first, but he'd insisted. Looking at him now, without his customary unruly mop of brown hair, she thought his bright, blue eyes looked even larger and, unfortunately, even more sad and soulful. She could see the aching struggle inside him.

"Eli—"

"It's all good, Ilsa." He came in, closing the door behind him and silently weaving through them on his way to his bedroom. "He knows what I did." Eli kept walking, and they watched him go. "I think I finally got what I deserve, yeah?"

"Sugar—"

It was Lyle's turn to place a restraining hand on her. "Let him be, love," he said softly. Eli entered his room and closed the door. They waited but didn't see the light come on under the door.

"Hang on. Is this about Dray and Alec or about Eli cheating on Bennett?" Tony asked, looking from Ilsa to Lyle in confusion.

Ilsa and Lyle turned stunned faces toward Tony.

ELI sat in his room, in the dark, thinking about Alec, thinking about Bennett, hating himself, and hating Dray. Someone knocked on his door.

"Not now, Ilsa. I'm fine," he said, kicking off his shoes and preparing to turn in early.

The door opened anyway. "Can I have a minute, mate?"

Though in silhouette, Eli could still identify him. "What is it, Tony?"

The artist stepped into the room and shut the door as Eli switched on his bedside lamp. "I've just been told," Tony said, approaching him, "that I lack a certain awareness of what facts are pertinent and important to be shared." Eli watched him warily as he took a seat next to him on the bed. "I know what happened between you and Dray."

"What? But how could—"

"I was at Rocko's the night Bennett went after Dray. It wasn't tough to figure out why."

Eli looked at Tony in disbelief. He had no idea Bennett had confronted Dray. "Tell me," he said quietly.

"You probably don't remember, but I was out of town the night you and Dray hooked up. When I got back, I headed straight for the nearest collection of hardbodies, and that happened to be Rocko's."

Eli nodded and waited anxiously for the rest of the story.

"A few good mates were going on about the show you and Dray had put on the night before, and before I could question them further, Bennett stormed in." Tony grinned. "I can smile about it now, but even thoroughly intoxicated, I could see the steam coming off him. He found Dray fairly quickly; he was on the dance floor, as always, the center of attention."

"I had confessed that morning." Eli closed his eyes, remembering. "He walked out on me. Went to work. I called him so many times that day, but he wouldn't take my calls, and he never came home that night."

"He was with me, getting drunk at the bar," Tony said, covering

Eli's hand with his. "And talking about you."

"Huh?"

Tony nodded. "After we pulled him off Dray and got that tosser some ice for his face, I took Bennett back to my table and bought him a drink." Tony sighed. "One of many, actually. Considering Dray's reputation, Bennett didn't have to pay for a drink the rest of the night."

Eli watched Tony's face for several moments. "What... what did he say?" he asked softly. Tony hesitated, and Eli saw it. "Tell me, please."

"He was angry, Eli. Angry and hurt." Eli nodded and stared at his hands resting in his lap. "I could tell the thought of Dray touching you made him ill, but we talked for hours." Tony squeezed Eli's hand, then reached out and lifted his chin. "For hours he ranted about you, about your stubbornness, your temper, and your selfishness." Eli grinned, remembering similar conversations with Bennett. "But as we sat there getting pissed, he started talking about your spirit, your energy, your laughter, the way he felt when you looked at him a certain way, and how you knew and understood him better than anyone on the planet."

Eli tried but couldn't stop the tears from coming, and he appreciated Tony pretending not to notice. "Bennett came to the conclusion, drunken though it was, that he didn't want to be without you. He loved you, Eli. And he forgave you." Eli welcomed the soothing feel of Tony's hand on his back as he sobbed silently.

"Now you have to forgive yourself and fight for your man." The artist cleared his throat and stood abruptly. "If you'll excuse me, all this sappy shite is making me itch." He headed for the door. "Besides," he said, pausing to smile at Eli, "Lyle still has a piece of his mind to give me."

As Tony opened the door, Eli immediately spotted Lyle just on the other side, trying frantically to peek around the artist. "What happened? Tell me what you said," he heard Lyle say breathlessly just before the door closed.

FOR the next few days, Eli followed a simple routine: after a night of very little sleep, he got up, got ready, and left to work with any clients he might have. He watched a lot of TV, sometimes with Ilsa and Casey but most often alone, much like he ate his meals—when he ate. He often found himself dwelling on Alec, imagining him with Dray, and then he'd shudder and find something else to occupy his thoughts, his attention. If he just kept busy, maybe he'd outrun that ache, an ache he'd brought on himself.

Mostly he'd just lie in bed, staring at the ceiling and contemplating a future without Alec. *I told him I needed time, and he's given it to me. He hasn't called or come by. Do I want him to chase me? Pursue me? Prove to me he really wants me? That can't be much fun for him.*

Alec had entered his life and rescued him, dug him out of the hole Bennett's murder had dropped him in. He brought him back out into the light and steadied him with his arms, his hands, lips, tongue—*hang on! Off track.* They'd been together nearly seven months and, truthfully, Eli didn't need rescuing anymore.

All recent evidence to the contrary, he had no intention of returning to that dark place where Alec had found him. He wasn't that person anymore. He wanted Alec and, he hoped, Alec still wanted him… his neurotic little pet. Eli smiled. *Maybe I should make an effort to show him how much I love him for a change.*

Eli's door swung inward, slamming into the wall, and the light came on, prompting him to burrow deeper under his covers.

"What the fuck?" he mumbled.

"Eli! Get up!" Ilsa commanded. "Now!" She moved about the room quickly: from the door to his dresser to his closet to the bathroom, grabbing clothing, his duffel, and toiletries. She dumped all the items unceremoniously on the bed at his feet. "Let's go!" Ilsa yanked the covers off of him.

"What the fuck are you doing?"

"Mopey time is over, sugar"

"I'll be up in a couple of hours." He reached for his covers.

Ilsa pulled them off the bed and dropped them in the floor.

"No! You have to get up right now."

"Why?"

"You have a flight to catch." Eli rubbed his eyes and blinked at her. "Alec needs you."

Chapter 30

ALEC knelt in the hospital corridor, hugging and kissing his niece and nephew. "I promise you'll see me later, guys."

Stacy wasn't satisfied. "Bobette won't be able to sleep without you!"

"The dog will be fine, dear," their father, Charles, said as he struggled to get his son, Chuck, into his jacket. The boy was at that age where he had the desire to do it all himself, but he lacked the motor skills.

"Are you going to be okay?" Deborah asked, looking into her husband's eyes, a slight smile playing on her lips.

"I will have them fed, bathed, and pajama'd before you know it, Deb." He smiled and kissed her good-night. "Might even throw in a bedtime story." The children cheered at that news.

"Shush! We're in a hospital. Inside voices, remember?" The children nodded. "You two be good for Daddy."

"We will, Mom," Stacy said, glaring at her brother, who was oblivious.

Charles zipped up Chuck's windbreaker with triumphant finality and sighed.

"See you later, Alec."

"Take care, Charles."

"How did the dog end up Bobette?" Alec asked after the family had disappeared into the elevator. "Yesterday her name was Camille."

Deb smiled. "Final name change. I promise," she said, raising her fists in a small celebratory gesture. "Stacy is obsessed with anything and everything French. Before you got here, the dog's name was Adèle, but last night as I was tucking her in, *your* niece—"

"Oh she's *my* niece now," Alec said, laughing.

"—decided the name should start with a B like her last name."

Alec thought about it for a moment. "Bobette Bellamy? I can see her point. It does have a certain ring to it."

They shared a laugh as they walked over to a bank of chairs in the waiting area to sit, but Deb continued to stand and pace.

"She's started a list of things she wants to do and places she wants to see. Of course France is at the top."

"Pretty ambitious for an eight-year-old." Alec smiled as he watched his sister pin her unruly curly black hair out of her face. It sort of reminded him of Ilsa, which led his thoughts to Eli. He frowned, but Deb didn't notice.

"True. I think she's going to be trouble when she gets older. She's a terribly curious child." She finally took her seat and looked into her brother's eyes. "For instance, she's asked me when you're going to get married." She took Alec's hand in hers.

"Does she know about—?"

"Mom has referred to your 'condition' enough times that Stacy finally asked what the hell she was talking about… not in those words, of course."

Alec laughed. "I would hope not." He tried to imagine the look on his mother's face if her granddaughter had used those words.

"Mom changed the subject immediately and hasn't mentioned you in front of her since, but I sat Stacy down and told her what I thought… about you and about her gran's bullshit—"

"Not in those words, of course."

They both began laughing, and Alec hugged his sister. When the hilarity subsided, Deb grew serious.

"How are you—you and…?"

"Eli."

"How's it going?"

Alec sighed. "It's a bit rocky at the moment."

"Sorry."

"We'll work it out. He's asked for time, and I'm making sure he gets it." Alec's gaze traveled everywhere but to his sister: the nurses' station, the elevators, and the door of his stepfather's room.

"You sound a bit peeved."

Alec shook his head. "I'm just… just—kinda tired, I guess."

"Sounds like he's being difficult."

"No… it's—he's been through a lot." Alec massaged the bridge of his nose. "I've told you about Bennett." Deb nodded. "Eli's got—"

"Issues?"

"Yeah," Alec said with a laugh. "Issues, and it's turned out to be more complicated than I expected."

"Do you love him?"

"Sis, you know my history." He stared at the nurses' station again. "What does that really mean?"

"So it's yes." Alec slowly nodded. "Have you told him? Outside of an orgasm, I mean."

"Jesus!"

"Where?" she asked, gripping the arms of her seat and looking around frantically.

They broke up laughing again.

"Well, I'm certainly glad to see the two of you are having such a lovely time while your father is in there waiting to die!" Eleanor Sumner had sneaked up on them.

"The ice woman cometh," Deb whispered, and Alec chuckled as quietly as he could. He stood and sighed. "Hi, Mom. You hungry?"

"Yes, you haven't eaten in quite a while," Deb added. "You should probably get something in your stomach. You want to be strong for Levi."

"You don't care about him… out here laughing your fool heads off. What if he were to hear you?"

"Then he would be conscious, and that would be a good thing," Alec said calmly.

She looked up at him, her eyes roaming over his features. "You're such a handsome boy." She reached for his hair. "I wish you'd trim this some. You look like a hippie. No woman is going to want—"

"Mom, I think you should stretch your legs." She moved to sit, but Alec caught her arm, keeping her on her feet. "Let's take a walk to the cafeteria."

He and Deb nodded to each other.

"No, I don't want to leave your—"

"I'll be with him," Deb piped up. "I have Alec's cell number," she said, wiggling her phone in front of them. "And if I need you, I'll call right away."

She watched Alec practically drag their mother toward the elevators. Deb gathered her sweater and purse to go sit with Levi but saw a nurse enter the room carrying the necessities of a sponge bath, so she sat back down and waited.

ELI watched the numbers light up as the elevator rose through Cabell Huntington Hospital. He had no idea what he'd say to Alec. Getting here had been a relative blur, with Ilsa the primary force behind his efforts. He was still shaking a bit from his rough ride on that tiny plane into Yeager Airport. He'd seen the runway from the air, and it appeared to be on top of a mountain—a mountain that dropped off abruptly.

The doors opened onto the fifth-floor nurses' station, and Eli stepped off. With his stomach churning and his heart thudding in his chest, he reached the desk but didn't realize how dry his mouth had become until he tried to speak.

"Pardon me, sir?"

"I wonder if you could tell me where to find Mr. Sumner's room."

"Are you family?"

Eli hesitated. "I'm… I'm a—family friend."

"Mr. Sumner is in Room 514, to your left. I believe the family is with him."

"Thank you." Eli turned to leave, but he stopped himself. "C-can you tell me how he's doing?"

"I'm sorry, sir, we're not allowed to give out that information."

Eli nodded and headed down the hall.

DEB checked her watch and glanced at Levi's room again. If her mother and Alec returned, and she was still sitting out here instead of in the room hovering protectively over her stepfather, she'd never hear the end of it. She looked up the hall toward the elevators when she heard the bell announcing the arrival of another car. The doors opened, but only one person exited.

No sign of them yet, thank God, but—the man exiting was about an inch or two shorter than her brother, with short, dark brown hair and using a cane. He stopped at the nurses' station and then looked toward her.

"Holy shit!" Deb sprang from her seat. She'd only seen one photo of him. In one of his letters, Alec had sent her a panoramic shot of the city from the London Eye. Eli was standing in the background, pointing something out to Alec through the window and hadn't known the picture was being taken. His hair had been longer, more shaggy. In the letter Alec had written, *Sis, that's him on the right*, and then drawn a heart.

"H-hello. Are you... Eli?" He blinked at her with large, beautiful blue eyes. Deb smiled. *Oh yeah, you're him.*

"I'm sorry. You—"

"I'm Deb, Alec's sister."

His smile lit up the room. "Oh yes! I've seen your picture. Alec has a photo of you and your family in his room."

They shook hands, and she led him to a seat next to her. "Is Alec expecting you?"

"Uh... no, I heard about—how is your father... uh, stepfather... uncle?"

"He's all those things," Deb said, laughing out loud. "I see Alec has filled you in on our colorful family history."

Eli nodded. "He told me that after your father died, your mother married his brother... that he had always loved her."

"True. He's doing fine, by the way, but don't let my mother hear you say that."

"What? Why not?"

"He had a bit of heart trouble, but they got him here in time and cathed his artery. He's just recovering, but Mom is a bit of a drama queen and appears convinced he's on death's door."

Eli smiled. "I'll try to remember that and show the proper, bleak concern."

Deb laughed softly, touching his arm and squeezing. "Oh, Alec'll be so happy to see you." Eli's expression darkened, and Deb stopped smiling. "What's wrong? You're here to see him, aren't you?"

"I came because I thought he might need—"

"He needs you."

"We need to talk some things out." Eli took her hand and squeezed it.

Deb looked toward the elevators and sighed as she saw Alec and their mother exit. "Yeah, that's what he said."

AFTER forty-five minutes too long with his mother, Alec had ushered her back onto the elevator to rejoin Deb on the fifth floor. He had stopped listening to her by the end of their meal and allowed her continued criticism and advice about his romantic life and "choices" become Charlie Brown's teacher in his head. By the time the elevator doors opened, he was nodding and smiling as if he'd actually heard everything she'd said. Then he spotted Eli talking to his sister. At least he thought it was him. His hair was so short, but there was no mistaking that face, that smile, and those eyes.

"Eli?" Alec gaped at him. Deb and Eli stood to face him and his mother.

"Deborah, why aren't you in there with your father?!"

"He's having a bath, Mom."

Eleanor couldn't say anything to that, even though it was clear she wanted to. She turned her eyes to Eli. "Who's this?" she asked, stepping forward to take Eli's hand.

Alec blinked. "He's my—"

"Friend," Eli said quickly. "I'm Alec's best friend from London, Mrs. Sumner." He took her hand in both of his and held it. He looked deeply into her eyes and with a sympathetic expression, he said, "I was so sorry to hear of your husband's difficulty. I simply had to fly over and see how my friend and his family were holding up."

Alec glanced at his sister and saw she was struggling to keep from laughing herself unconscious, but their mother appeared to be buying it all.

"Oh, well, thank you, thank you so much, Mister...."

"Burke, Eli Burke." He led her to a seat and sat next to her, still holding her hand and occasionally smiling and nodding as she recounted the horror of finding her "beloved" husband sprawled out on the bathroom floor.

"I thought Levi was in the kitchen making a sandwich, Mom." Deb glanced at Alec, who eventually dropped into a seat beside his sister, still gaping at Eli.

Eleanor ignored her daughter, apparently finding Eli and his accent distractingly charming. "You didn't tell me you had such nice friends, Alec."

"Didn't I?" Alec grinned slightly. He watched his mother's fluttering eyelashes, saw the color rising to her cheeks, and in complete bewilderment, he leaned over to his sister. "Is our mother flirting with my boyfriend?" he asked, shuddering visibly.

Mrs. Sumner dabbed at her eyes with her handkerchief. "I should really freshen up before I go back to Levi's room." She and Eli stood, and he released her hand. "If you'll excuse me."

"Of course."

She walked off, Deb following in her wake after glancing between Eli and her brother. They stood alone now, looking everywhere but at one another.

"You look tired," Eli said.

Alec shrugged. "How was your flight?"

"Good, good. A bit rough coming into your airport, though."

Alec smiled. "Yes, I can imagine."

They fell silent again.

"Your sister tells me your stepfather is going to be all right."

"Yeah. The doctor expects a full recovery."

"That's good."

"Of course, he'll have to watch his diet and increase his exercise."

Eli nodded and the silence quickly became oppressive. Alec looked around the brightly lit waiting area. "Would you like to meet him?" he asked.

Eli looked at Room 514. "Uh... okay."

They walked over, and Alec knocked.

"Come in," the nurse said. He pushed the door open slowly and saw her covering Levi with a blanket, tucking him in and making sure he was comfortable. "I'm all done." She checked the readings on his monitors and then carried a small basin of water into the bathroom and emptied it in the toilet. "He's all yours."

"Thank you." Alec said, holding the door for her as she left.

For all intents and purposes, they were alone again. Alec and Eli stood there staring at Levi Sumner. The only sounds in the room were their breathing and the barely audible conversations coming from the wall-mounted television.

"I missed you," Alec whispered.

"Alec—"

"I know. Not now." He didn't speak for a few moments. "Did Ilsa tell you where I was?"

Eli nodded and then grinned. "She practically packed my bag and threw me out of the house."

"I'm glad she's not angry with me anymore."

Eli looked at him. "Alec, no one is angry with you."

"You seemed pretty angry the last time I saw you."

"I was mad at myself, not you, and I was... ashamed." Eli continued to watch the elder Sumner breathe. Alec moved closer, but Eli started talking again. "I'm sorry I lied to you. I'm sorry I messed things up."

"Eli, you didn't mess things up." He took Eli in his arms, but Eli resisted, pushing against him to free himself.

"I know you had Dray over—"

"What?"

"And that's—"

He silenced Eli with his mouth, kissing him long and hard, parting his lips with his tongue until Eli's struggles weakened, and he clung to Alec, pressing the full length of his body against his.

"Stop it!"

They parted abruptly, their heads swimming. Eleanor Sumner stood in the doorway glaring at the two of them. Deb stood behind her, smiling like it was Christmas morning.

"In the hall, now!" Eleanor hissed.

Before following her, Alec glanced at Eli, but he nodded that he'd be okay, and Alec walked out.

Deb smiled apologetically at Eli. "I'd better referee," she whispered. "You have a seat. Read a magazine or something." Eli nodded at her and smiled, and then she was gone.

HE LOOKED at the elder Sumner lying there. The monitor beeped steadily, and his chest rose and fell smoothly. All seemed well. Eli sat down, opened a magazine, and waited. He was almost lost in an article when he heard raised voices in the hall. He looked at the door, but he couldn't make out anything that was being said. However, he could imagine. The voices quieted, and he tried to find his place in the article again.

"You… you mustn't blame her," Mr. Sumner whispered. Eli jumped, the magazine sliding to the floor at his feet.

"Sir?"

"Don't blame her, please." Eli didn't say anything. He glanced at the door, thinking that perhaps he should summon someone. "It's all right. I pretend to sleep when she's here." Eli grinned. He could understand that after only just meeting Mrs. Sumner. "Who are you?"

"I'm… I'm Eli, sir. Eli Burke."

"Limey, huh?" he asked. Eli nodded. "You with Alec?"

"Yes, sir."

He sighed deeply and stared at the ceiling. "My wife… she likes things, her life, a certain way." He looked back at Eli. "She tends to come undone when things don't fit like she thinks they should—doesn't know how to function." Eli waited. "One day Alec—our boy, he just didn't fit anymore."

"That must have been painful."

Levi nodded and closed his eyes. His expression twisted, and thinking he might be in pain, Eli stood. "Can I get someone? Do you need anything?"

"Water."

Eli looked around the room and saw a water bottle with a straw on a cart against the wall. He went to it and brought it to Mr. Sumner. He held the straw to the man's lips while he took a few tentative sips and sighed.

"Good?"

"Yes, thank you." Eli returned to his seat, setting the bottle on the table next to him. Mr. Sumner was watching him. "How old are you, boy?"

"Twenty-six, sir."

"What you need a cane for?" Eli opened his mouth to speak, but wasn't sure how to begin. He closed his mouth. "Sorry," Mr. Sumner said, turning away. "None of my business. Didn't mean to embarrass you. Guess you might have been born that way."

"Actually, I was born just fine," Eli said, the anger flaring in him. Sumner stared at him, waiting. "Almost three years ago I ran into a group of men who thought my partner and I probably shouldn't exist."

Sumner was silent for a few moments, watching Eli's face. "They hurt you?"

Eli closed his eyes and sighed. "More than I can explain."

"And your... your... man?" They looked at each other, the silence stretching out between them until Sumner turned away. "Too much hate in this world."

"Yes, sir."

"But then you met my boy."

Eli smiled, and when he looked up at Sumner, he was smiling too. "Yes. I saw him waiting outside a coffee shop holding a green handbag. You don't forget that."

"You love him?"

"Very much."

"Then you'll be fine. He's grown into a good man. I'm proud of him."

"You should probably tell him that, sir."

"I will... first chance I get," he said, yawning. "And don't let that wife of mine scare you."

"She doesn't."

Sumner laughed. "Then you're the only one, son." They both laughed.

AFTER Levi was settled for the night, Eleanor, Deb, Alec, and Eli left the hospital. First stop was dropping Eli off at his hotel.

"Thanks for the ride, Alec." Eli grasped the door handle to exit the car.

Alec looked out the window at the hotel. "I've never stayed here. Is it nice?"

Eli glanced at the nondescript building and then smiled at Alec. "It's fine. Very comfortable." He opened the door. "Thanks again."

"You hungry?" Alec asked quickly. "I'm sure we could find some place still serving over at Pullman Square."

"Alec, we really should be getting home," Eleanor said from the back seat. "I was hoping you'd spend the night at my house. I'd hate to be there all alone."

Alec glanced in the rearview mirror at his mother and Deb. He and Deb rolled their eyes in unison. "Mother, I haven't been staying with you the two days I've been here," Alec said. "Why do you need me so desperately now?" Eleanor had no response to that, and Alec turned back to Eli hopefully. "We could try Uno's or Five Guys... they're probably still open. What do you say?"

"I'm not really hungry, Alec. Thank you. I think I'm just going get some sleep. Still haven't quite recovered from the flight."

Alec nodded, and they ran out of things to say. But then Deb hopped out of the backseat and gave Eli a hug. "I hope you'll come to dinner tomorrow, Eli."

"Deborah, I don't think—"

"Mom!" Alec and Deb shouted in unison, and Eleanor quieted, averting her eyes.

"Would you, Eli?" Deb said, replacing him in the front passenger seat as he held the door for her. "Come to dinner, I mean?"

He thought about it, looking at Alec and seeing the hope in his eyes. "Yes, thank you, Deb. I'd like that."

Alec visibly relaxed, just as his mother tensed and puckered further.

Chapter 31

STACY stood by the dining room table holding as much silverware and napkins as her smaller hands would allow. Bobette, their Bichon Friese, walked around her and under the table, searching for attention. When she didn't get it, she disappeared into one of the back bedrooms. She'd made the circuit at least twenty times already. After her father had placed all the plates, Stacy studied the table. "Who's coming to dinner, Daddy?" she asked as she straightened a butter knife on a napkin beside a plate.

"Your uncle's boyfriend, Eli."

She continued to help her father set the table, carefully laying out another place setting of silverware in the proper order. "Is he nice?"

"I haven't met him yet, honey, but I think if your uncle cares about him, he must be."

"What does he do?"

"I think Alec told us he was an interpreter for the deaf."

Stacy paused in her duties, her eyes widening. "We have a couple of girls at school who can't hear. They have people with them who talk with their hands. That's what he does?" Charles nodded and smiled at his daughter. "They always sit with each other at lunch. Maybe I could learn to talk to them."

"Maybe you could, dear, but it takes a long time to learn another language."

Stacy nodded thoughtfully. "Are they going to kiss?"

Charles paused in putting out the drinking glasses and stared at his daughter. "Who?"

"Uncle Alec and Eli."

"What do you know about kissing?"

She shrugged. "Tommy Piper tried to kiss me last week."

"What?" Charles asked, standing up straight in shock. He turned to his wife who entered the room with Chuck in tow. "Deb? Stacy says some boy tried to kiss her last week."

"Uh-huh."

"Uh-huh? What the f—"

"Dear… let's not get worked up about that. Okay?"

"She's eight!" Charles roared.

"Precisely."

"But—"

Deb held up a silencing finger and turned to her daughter. "Stacy?"

"Yes, Mommy?"

"What did you think of that boy trying to kiss you?"

Stacy's face twisted in disgust. "Ewwww!"

"What did you do?"

"I punched him," Stacy declared, imitating the move, punching the air with her fist. Deb smiled knowingly at her husband, and Charles appeared relieved. "I punched him right in the nuts!"

The horror returned to Charles's face. "Nuts?!"

"Who's having nuts?" Eleanor asked, entering the room.

Stacy turned to her grandmother. "I was telling Mommy and Daddy that I—"

"Stacy, come help me in the kitchen, dear." Stacy dropped the remaining utensils and dutifully followed her mother into the kitchen.

Eleanor scooped up Chuck and began tickling him. He squealed with delight, but his kicking feet startled her, and she quickly put him back down. Chuck waddled over to a blue toy truck and began scooting it along. Eleanor turned to Charles, who was finishing setting the table.

"Do you really think this is a good idea? Having this *man* over for dinner?"

"Oh? Deb told me you seemed quite taken with him until you caught him kissing your son," he said with a smirk. Before she could object further, Charles raised his eyes to meet hers and said, "Alec cares about him, and therefore he's welcome in our home."

"But surely—"

Charles pointed his finger at her, silencing her effectively. "You should know that if you say anything inappropriate regarding Alec and Eli, I will not stop Deb from throwing you out of this house. And don't call me Shirley."

"Ha! Good one," Alec said, strolling into the room, straightening his collar, Bobette in his wake. The tiny dog made a beeline for Chuck. The toddler burst into a fit of giggles as the tiny dog nuzzled him.

"Where have you been, brother?" Charles asked.

Alec blushed slightly. "I was just… um—"

"Checking yourself out in the mirror?"

Alec didn't say anything, but his mother glared at him and mumbled, "I hardly think I would be the one offering an inappropriate—"

"Mother!" Deb said, entering the room and placing a casserole dish on the table. "We'd rather our children not be exposed to your hateful, ill-informed bullsh—"

A knock at the door gave them pause. "I got it!" Alec rushed to the door, but before opening it, he turned to his mother. "Be good." She harrumphed and looked away as he opened the door.

Eli stood there holding a bottle of wine and smiling. He wore dark jeans, a blue button-down shirt, and a lightweight navy jacket. He and Alec gazed at each other. Deb stepped forward quickly, as Alec seemed tongue-tied.

"Come in, Eli," she said, taking the wine.

"Thank you." He looked around the room. "Alec," he said, nodding. "Mrs. Sumner. Good to see you again."

"Mr. Burke." She nodded coolly, staring at his cane.

"This is Charles, my brother-in-law," Alec said.

"Hey there," Charles said, coming forward to shake Eli's hand. "You're here just in time."

"Hi," Stacy said, suddenly appearing and taking Eli's hand to lead him to the table. "I'm Stacy. You sit next to me."

Eli glanced nervously at everyone, but he allowed himself to be drawn forward and into the dining room. Stacy sat him in a chair and dropped down next to him. "Uncle Alec, you sit on the other side of Eli," she instructed.

"Yes, ma'am," Alec said with a grin.

Eli jumped when Charles whistled sharply, opening the sliding patio door for Bobette. The dog obediently exited, taking up a position directly on the other side of the glass so that she could watch the goings-on at the dinner table. Though the family had quickly become immune to the tiny, fluffly, white dog's pleading, dark gaze through the patio door, it was clear Eli and Alec were moved whenever Bobette lifted one tiny paw to the glass.

"Ignore her," Deb said with a laugh. "She's playing you."

Deb took her seat next to Chuck and his highchair, while Eleanor sat on the other side of it. At the head of the table, Charles prepared to fill everyone's plates.

"Eli?" he asked, holding up a plate, his serving spoon hovering over the mashed potatoes.

"Oh, a little of everything, please."

Charles began dishing out the food. Once little Chuck's plate was ready, Deb cut his pork chop, carrots, and broccoli into tiny, manageable pieces, while she maintained control of his mashed potatoes and applesauce to avert total disaster.

Eli watched Stacy cut her food just as her mother had done with Chuck's and daintily spear and eat a piece of her pork chop. "My, you're quite the little lady, aren't you?"

She beamed up at him. "Uncle Eli—"

"Oh, he's not your—"

A look from Charles was all it took to silence Eleanor, and she went back to focusing on her dinner.

"What were you going to say, Stacy?" Alec asked her.

"Uncle Eli, how far is France from England?"

"Um, just a few hours by train, but on very clear nights, there are places in southern England where you can see lights from France."

Stacy's eyes grew wide with wonder. "You mean if I came to visit you and Uncle Alec, I could see France?"

Eli looked nervously from Alec to Deb and Charles. "Uh... I think your mum and dad would have to—"

"Stacy, if you came to visit me, I'd take you to France," Alec said quickly. He looked to Eli for help. "There's a special train... right?"

"Oh, yes." Eli smiled at Stacy. "It's called the Eurostar, and one

runs every hour between London and Paris. It goes about 300 kilo—"
He scrunched his face in concentration. "Uh, 186 miles per hour. The
trip only takes a bit more than two hours."

"That's impossible!" Stacy said, beginning to giggle. "You're
making that up. My daddy's an engineer. He knows." She turned to her
father. "Isn't he making that up, Daddy?"

Charles shook his head. "Nope, sweetie. It's true. All of it." He
smiled as Stacy's eyes got so big and round that they looked ready to
pop from her skull, her mouth forming a silent, *Wow!*

"Can our car go that fast?"

"Not on its best day, hon," Charles said, laughing.

With no further snide remarks from Eleanor, dinner was a
complete success, with plenty of laughter, delightful conversation
around the table, and delicious food. Eli talked about when he first saw
Alec on the street and how he had shown him around London. Charles
asked some questions about sign language and how Eli got into it,
which Stacy listened to intently.

Eli showed her how to introduce herself to the girls at school.
"And I suggest you get a book that shows you the alphabet. It comes in
handy because there's not a sign for everything, and knowing how to
spell will save you."

When Chuck's head fell forward, jerking him awake for the third
time, his father hopped up from the table. "I've got him, honey."
Charles freed him from the highchair and carried him to his crib. "Let's
get your pajamas on, little man. Come on, Stacy. You too."

"Awww! I want to talk to Eli some more." Stacy stretched up to
Eli's ear and whispered, "I like the way you talk." Eli blushed and
smiled at Deb and Alec.

"Time for bed, sweetie," Deb said.

"Okay, I'll go," Stacy said, stomping toward the hallway. "But I
got one more question." She had stopped and turned to face the table,
her hand on her hip. It was all the adults could do not to laugh at her.

"What is it, honey?"

"Eli, what happened to your leg?"

Their smiles faltered, and Eli stammered, "Oh, uh… well,
Stacy…." She was still watching them, waiting for an answer,

completely oblivious to the discomfort she'd caused.

"Honey, that's not really an appropriate question," Eleanor said, but she looked at Eli with obvious interest and hope in her eyes that he would answer.

"I'm sorry," Stacy said, lowering her eyes.

"No, Stacy," Eli said quickly. "It's fine. A long time ago, my leg got injured. The doctors worked on it for a long time, but this is the best they could do. I go to the gym three times a week to make sure it stays strong and continues to work for me."

"I'm sorry you hurt your leg, Uncle Eli." Stacy came over to him, threw her arms around his neck, and kissed his cheek. "Good night!" She repeated the same maneuver on Alec, her mother, and her grandmother before rushing to the patio door to let the dog back in. Bobette trotted by her, heading for the bedrooms, and Stacy followed her.

Alec began clearing the table, urging his sister to have a seat and some wine.

"Let me help," Eleanor said, grabbing some dishes and following him into the kitchen as Deb and Eli moved into the living room with their wine.

"Alec?" Eleanor set her dishes on the kitchen counter.

"Yeah, Mom." His back was to her as he began scraping the food scraps into the garbage.

"What… what happened to his leg?" Alec looked at her sharply, and she lowered her eyes. "I was… I was just curious," she said softly. "I was… I guess, too charmed… and then too angry at the hospital to think about it."

Alec watched her conflicted expression for several moments, and then he told her exactly what had happened to Eli's leg.

Chapter 32

AS THEY dropped off Eleanor at her posh Ritter Park home, Eli had expected further stalling tactics on her part. He believed she'd try just about anything to stop her son from being alone with him, where God knows *what* could happen. But he had been pleasantly surprised when she simply thanked Alec for the ride and then paused by Eli's window to say good night and tell him how nice it was to meet him. After she'd gone inside, he turned to Alec, and they stared at each other in shock before sharing a smile and driving away.

Alec took the long way round to the hotel, and Eli listened politely as he described his hometown. When they neared his old high school, Alec explained, "They made it into apartments for the elderly." Eli strained to make out the pale, massive structure, and even in the failing light, he could see how elegant and beautiful it was, with matching staircases curving toward each other and creating an arch. "The city wanted to save the architecture."

"It's beautiful," Eli said as Alec pulled the car over and parked.

Alec turned excitedly to face him. "It was even in a movie once— a horrid movie," he said, closing his eyes, shaking his head, and smiling sadly, "but a movie nonetheless." Eli smiled as Alec struggled between being thrilled and being disgusted. "It was called *Teen-Age Strangler*. Made back in 1964." Alec gazed out the window at his old school. "It was on an episode of *Mystery Science Theater 3000*—"

"That program that makes fun of bad movies?"

Alec nodded and laughed. "In one of the scenes, I recognized my school. I just about choked on my pizza."

"So where's the new school?" Eli asked.

Alec grimaced. "The city consolidated Huntington High and Huntington East High years ago." His expression told Eli a lot about how Alec felt about that decision. Alec sighed and pulled away from the curb. "Well... I'd better get you into bed—I mean... I mean... back to your hotel."

Eli smiled to himself, and they were soon parking in front of the Holiday Inn Express. Alec cut the engine, and they sat in silence for a few moments, both apparently unsure about what to do or say next. Eli sighed and took hold of the door handle, which prompted Alec to speak up.

"How long will you be in town?"

"I'm thinking about leaving tomorrow."

"Oh."

Eli looked at Alec. "Your stepfather is doing well, and you all seem fine. You have your family around you—they're great, by the way—but there probably wasn't any real need for me to come."

"I needed you." Alec's hand found Eli's thigh. "I'm glad you came."

Eli looked at the hand and imagined it moving elsewhere on his body, remembered it moving elsewhere. "I... I was worried... about you. I had to see that you were okay." Alec leaned over and kissed him gently, lingeringly, and Eli responded, leaning as close as he could in his awkward position. "I'm sorry, Alec. I'm sorry for so much."

"You don't have—"

Eli closed his eyes and held up a hand to silence him. "I do have to," he said. He opened his eyes and held Alec's gaze. "I'm sorry I lied to you about Dray, but mostly I'm sorry I've been so much work."

"I'm not going to say it's been a cakewalk, Eli, but I believe you're worth it."

Eli looked out his window at the welcoming lights of the hotel entrance. He sighed, not knowing how to go on. Luckily he didn't have to as Alec reached over and gently ran his fingers over his hair, sending shivers through him.

"I think I'm going to need time to get used to this hair," Alec said, smiling. His hand continued to stroke Eli's head. "Why'd you cut it?"

Eli shrugged and looked at him. "It was one, quick, easy way to simplify my life a bit. I was always fussing with it, trying to get it to behave, so...." Alec couldn't seem to stop rubbing his head, and Eli began to respond, his eyes growing dreamy. It had been about a week since their date, that fantastic night that ended so horribly the next day. He leaned into Alec's hand, and then their lips met again. Beginning gently, the kiss soon became more demanding and desperate.

"Do you remember the first time you put your hands on me, Eli?" Alec whispered.

"Huh?" he uttered as he went for Alec's earlobe, and his hands slid beneath Alec's shirt. They continued kissing and groping for each other, fighting the steering wheel and console between them.

"Remember?" Alec said. "We were in the backseat of Ilsa's car?"

Eli paused, allowing both of them to catch their breath. "Y-yes, I... I remember. Why?" Alec smiled and glanced to the backseat and then back at Eli, who laughed, "Alec, we're not a couple of teenagers."

"Come on," Alec pleaded, flashing a wicked grin.

Eli glanced nervously at the hotel and then through each window of the car. "What if... someone sees us?"

"I'm willing to take that risk."

"And what, precisely, are the sodomy laws in this state?"

"Repealed in the 1970s." Alec wriggled his eyebrows at him enticingly.

Eli grinned, and they quickly exited the car—Alec pausing only to hit the button on his door that unlocked all the other doors—then scrambled into the backseat, both breathless, turned on, and nervous. However, as Alec pulled Eli to him, guiding him to straddle his lap, Eli became a bit more than nervous.

Between hungry kisses and frantic rubbing, he experienced flashes of breath-stopping terror. The memory of his lover's murder kept coming to him—chilling him despite the lust-fueled fever he was in. He tried to shake it off, tried to forget that they had only been walking together, chatting, and holding hands when they were cornered. What would happen if he and Alec were discovered engaged in window-steaming sex?

Alec soon had Eli's shirt undone, and when his lips closed over Eli's right nipple, all Eli's ghostly memories fled the car. He tangled his hands in Alec's hair and pressed himself against his mouth. Alec seemed to accept his mission, because Eli could feel him smile against his chest before his tongue and teeth went to work. Eli whimpered as a shiver ran through him. Alec's fingers found Eli's belt buckle, quickly undoing it, and then performing the same action on his jeans. When Alec's hand found him hot and hard, Eli jerked forward gasping Alec's name before bending to take his lips.

"I remember, Eli," Alec whispered between kisses. "I remember your lips and teeth on my ear."

"What did I say?"

"You… you said I smelled good."

"Mmm-hm, you still do," Eli said with a smile. "I remember you trying to fend me off. You should know that only served to excite me more."

Alec chuckled, took Eli in hand, and began stroking him. "Come for me, baby," he hissed. Eli trembled as Alec's hand moved on him, wrapping his arms around him, pressing Alec's mouth against his collarbone. His hand tugged Alec's hair, and then he playfully bit his ear, causing him to cry out.

"*Yes,*" Eli whispered. "*Yes, Alec.*" He was so close, so ready to let loose—then the parking lot lights came on, illuminating the inside of the car and the two of them.

They froze for mere seconds before leaping away from each other and laughing hysterically as they frantically put themselves away and straightened their clothes. Moments later, red-faced and breathless, they strolled through the doors of the hotel and headed for the elevators.

"Excuse me, Mr. Burke?" the front desk clerk called, appearing out of nowhere.

Eli stopped and turned slowly, trying to keep his face calm and disinterested. "Yes?" he said as he motioned for Alec to continue to the elevator.

The clerk turned and pulled a note from beneath the counter. "I have a message for you," he said, sliding the paper across to Eli.

"Thank you."

"Have a good night, sir."

Eli nodded and joined Alec on the waiting elevator.

WHEN the door to the room clicked shut, Alec locked it and approached Eli, who was standing in the middle of the room staring down at the note in his hand. He gasped when Alec's arms wrapped around him.

"Now, where were we?" Alec nibbled his neck as he reached around and began loosening Eli's jeans again, trying to get at him. But Eli squirmed free.

"I just need to call Casey," he said, smiling and holding up a finger as he turned and backed away. "One moment."

"Is everything okay?" he asked as Eli whipped out his cell and turned it on.

"She just asked that I call her as soon as possible." Eli sat on one of the beds and waited as the phone rang, glancing at the clock on the bedside table. Alec stood by, looking down at Eli, at his features, and mulling over the haircut and how it set off his eyes so well.

"Hello. Casey… Sorry it's so late. Yeah, he's fine…." He looked up at Alec. "She says 'hi'."

He smiled and joined Eli on the bed, gently squeezing his boyfriend's leg as he listened to Eli's side of the conversation and watched his changing expression. Alec grinned when Eli gently readjusted himself to accommodate his stirring erection.

"What?!" Eli exclaimed, and Alec's hand paused on its trip up Eli's thigh. "Of course we didn't forget!" Eli covered the receiver and looked at Alec. "We forgot about Ilsa's surprise party," he whispered.

Alec's eyes widened as he sighed and fell back on the bed.

"Sorry?" Eli resumed listening to Casey. "Oh, yeah, definitely. We'll be there." Eli glanced at him again. "Or, at least, I'll be there for sure. I'll have to check with Alec." He listened again. "Take care, love."

Eli ended the call and promptly stretched his body out on top of Alec's. They both sighed into each other, and Alec's hands cupped Eli's bottom, kneading possessively.

"What's the verdict?" he asked.

"I need to leave in the morning," Eli said softly. Alec looked away from him in an attempt to hide his disappointment. "I'd like to get back early enough to be of some help. Casey's working later at the hospital than she'd planned—somebody's ill—but Tony and Lyle are taking up most of the slack."

He smiled at Eli, stroking his face. "I'm coming with you."

"Your family—"

"I'll catch a later flight. I'll make sure to check in on Levi and tell them all goodbye." He kissed Eli. "I'll be right behind you," he said softly before suddenly flipping Eli and pinning him to the bed. In a flash, his hands were under Eli's shirt, stroking his warm skin, and his lips were on Eli's mouth, searching for his tongue.

"Hang on! Alec, I think we should talk about Dray."

Alec groaned, rose up, and stared at Eli. "What the hell for?"

Eli propped himself up on his elbows. "I know you had him over to your place." Alec just stared at him until Eli averted his gaze. "Tony ran into him on his way up. Said he had a bottle of wine and a... a self-satisfied air about him."

"Let me explain."

Once again Eli squirmed free of Alec, much to his disappointment. "Look, I know I have absolutely no right to have any feelings about this whatsoever—"

"Yet, you do," Alec said, grinning slightly.

Eli got off the bed, grabbed his cane, and walked across the room, putting a bit more distance between them. "After what I did... to Bennett and... and after what I've done to you."

"To me?"

"Since we've been apart, I've been thinking," Eli said, beginning to speak more rapidly, "thinking about all you've done for me, all you continue to *try* to do for me. And I realized I haven't been there for you like I should be."

"Eli—"

"You know how I was when we met." His gaze flicked to Alec and away again. "And then when we got together... Alec, it was great. I thought I could move on, move forward with you, but the longer we were together and the happier I became—"

"The more guilty you felt about cheating."

"I didn't think I deserved to be happy." Eli ran his hand over his head and appeared quietly surprised not to find more hair there. "I lashed out at Dray. I lashed out at you for talking to Dray. And the entire time…." He shrugged and sighed. "I was just angry at myself for what happened with Dray."

Eli turned his back to him and leaned on the dresser. To Alec he looked like he was examining the striking contrast between the dark wood and his pale hands.

"I want you, but I know you deserve better," he whispered. He looked in the mirror above the dresser, meeting Alec's eyes over his shoulder. "I don't know what to do."

Alec was off the bed and closing the distance between them before Eli could say anything more. He spun Eli around to face him, pinning his arms to his sides.

"Leave off!" Eli struggled but couldn't free himself.

"Eli… Eli, stop it! Listen to me." Alec looked into his eyes until Eli stilled himself. "I have something to ask you."

ELI could feel the heat of Alec's body passing through his cotton shirt. He smelled his skin—that chocolate-vanilla-sandalwoody bodywash he used—a scent that never failed to comfort him. And he felt Alec's muscles working as he held him in place. His eyes fluttered closed from the sensations washing over him. His mind spun with the thoughts and images dancing behind his eyes.

"I can't think clearly with you pressed up against me like this. C-couldn't you have asked me from where you were?"

"No." Alec loosened his grip and slowly turned Eli to face the mirror. "I didn't think you'd stand still for it." Eli opened his eyes and saw their reflection staring back at him: Alec holding him from behind and resting his chin on his shoulder, his cheek against Eli's. "What do you see?" Alec asked. Eli stiffened and tried to pull free of him, but Alec held tight, and he eventually stopped struggling but averted his eyes. "Tell me," Alec urged.

Eli looked into the mirror again. "I see you."

Alec grinned. "What about the man I'm holding in my arms? What do you see when you look at him?"

"This is ridiculous!" Eli tried in vain to break free again.

"Possibly, but I'm not releasing you until you answer me—and honestly."

He reluctantly focused again on the mirror. He stared at himself for several moments and sighed. "I see a cheat and a liar. I see... damage." Eli looked away.

Alec frowned slightly but didn't release him. "I see a strong, intelligent, handsome man with a beautiful spirit, a great sense of humor, and the loveliest eyes I've ever seen."

Eli smiled hesitantly. "I'm not surprised that's who you see when you look at yourself."

Alec chuckled, and Eli joined him. "Thank you, but you know who I'm talking about." As their laughter faded, Alec became serious again. "I see the man I love." The pleasant grin on Eli's face faltered, and he tensed. "I love you, all of you—the wonderful and the damaged, the compassionate and the heartbroken, your silence and your chaos."

Alec pressed him forward into the dresser as his fingers slid beneath Eli's shirt and up along his back, stripping it off over his head and tossing it to the floor. Then Alec's hands caressed the back of Eli's neck, sliding into his hair and causing him to shiver. Eli watched their reflection as he leaned his head to give Alec better access to his neck. He moaned, feeling himself grow harder as Alec kissed and nibbled at him, all the while grinding his own erection against him from behind.

"I didn't sleep with Dray," Alec panted between kisses.

"No?" Eli asked, pressing backward as Alec began undoing Eli's jeans again. He unceremoniously shoved Eli's pants and briefs to his ankles, and then he roughly bent him over the dresser. Eli's cane hit the floor as he took himself in hand, making sure nothing of import got caught or squashed in the coming frenzy. Alec peeled off his shirt and shoved his jeans just to his thighs.

"No," Alec assured him as he yanked open a small, top drawer on his right, discovering a small complimentary first-aid kid. "If Tony could have seen Dray storming out of our building, he would have known he hadn't gotten what he'd come for." Alec popped open the kit one-handed and, after rummaging through it briefly, produced a tube of Vaseline lip balm. He smiled and held it up so Eli could see in the mirror. "It's got aloe."

"Brilliant," Eli moaned. His gut tightened with need, and he pressed backward even harder against Alec's cock. He ached to have Alec inside him, but he waited patiently as Alec prepared himself. Eli tensed involuntarily when he felt Alec spread him, his slick fingers playing against his opening. When two fingers breached him, Eli's entire body spasmed, and he grunted, gripping the dresser to steady himself.

"Sorry."

"No... no w-worries," Eli said, breathing heavily, struggling to relax enough to accommodate.

ALEC looked at their reflection, and his dick twitched at the aching, lustful grin on Eli's face. He worked his fingers within Eli, watching Eli's reflection buck and squirm in response. Then he removed his fingers and spread Eli, positioning his cock at his opening and slowly sliding into him. Eli groaned, and his right leg buckled, but Alec's arm quickly encircled his waist, holding him fast and upright as he began rocking into him.

"I've got you," Alec whispered.

Alec was thankful the mirror was mounted on the wall above the long, low dresser rather than attached to it. Otherwise Eli's moaning would be punctuated by a rhythmic thumping against the wall, and they might expect a call from the front desk about complaining neighbors. As it was, there were only Eli's ever-vocal responses as the top of the dresser became slick with his sweat.

"Ahh-Alec...," Eli moaned. "F-fuck *meee.*"

Alec slowed and, several times, pulled almost free of Eli before slowly pushing back in, thus drawing out the sensations for both of them. This soon had Eli whimpering, and Alec was unsure of how much longer he could last, so he changed his angle a bit, gripping Eli around his chest, pulling him up and back, against his own chest.

"Look," he instructed as he took hold of Eli's cock, stroking it. They took in their reflections together. Alec could see Eli's eyes widen and a smile play at his lips, parting in a gasp. "Look how beautiful, how perfect you are. Look at me loving you," Alec rasped, striking that sensitive spot within his boyfriend.

Eli shouted something inarticulately profane and went rigid in his arms as ribbons of come hit the mirror. His inner muscles undulated around Alec, bringing him along right behind him. When Eli's leg gave out again, they both collapsed onto the carpet in a sweaty, breathless, laughing heap.

Chapter 33

ELI dropped his duffel by the door and walked over to Alec's sleeping form. He quietly set the alarm to go off in ninety minutes, and then he pulled on a fresh shirt before finishing a quick towel-dry of his shorter hair. Alec stirred in his sleep, and Eli went quickly to the dresser, wiping away the evidence of their activities from last night with the damp towel. He smiled at the memory.

He carefully sat on the bed and watched Alec's chest rise and fall peacefully; his dark hair had fallen over his eyes.

"You look exhausted," he whispered as he reached out and brushed the hair off Alec's face before kissing him goodbye. "See you at the party, love." He slipped on his suit jacket and left the room, leaving a "do not disturb" sign on the door.

ALEC flipped through the in-flight magazine and considered watching the movie provided. Earlier, when he woke up alone, there had been a moment of panic and disorientation, but then he'd realized Eli had set the clock for him, leaving time for him to say his goodbyes and catch his flight to London. He glanced at his watch. He'd make it to the party later than he'd hoped, but he'd be there, back among his friends and— he smiled—back with Eli.

His mother had surprised him again by not raising a ruckus over his leaving. When he told her goodbye, she'd hugged him for a very long time and kissed his cheek. There was a softness in her eyes that he'd never seen before. It gave him pause.

"Mom? Are... are you okay?"

She'd smiled and nodded. "I'm fine, dear, but... call me more often, please."

Alec had just blinked at her in disbelief. "Mom?"

She put a hand on his shoulder. "I saw the way you looked at each other." She fell silent for a moment, then, "I'm not saying I've accepted your choice—"

"It's not a choice, Mom."

She raised a hand to silence him, her eyes closing as she struggled. "I... I hear you." Her eyes opened again, and she looked into his. "Just... just call me more often, please. Tell me how you are. Okay?"

Alec had promised he would, and he hugged her again.

Levi was doing well, sitting up in bed and trying to argue with his wife. Deb had been thrilled to hear things were better between him and Eli, and after hugs and kisses for his niece and nephew, she'd shooed him on his way.

Alec gave up on the movie and put away the magazine, deciding instead to sleep as best he could during the direct flight from New York City. He closed his eyes and sighed. He wouldn't be far behind Eli.

"WHAT'S left?" Eli asked as he and Tony looked over the living room.

"I don't think Lyle's left much for anyone to do." He grabbed a pillow from the sofa and fluffed it. "He's operating in crisis mode."

Just then Lyle appeared carrying two stepladders in one arm and a roll of some type of paper in the other. "Gents, I need help with this banner." They sprang into action, Tony and Lyle ascending the ladders in tandem while Eli eyed the positioning of the HAPPY BIRTHDAY, ILSA! banner. They taped it in place, then Lyle scrambled back up each ladder and stapled it to the arch leading into the dining room.

Tony grabbed the ladders and, without being instructed to do so, carried them back down into the cellar. Eli watched Lyle as he looked over the rooms, his friend absently tapping a thoughtful finger to his lips.

"What do you think?" he asked.

Lyle glanced at him as if he'd forgotten Eli was there. "Oh, it looks great... don't you think?" Eli nodded. "I just don't want to forget anything."

"Lyle, the house is clean. You've cleared space in the kitchen for the food and drinks." He turned to a corner of the living room and held his hands up like he was framing a scene in a movie. "You've designated a spot for the presents to accumulate. And the breakables are safely tucked away." Lyle nodded and grinned, and Eli turned back to face him. "What else is there?"

"We need to shower and change before the guests start arriving."

"Good call," Eli said. "I'll cover the door until you two are done."

Lyle headed for the hallway, and just as he reached it, Tony reappeared from the cellar.

"Tony, follow me!" Lyle commanded, running up the stairs.

The artist looked lost and glanced at Eli. "What?"

"Shower."

"Ah!" Tony dashed up the stairs behind Lyle, beaming from ear to ear. "Coming, dear!" Eli chuckled as he watched them go, and he wondered how long that shower would take.

THE taxi driver looked curiously out his window. "What's going on here, mate?"

"Birthday party," Alec said, paying him and exiting, dragging his suitcase behind him.

"Anyone need a safe ride home, tell 'em to give us a call, yeah?"

"You bet. Good night."

"Cheers!"

Alec headed up the walk.

"Dr. Sumner?" a young man shouted, rushing up to him, Lincoln following in his wake.

"M-Mickey?" Alec looked the man up and down. He looked so different out of his waiter gear and... smiling. "How are you?"

"I'm good, thanks." Mickey reached behind him and grasped Lincoln's hand.

"We're both doing fine," Lincoln said softly. It was dark out, but Alec could swear he was blushing.

"What are you doing out here? The party's inside."

"We could ask you the same thing," Mickey said.

"Just getting back from the States."

Lincoln held up a cigarette. "Fags."

Alec noticed Mickey glancing sideways at the house, taking in the lights and music and raised voices pouring out of it. "You been here long? There's a deck out back and a big back yard where you could smoke."

"Oh, yeah?" Mickey asked. He looked at Lincoln. "Sound good?"

"Let's go."

"Just go to the right and follow the path."

"Thanks. See you later."

Alec smiled, watching them disappear hand-in-hand around the house. He looked up and smiled at the multitude of shadows passing by the windows. When he opened the door, he was assaulted by the music and the living, breathing bodies casting those festive shadows.

"Alec!" they shouted. There were too many to take in, too many faces to match to too many names.

"Hi!" he shouted at everyone, his eyes searching for one particular face. He fought his way through the hall to the closet and dropped off his suitcase, then turned to fight his way into the kitchen. If he knew Ilsa, that's where she'd be holding court, and perhaps Eli would be nearby.

He was partially right. He walked into the kitchen to find Ilsa at the island organizing the food and chatting with friends, some of whom Alec recognized, some of whom he didn't.

Ilsa squealed and rushed into Alec's arms, knocking shocked laughter out of him. "Were you surprised?"

"Completely." She beamed up at him.

"Why are you working at your own party?" he asked.

"We asked her the same thing," a young man with light brown hair said. "It's her night, and she's in here making sure the food is orderly." He chuckled.

Alec turned to him and smiled. "Bishop, right?" They shook hands. "You're with DI Albee?"

"Please, call me Keith," Albee said, sweeping into the room, carrying two drinks. "I met you at the planning stage for this spectacular event, right?" His powerful hand took Alec's and shook it vigorously.

"That's right." Alec watched as Keith took his place at Bishop's side and passed him his cocktail. "How did you two meet?"

"He handled Mum's estate when she passed two years ago," Keith explained.

"Oh, I'm sorry."

"Thank you, though something beautiful came out of losing her. She'd be happy for me. Always worried herself over me being alone once she'd gone, and now I'm not." Bishop and Keith kissed, and Alec smiled as he watched them.

"I hear Eli met your family," Ilsa said playfully as she tickled Alec's ribs.

He grabbed her hands to still them. "*Yes* he did, as a matter of fact. We had a great time, and my mother became strangely...."

"Yes?" she asked as the others looked on.

"Strangely receptive." Alec looked into her eyes. "If I had to guess, I'd say Eli truly charmed her."

"He can do that."

"Oh, happy birthday."

"Thank you, Alec." Ilsa hugged him tight. "I'm glad you're here."

"Sorry I'm late, but it looks like the party all went off without a hitch."

Keith nodded. "That it did."

"Did I miss anything?"

"The Brandts were here earlier, but it's past their bedtime, I think," Ilsa said.

"Has anyone seen Eli?" Alec asked. "I haven't spotted him yet."

"Last time I saw him," Bishop offered, "he was putting as much distance between him and Shana as possible."

Alec chuckled at the image.

"She's harmless," Ilsa said dismissively. "But good luck finding him in this multitude." Ilsa patted his tummy and went back to the island to fill a plate for him. "You should eat something."

"I'm good, Ilsa, thanks. I ate on the plane." He looked warily at the undulating mass of bodies. "I'll talk to you all later. If you see him before I do, corner him for me."

"You've got it," Bishop said, wrapping his arm around Keith and pulling him closer. "You could shout, but he wouldn't hear you over the music."

"I could send up a flare," Alec said, laughing.

ELI sat on the arm of the sofa in the living room, right next to the pile of gifts for Ilsa, chatting and drinking with several guests.

"Eli, right?"

"Yes." Eli reached out to shake hands. "Conley?"

"You got me, mate. Good to see you."

"How did the team do without Alec?"

"We squeaked by, squeaked by," Conley said, laughing. "Speaking of your beau, I haven't seen him tonight."

"He was taking a later flight from the States, but," Eli said, glancing at the clock on the table by the sofa, "he should be here by now." His eyes searched the room and the dining room, and Conley looked around as well. Eli thought he looked a bit anxious. "Everything all right?" he asked.

"Oh, yeah. I just need to talk to him." Eli cocked an eyebrow, and Conley laughed nervously. "It's just team stuff. No worries."

Eli watched him for a few moments, then reluctantly asked, "How's Dray?"

"Huh?"

"Dray? You came together, didn't you?"

Conley's expression clouded briefly. "Yeah, we came together, but...."

"But?"

"I don't think we're long for it," Conley said, shaking his head.

"It's been fun, but lately… it's just been weird."

"Sorry."

Conley brightened suddenly. "I think I'll go try to scare up your man."

"If you find him, point him in my direction, will ya?"

"You got it."

ALEC poked his head out the back door and did a quick inventory in search of Eli. He spotted Mirabell, Tony, Mickey, and Lincoln. Mirabell and Tony paused in their smoking and laughing to smile and wave at him. He returned the gesture but noticed that Mickey and Lincoln—their hands in each other's back pockets—were too busy staring into each other's eyes to acknowledge him. Alec understood.

"Anyone seen Eli?"

"I think he's in the living room," Mirabell said.

"Thanks. Tony, where's Lyle?"

The artist took a gulp of his drink and said, "I'm sure he's busy cleaning up behind people. The man is unstoppable. He's been collecting empties and demanding coaster usage all evening."

Alec laughed. "If I see him, I'll try to get him to give it a rest and relax."

"Much appreciated, sweetie," Tony said, raising his glass in toast.

"I haven't seen Casey," Alec said.

"She got here about an hour before you," Tony said.

"She's in the shower," Ilsa offered, coming up behind him and smacking his bottom hard. He yelped, and they all laughed.

Then Ilsa yelped as Casey smacked her on her ass. "Out of the shower, love." They quickly wrapped their arms around each other and kissed long and deep. "Happy birthday, honey," Casey said softly. "You having fun?"

"Tremendous fun." Ilsa's eyes twinkled.

Alec laughed. "I'm missing Eli."

"Go and find him, then," Mirabell instructed, shooing him away theatrically. "Go on, abandon us. Go find your *luvah*." Alec snorted at his friend, then turned to head back into the house, the group chuckling in his wake.

He paused at the kitchen island and snagged a couple of *hors d'oeuvres*, then walked into the dining room. He saw Ilsa's exes, Shana and Lori, chatting with several other women and men at the dining room table. They seemed to be engaged in a heated discussion about something, but there was occasional laughter as well, so he figured nothing was about to be broken. He glanced into the living room and spotted his target, Eli, sitting on the arm of the sofa.

They caught each other's eye and smiled, holding the gaze. Alec made a beeline for him, but Conley waylaid him before him could even make it beyond the dining room.

"Can I speak to you?"

"Uh, actually, Conley, I'm heading for...." He spoke around the *hors d'oeuvre* in his mouth and pointed at Eli with the other one before popping that in his mouth as well.

Conley glanced over his shoulder and then back at Alec. "I understand, but I need to talk to you about Dray."

After chewing and swallowing rather quickly, Alec asked, "What about him?"

Conley grabbed him by the arm and pulled him to the side so Eli couldn't see them. "What happened between you two?"

"What? Me and Dray?"

"Look, you called me for Dray's number, told me you needed to talk to him. The next time I see him, he's... he's—"

"What?"

"He's not making sense and so... so quiet it's... I don't know... unnerving."

"Well, he was upset when he left my place, but I—"

Conley wasn't really listening. "For days he's not himself, then he calls and invites himself along here as my date, like nothing's happened."

"Where is he?" Alec asked.

"No idea. I lost track of him after our first hour here."

ELI saw Alec appear, and when their eyes met, he had to admit his pulse quickened. But their gratification was delayed by Conley and some silly football business. He felt himself swell a bit, remembering their last bit of time together. He tried to recall if Alec had a dresser at his flat like the one at the hotel. He smiled to himself; he certainly hoped so.

He sighed and tried to readjust himself subtly before deciding that maybe delaying gratification wasn't such a bad idea. He could just make out Conley speaking urgently to Alec, who he had backed into the corner just beyond the arch leading into the next room. Eli couldn't see anything but Alec's hands. He loved those hands.

He glanced to his right, into the hallway. "Excuse me," he said to the small group around him. "If my boyfriend comes looking for me, tell him I said to *find* me." He winked at the group, then watched Conley and Alec, making sure he wasn't spotted leaving the room. His friends' conspiratorial laughter followed him out of the room as he headed straight for his bedroom.

Eli rushed to close the door behind him, hoping as few people as possible saw him sneak into his room. He turned on the light and discovered Dray Jenkins sitting in the chair by the bed, sipping a drink, and holding a picture of Bennett in his lap.

Chapter 34

"WHAT the fuck are you doing in here?" Eli asked. Dray didn't say anything, just looked him up and down and sipped his drink. "Oh. I see. Still after Alec, eh?"

Dray laughed, but there was no amusement in it. "I wasn't looking for Alec." He stood and crossed the room to return the photo to its proper spot on the shelf. He smiled at Eli. "He's made his feelings perfectly clear."

"Yes, months ago, but that hasn't slowed you down any, has it?"

Dray made his way toward him, pausing at the closet and feeling the lapel of a suit jacket hanging on the back of the door.

"Ya know, Erby, I've been in here for the past hour, going through your things, trying to figure out just what it is about you." Eli watched him, trying to pinpoint what was different about him. Something was, but he couldn't name it. "Why Bennett and now Alec are so into you." Dray smiled wickedly. "I have to say, I just don't see it, and I thought when our handsome American friend found out we'd slept together, he'd surely break it off with you."

"Why? Bennett didn't."

"True, but you'd been with him longer. You and Alec are just starting, and I'm sure you've already filled his head with all sorts of horror stories about me and my conquests," he said, looming over him. "So if you were one of them, what would that say about you?" Dray reached out and curiously rubbed Eli's new haircut. He seemed amused. "Cute."

Eli pulled away from the contact. "Alec can see for himself who and what you are. He's a big boy."

"Yes, a big, beautiful boy," Dray said. "Just like me." He turned slightly away from Eli. "But he only seems interested in figuring me out." He looked back suddenly. "Did he tell you that? He asked me up

to his place to *analyze* me? To understand why I was so fucked up?"
Dray stared into Eli's eyes. "There. Is. Nothing. Wrong. With. Me!"

Eli grinned. "You keep telling yourself that." He turned away
from Dray. "Now, if you'd be so—ah fuck it! Dray, get out of my
room!"

Dray caught his arm and jerked him back around to face him.
"They both chose you over me. That doesn't make sense."

"I'm sure it doesn't." Eli smiled. "The truth is, for the longest
time, I didn't understand it either, but there it is."

"There what is?" Dray asked, downing the rest of his drink.

"I offered them something more than a quick shag. I loved them."

The two of them stared at each other for a few moments, Eli
unable to read Dray's changing expressions. Suddenly Dray grabbed
him and kissed him. Eli was too stunned to react at first but then broke
free in sputtering disgust.

"Are you out of your bloody mind?!" he asked, wiping his mouth.

Dray chuckled. "Come on, Eli. We had fun once. There's no one
around. We could again."

"You nutter. What happened before was the worst mistake of my
life! And…," Eli said, beginning to laugh, "*you* are the last man on this
planet I want in my bed. You're just too drunk and self-absorbed right
now to notice." He went to the door and pulled it open, but Dray
reached around him and slammed it shut.

"You're laughing at me now?"

"How can I not?" Eli reached for the doorknob again. "Get out,
get sober, and I promise never to bring this up again." He opened the
door again, and Dray slammed it shut again, this time stepping into Eli
and pressing him back against the door with his own body. *Oh, this is
pathetic*. "What are you—?"

"Shut it!" Dray threw down his glass, and Eli flinched as Dray
began to feel him up, exploring his body as he kissed Eli's neck and
ground against him. He put up with it, standing there, arms at his sides,
waiting for the drunken idiot to realize he wasn't working him into
some wanton sexual froth. "You remember how good it was with us
that first time, right?" Dray asked, his breath steaming up Eli's
disinterested ear.

"Not really." He looked Dray in the eye. "I was drunk, remember?"

Dray growled low in his throat and punched the door right next to Eli's head, denting it. Eli gulped as he looked at the damage and then into Dray's rage-filled eyes. *That,* he recognized. He felt fear-fueled iciness run over the surface of his skin as Dray pressed him harder against the door. Eli could feel him, rock hard and huge against his thigh.

"Let me remind you," Dray said, grabbing him by the arm and throwing him to the floor by the bed.

As Eli struggled to his feet, he saw Dray lock the door. He did remember that night. If he hadn't been ready, sufficiently drunk and relaxed, Dray would have really hurt him. He also remembered their fucking had begun gently and become rather rough, the way Dray liked it. Now his mouth was dry with fear, and he hated feeling afraid—afraid and not strong enough, like he had in that alley years ago.

He eyed the door behind Dray, and he knew he wouldn't be heard above the music that pounded through his walls. As Dray approached him, Eli back away and braced himself, squaring his stance and repeating *put him down, put him down* over and over in his head as he searched for Dray's soft spot—although he really didn't appear to have one. Dray came at him, and Eli slammed the head of his cane into Dray's gut, just below his ribs.

WHEN he came to, he was shirtless… in his bed… a weight on top of him. Dray was biting his neck, pressing him into the mattress, and massaging his cock through his pants. Eli moaned and tried to squirm free as his head swam and throbbed. Dray's looked at him and smiled.

"There you are, Erby," he chuckled. "Thought I'd killed you."

"Yet you're still trying to fuck me… charming." Eli tasted blood, and his lip was swollen.

"I didn't mean to hit you that hard, but you *did* hit me first."

Eli tested his jaw to see if it was still hanging properly, and Dray began unhooking Eli's belt.

"Hang on! Stop it, Dray!" He tried to stall Dray's busy hands with his own.

"Now, Erby, just relax. I'm not angry anymore. I'll be gentle."

"Get off!"

"I'm trying to," Dray chuckled.

He shoved on Dray's massive shoulders with all he had, but the behemoth wouldn't budge.

"Son of a bitch!"

"How'd you know?" Dray asked.

Eli punched him in the face, and Dray's head snapped right. He hadn't expected that. Angry again, he captured Eli's hands and pinned both above his head with only one of his, then he kissed him as he slid his other hand across Eli's chest and down his front. Eli turned away from him, sucking air past his teeth as Dray took hold of his cock.

"St-stop it."

Dray didn't. He began to stroke Eli slowly while watching his face. Dray smiled as Eli began to respond, despite his best efforts to resist.

"There we go. That's more like it, Erby."

"You sick, twisted s-sack of shite!"

Dray laughed.

"Why such venom? I'm not such a bad bloke." He was back to solicitous, charming Dray. "Haven't I been careful with your bad leg?" he asked in a singsong, light voice. "Last time we did this, you weren't crippled." Dray smiled. "I've never fucked a gimp before."

Eli's heart began to race. He felt like he couldn't fill his lungs, and he looked around for something within his reach that—if his hands were free—he could use to get Dray off of him. He glanced down beside the bed and saw his cane, the one Alec had given him, lying in two pieces on the floor. Eli cried out and began to struggle again, but his hands were still pinned, and he couldn't lift Dray with his legs alone. It was like trying to wriggle free of a boulder.

"If you wanted me all this time, w-why go after Bennett and Alec?" Eli asked.

Dray laughed out loud. "I never wanted you, you little fuck!" He squeezed Eli's cock until tears came to his eyes. "I wanted Bennett, and you were in the way. I want Alec, and here you are in the way again. I never wanted you, Eli. I hate you!"

They locked eyes and fell silent. The only sound was Eli's panting and the thumping music spilling through the walls. Then someone knocked on the door. Eli opened his mouth to shout, but Dray grabbed him by the throat and squeezed until he couldn't make a sound. His hands free, Eli pushed against Dray, his face, his chest, but he still wouldn't budge. Dray was listening for another knock. Eli punched him in the face again, and suddenly Eli could barely breathe.

"You hit me again, Erby, and I'll snap your fucking neck!" Dray hissed, then he tentatively licked a bit of blood from his own lip.

"Eli?" *Alec!* Eli struggled harder to free himself and shout, but Dray's hand tightened around his throat, and the room began to grow dark. "Eli, I've been thinking about you all day." The doorknob turned uselessly. "Can't wait to get my hands on you again."

Dray was waiting and listening so intently that he didn't notice Eli's struggles had stopped. He loosened his grip, and Eli coughed and sputtered back to consciousness.

"Oops, sorry about that, Erby," Dray said, laughing.

"A CACKLING group of your friends told me I should 'find you', and I'm betting you're in there," Alec said. When there was still no answer from within, he rested his head against the door and closed his eyes. "Fuck! Where are you?"

He glanced at the stairs, but decided Eli wouldn't try that, especially not if he'd been drinking. Alec looked down the hall and into the kitchen, thinking maybe he had moved through there and out onto the deck. This hide-and-seek was going to be the death of him. He walked away, entering the kitchen.

"Did Eli come through here?"

"No luck yet?" Casey asked. She had Ilsa pressed up against the sink.

Alec shook his head. "I tried his bedroom, but the door's locked."

Ilsa laughed and pried herself free of Casey, leaning over to the side of the refrigerator. "I've got an extra key here somewhere," she said, fiddling with a magnetic key rack. "Let's see, backdoor, bedrooms: four, three, two, and—here you go." Ilsa handed Alec the key. "He's probably just playing games. Go get your man."

ELI winced as tears of anger and frustration spilled from his eyes. He couldn't move. He couldn't stop Dray, just like when he was facedown in that alley so long ago and unable to help Bennett... helpless. He wanted to scream, but he didn't want to give Dray the satisfaction.

"When I get free, Dray, I'm going to kill you," he rasped.

"You're welcome to try, Erby. Now—*come* for Daddy."

THE door opened, and Alec stood there, transfixed long enough to see the broken cane on the floor, Dray's glass on its side by the bureau, and Eli's swollen face. His body went rigid as he realized what was going on. He moved toward them with images filling his head of the shovel in the cellar and the freshly turned earth in the back garden. He knew just where to put Dray after he'd beaten him to death. He grabbed him by the back of his belt and lifted him off Eli with one hand, throwing him to the floor.

Dray scooted away from him as he advanced. "Now, Alec, you don't want any of this, love."

"Never have. Never will," Alec said, continuing forward.

"I'm just saying," Dray said, getting to his feet, still amused. "I'm a lot bigger than you."

Chapter 35

ILSA, Casey, Bishop, and Keith stood chatting around the kitchen island, but their conversation stalled when they heard a crash. Even above the music, they could tell something was very wrong. They listened... waited... and were rewarded with another thump and crash. Following the sound, Ilsa slowly walked around the island and headed for the hall, the other three in her wake. As she neared Eli's bedroom door, there was another thump, and the pictures lining the hallway rattled on the wall. The three of them looked at each other and recoiled in unison as a crack appeared in Eli's door.

The door was yanked open, and they watched Dray Jenkins seemingly fly through the air, his shiny, black, bald head cracking two railings in the staircase banister before he landed on his ass on the hardwood floor,.

"Size doesn't always matter," Alec said, stepping into the hall and grabbing Dray by the collar, "not when one man intends to kill the other."

That was it. The K word. Keith sprang into action, grabbing Alec and pinning his arms behind his back before he could land another blow. He quickly twisted Alec and pressed his face against the wall. Casey ran to the back door and shouted to Lyle and Tony. The artist stood up so quickly, he almost tossed Lyle off his lap and onto the deck. Lincoln and Mickey stopped kissing and decided to follow the commotion instead.

As Tony passed the dining room, he spotted Mirabell slow-dancing with Buddy and shouted for her to follow them, which she did after shutting off the music. Unfortunately, this created a bottleneck at the kitchen door, and not everyone could see what was going on in the hall. Suddenly Mirabell appeared above them all as Buddy lifted her in his arms. She gave him a blow-by-blow account of what she saw.

At the front of the group, Ilsa stood, her mouth agape. She didn't think she'd ever seen Alec so angry. As she looked around, she wondered what Dray could have done.

"Hang on! Where's Eli?!"

Eli answered her question by coming out of his room swinging his old, battered, metal cane like a baseball bat aimed directly at Dray's skull. The man ducked just in time, and it simply splintered another banister railing.

"Eli!" Ilsa shouted, stepping between them and raising her hands.

"Move, Ilsa!" Eli said. "He wouldn't let me go! He wouldn't stop! I couldn't breathe!" He raised the cane again. *"I couldn't move!"*

Ilsa looked into Eli's eyes and saw tears there—not tears of sadness and fear like following a nightmare of Bennett's murder—but tears of murderous fury. Before he could get his second swing going, however, Bishop caught hold of the cane. Happily, no one had hold of Ilsa. She rounded on Dray, who had finally struggled to his feet, and kneed him in the crotch. His lungs seized up, and he dropped back to his knees, clutching himself.

"You filthy son of a bitch! You ever come near Alec or Eli again, I'll chop you into a stew!"

Other partygoers had started filtering in from the living room, and all eyes were on Dray as he fought to catch his breath and get up. He clutched blindly at the railings on the stairs for assistance, but he kept grasping broken ones. Finally he found a solid one and hauled himself to his feet. He tried to smile, but it seemed to have lost some wattage.

"Eli and I were just having a little alone time," he said lightly but with a grimace.

Eli howled and tried to get around Bishop, but he held him off. They vanished back into the bedroom, and the crowd in the hall heard things smashing above Bishop's calming voice.

"Let me go!" Alec shouted to Keith. "Let me go!"

"You have to promise not to go after him again," Keith said.

"Wait... uh, let me just head out before you..." Dray said, heading for the door. Tony and Lyle dashed into the dining room, heading for the living room.

"What's going on out there?" Shana shouted as they passed.

Tony turned, but he didn't stop moving. Bumping into curious guests as he walked backward, he said, "Dray attacked Eli, and he's trying to leave." The two men stepped into the hallway, blocking Dray's exit, then Shana strolled up and took a position behind them.

"Not likely," Tony said.

"You're staying put, mate," Lyle added, "until the coppers tell us otherwise."

"I'm good, Keith. I won't touch him," Alec said, his speech a bit mangled as his face pressed into the wall. "I just need to get to Eli. Please." Keith released him, and Alec tossed Dray a final glare before entering the bedroom and tapping Bishop on the shoulder. "I got this," he said.

The young solicitor stepped out of the room, and Alec closed the door. Eli's rage-filled voice continued, occasionally punctuated by something smashing and the guests flinching when further breakage occurred. Dray himself flinched when the bedroom door rattled under a fresh onslaught from Eli.

Ilsa stared at the door and prayed Alec was all right.

"Okay, people, I think this party is over," she said, clapping her hands in front of her. "Thank you for coming."

The guests snapped to, gathering their belongings and rushing out the door. Conley paused on his way out. Dray looked at him in search of sympathy, working his swollen eye and split lip for all they were worth, but he was greeted with, "You sick fuck." Then Conley was gone.

Mirabell paused in the doorway while Buddy helped her into a bright orange jacket. "Tell Alec to call me if he needs me." Ilsa nodded, smiled, and waved goodnight.

Tony and Lyle hovered near Eli's bedroom door, listening, while Keith and Bishop dragged Dray into the living room and deposited him onto the sofa.

"How long am I going to have to wait here?" Dray asked.

"Until Eli decides if he wants to press charges," Bishop said.

"He won't. The authorities won't give a shit about this," Dray said with a smile. "They don't care if we kill each other off."

Keith stepped forward. "I assure you, Jenkins, the coppers at my station give a shit."

Dray smiled more brightly, spit blood onto the floor, and shook his head. "They'll just call it a lover's spat, and I'm not saying different." He sighed, looking them in the eye. "Me and Eli, we've got history. I've shagged him before. He won't deny it." Dray shrugged. "And even if he does? It's his word again mine—"

"And ours," Casey said walking into the living room and wishing him dead with her eyes.

"And mine," Mickey said, stepping into view. Dray's eyes widened, but he recovered.

"Who the hell are you, mate?"

"Who the hell am—?"

Mickey rushed forward, leaping onto Dray and pounding him about the head.

"Michael!" Lincoln shouted, taking hold of him and trying to pull him off Dray.

Mickey fought him desperately. "No! No! Let me... he... he did it!"

Lincoln pulled Mickey into his arms despite his struggles. "He did what?" Lincoln grabbed the sides of Mickey's head and forced him to look him in the eye. "Mickey?"

"All right! That's it!" Dray shouted, wiping his bloody face. "He broke my fucking nose!"

"Shut it!" Keith shouted at Dray, quickly turning to watch Lincoln and Mickey closely.

"No! You coppers can't just hold me here like this, not and let every nutter have a go at me!"

Mickey kept trying to turn his head toward Dray, his eyes darting to the right repeatedly until they settled on Lincoln.

"He... he's the one who hurt m-me," he said softly, and then he began to cry silently. Lincoln embraced him, all the while looking at Dray like he wanted his turn at him.

"Bishop?" Keith said.

"Got it," Bishop answered, tossing his cell to Keith. He hit speed-dial. "I need transport for a suspect," he said, walking briefly into the hall to finish his call. Shana took his place, arms folded across her chest like some Amazon warrior, while Lori waited for her by the door in silent admiration.

Ilsa turned on her heel and headed for the kitchen.

"Wh-where are you going?" Casey asked.

"To get my butcher knife and put on a big pot to boil."

Casey turned back to Dray and smiled. "I'll help," she said.

Dray watched them go.

"I left some plastic drop cloths in the cellar if you need them, Ilsa," Tony announced.

"Here, here! That's not right," Dray said, struggling to his feet. "Are you hearing this?" he asked Keith as he re-entered the room.

"I don't hear a thing, but don't get all worked up, Jenkins," the officer said over the sound of Ilsa expertly sharpening her knives against each other; it was a distinctive, disconcerting sound. "My mates will be here soon to cart your arse to jail. And I'd advise you to sit back down, or I'll put you down myself."

Lyle walked to the front door and locked it. He smiled at Dray as he passed the living room, and Dray gulped and finally fell silent.

Chapter 36

ALEC stood watching an exhausted Eli sway in the center of the bedroom. Surrounded by chaos and destruction, he hadn't shouted or howled or spoken or smashed anything for nearly three minutes. He looked lost, spent, and disoriented: dragging the head of his cane on the floor, his hair wet, and sweat dripping down his face. Alec waited for the right moment, and when Eli went, he rushed forward to catch him. They dropped to the floor in a tangle and clung to each other as Eli sobbed against him.

"It's all right, it's all right," Alec whispered over and over, stroking his hair.

Eli didn't say anything for a long time and then, softly, "I need a new bed."

"I understand."

"I can't sleep in that bed again. I need a whole new set, maybe."

"Mm-hmm."

"Bennett and I picked this set out."

"I know."

Eli pressed his face into Alec's chest, breathing in his comforting scent. Alec looked around the room. He didn't see much that was salvageable. Eli had put two holes in the wall and another crack in the door. He had torn several drawer fronts off and dented most of the others. And one of the last things he did was shatter the mirror hanging on the back of the closet door.

All of this couldn't be put at Dray's feet. He knew Eli was expressing everything he hadn't when Bennett was killed, and Alec was even more thankful that he'd come in when he did. If not, Dray would have had his way with Eli and—amused with himself—turned his back on him. Eli would have killed him. Alec was sure of it.

"I used to talk to him," Eli said in a whisper.

"What, sweetie? Talk to who?"

"Bennett... after... he died... I used to talk to him." Alec remained silent, allowing it to simply come. "Whenever the anniversary rolled around, I'd talk to him more and... and he... he would talk to me." Eli looked up into Alec's eyes suddenly. "I wasn't crazy." He lowered his gaze again and closed his eyes. "I mean, I knew it was just me... my thoughts, but it made me feel better. And sometimes he would help me work things out."

"I understand."

He looked up at Alec again. "He helped me work out my feelings about you."

"Then I'm in his debt." Alec continued to stroke Eli's head. "Do you still talk to him?"

Eli shook his head as it rested against Alec's chest. "No. Not since last November, when I came back from his family's place." Alec smiled and kissed the top of Eli's head. "Not since I came back to you."

Suddenly Eli inhaled sharply, and Alec thought he was in pain, but then he realized he was reacting to Alec's injuries.

"Your hands!" He gingerly touched Alec's knuckles and grimaced at the dried blood and bruising. Eli tried to get up, but Alec pulled him back down into his arms. "We should get Casey to look at these. You could have broken something."

"I'm fine, Eli," he said.

"You should ice those. Can you wiggle them?"

Alec looked at his hands and wiggled the fingers so Eli could see. "Nothing's broken, and I'll ice them once you're taken care of."

"I love you, Alec."

It was a simple statement—a statement born out of exhaustion and truth.

"I love you, Eli," he said, trying to keep the tears out of his voice and holding his man more tightly. *My man.*

"D-don't leave me."

"Leave you? Eli, why would I leave you?"

"I'm a mess."

Alec laughed. "You're *my* mess, babe."

Eli looked around the room. "I've made a mess." They laughed together.

"YOU shouted for me?" Casey asked when she opened the door.

Alec nodded, and she and Ilsa entered. "He's in the shower," he said.

"Still?" Ilsa asked as she looked around at the devastation.

"Yep. He's vomited a couple of times, but he's better. I just wanted Casey to look him over... maybe we can find something to help him sleep, and I'll take him to my room—my old room—for the night."

"Sounds good," Casey said.

Alec sat on the bed and began to rub his eyes. "What's going on out there?"

"They took Dray away." Ilsa glanced at the bathroom door. "How did Eli do?" Alec looked at her with exhaustion and confusion in his eyes. Ilsa sat on the bed next to him and placed her hand on his knee. "With... with Keith gathering the evidence, his statement, the pictures and... and all?"

Alec shuddered. "Actually that sent him into the bathroom the first time, but he came back and finished up." He looked up at Casey and then Ilsa. "But I don't know if Eli wants to prosecute."

Ilsa shook her head and smiled. "Doesn't matter. Mickey charged Dray with sexual assault."

"What?!"

"Apparently Dray wouldn't take no for an answer from him, either."

Though stunned, Alec nodded thoughtfully. "He *was* at Tony and Lyle's party the night Mickey freaked out."

"Get this," Ilsa said. "Dray heard Bishop was a lawyer and tried to secure him as counsel."

"You're joking."

"Nope," she said, smiling. "Bishop calmly told him that he was unable to defend him, but he would be happy to handle his estate were he to die in prison."

"Ilsa!" Casey said. She tried but couldn't stop herself from smiling.

Ilsa continued as if her girlfriend hadn't said anything. "And before they took him away, he was mouthing off, saying, 'they'll never convict me' and 'Eli wanted it'."

"How cliché," Casey said.

"That son of a bitch!" Alec added. He tried to make a fist, but his fingers were too stiff.

"I told him he had better be convicted, because I have an ex-girlfriend with a hog farm just outside the city." Alec just stared at Ilsa, not understanding. "They'll eat any and everything," she assured him.

The ensuing laughter covered the sound of the shower shutting off, so they were surprised to see Eli standing in the bathroom doorway, a towel wrapped around his waist, watching them.

"Oh, sugar!" Ilsa said, rushing over to him. Casey joined her, examining and frowning at the dark bruise and other marks around Eli's neck.

"Here, come sit on the bed," Casey said as she walked him over to Alec, "Scooch over!" she commanded, and Alec did as he was told while the women hovered around his boyfriend.

"Could someone get ice for Alec's hands, please?" Eli asked.

He sounded exhausted.

"Mmm, you smell good," Alec said, wrapping one arm around Eli as they began to ascend the stairs to the attic room.

"I used your soap," Eli said. "That sandalwoody-chocolate-vanilla stuff." His eyes were droopy, and he leaned heavily on Alec for support as they slowly made their way up. "You left some in my bathroom last time you showered there."

"Mmm, then I *do* smell good," Alec said, and Eli smiled.

Ilsa stood at the foot of the stairs watching them go. She was soon joined by Tony, Lyle, and Casey.

"Where do you need us, Ilsa?" Lyle asked.

She looked at him and then at Casey and Tony as they stood waiting.

"Eli's room."

They all stood their ground until Eli and Alec were out of sight. Then they moved into the room and began cleaning up.

ELI lay in bed listening to Alec in the shower and watching the steam sneak under the door. He glanced at his bruised knuckles from where he'd struck Dray. His hands were nothing compared to the way Alec's looked. He remembered watching Alec beat Dray. He was afraid he was going to kill him; after all, Eli certainly wanted to when he'd come back to himself. He shivered and glanced at the bathroom door again, wishing Alec would finish and come to bed.

The water cut off, and he heard the glass door moan as it opened. Shortly after, Alec exited the bathroom with a towel around his waist, vigorously drying his hair with a smaller one. Eli smiled at the gorgeous man before him.

He couldn't believe he'd almost let Alec get away by being stubborn over the idea of finding their own place and lying to him about Dray. A flat all on one level and a bed and bedroom he could share with Alec every night was terribly appealing.

"I thought you'd be asleep by now," Alec said.

"I wanted to wait for you," he said, watching Alec remove the towel from his waist and slip into a pair of sweat shorts before climbing into bed next to Eli. He snuggled down under the covers and tangled his feet with Eli's. They kissed, and Eli's hand lingered on Alec's waist. "I've been thinking," he said, drawing his fingers along Alec's side, making him shiver.

"About?"

"Me moving in with you."

"I thought you were against that."

"Just fear talking," he said as he pushed Alec onto his back and slid on top of him. "The fear of things changing, fear of the unknown, but lately, I've realized what I fear most is losing you." He stroked Alec through his shorts and kissed him until they were both breathless. "Make love to me," he whispered.

Alec grabbed Eli's arms and held him at arm's length. "No."

"What?"

Alec stared into Eli's confused eyes, then gently drew his finger across the bruise on his neck. Their eyes met again.

"I need you to understand something," Alec said softly. "You're not going to lose me, whether you live here with Ilsa or not. I'm not going anywhere. Do you hear me?" Eli nodded. "I understand you have a lot of history here… history with Bennett and Ilsa, and I don't want you to let go of that until you're ready."

"I'm ready."

"Hear me out—"

"Alec, I dread the thought of sleeping in that room again, and, honestly, I'm not sure I left much of it standing." Alec laughed. "I'm tired of sleeping without you, and you can't drag me up these stairs every night."

"If you're sure—"

He leaned in again for a kiss, but Alec held him off.

"What is it?" Eli asked.

"I will happily hold you all night, but that's all."

He pulled back and stared at Alec. "Why?"

"I don't want what happened tonight mixed up in your head with you and me. Can you understand that?"

He didn't like it, but he understood it. "You're the psychologist, love."

They wrapped up in each other, and Alec laughed to himself a few moments later when he realized Eli was sound asleep. He pressed his lips to his head, breathed him in, and then drifted off.

Epilogue

ELI let the hot water cascade over him, pounding loose the tension and fatigue his body held and rinsing them down the drain. His day had started early with a new client and several of the student's classes, which involved introducing himself to and chatting with each instructor afterward. Then he worked out at the gym and grabbed a quick lunch before joining Alec, Stacy, and Chuck for a trip to St. James Park.

He had sat on a bench and watched Alec run himself ragged chasing and playing with his niece and nephew, the children giggling themselves into limp-bodied hysteria. When his boyfriend was properly exhausted, he joined Eli on the bench to marvel at the boundless energy of the two youngsters.

Unfortunately, a call from Hammersmith Hospital had ended their fun. Now on the call list for sign language interpreters, they apparently needed Eli's skills right away, so the two men had kissed goodbye, the kids got hugs from their Uncle Eli, and Alec took the little ones back to Ilsa's to hand back over to their parents.

The family had settled nicely into the one guest room Ilsa and Casey had completed for their bed-and-breakfast project. There was much more work to be done throughout the property, but with Lyle and Mirabell pitching in, they'd be officially open for business in a couple of months. Ilsa and Casey had both cut back on their hours to devote more time to the endeavor. Eli had never seen them so excited, especially Ilsa, as now she would have a continuing stream of people to take care of and cook for—an ever-changing family.

He smiled to himself as the soothing hot spray washed over him. The novelty of the different shower settings had worn off after three weeks, but he had his favorites. He wasn't expecting Alec home for a while because, after taking time out in the middle of his day for their get-together in the park, his boyfriend—his partner—still had paperwork to finish at the university.

Eli slowly began to soap himself, meditating on the various contours and textures of his skin: the smooth, unblemished areas, the coarse hair, the scars, the hard muscle, and his stubbled face. He closed his eyes and imagined Alec touching him in all his favorite places, grinning as his hands wandered over his skin, eventually lingering between his legs, where he quickly grew hard. He raised his face to take the shower's blast directly and sighed again, but when his leg twinged—still disagreeable from his workout—he bent to massage the stiffness out of it.

Surrounded by the hot steam and warmth within the giant glass box, he suddenly felt a temperature drop at his back, but he didn't turn around. He simply rose up, holding his breath and waiting in nervous anticipation.

"Hi, babe," Alec whispered in his ear as he wrapped his arms around Eli, pulling him back against his chest.

"Hey!" Eli started with a laugh. "You're still dressed, you nutter!" He spun in Alec's arms to face him. "What the hell are you doing?" He couldn't stop grinning as he watched Alec's shirt and trousers become completely soaked through, his hair hanging wet and limp under the onslaught from the showerhead. Eli reached up and lifted Alec's hair out of his face so he could see his eyes.

"I took my shoes off," Alec explained, pointing down, "but I didn't want to miss this opportunity." He reached for Eli again and pulled him in for a quick kiss. "My family's only been here since Sunday, but I'm already dragging." Eli shuddered as Alec's belt buckle—still cooler than the surrounding heat—brushed against his tummy. They kissed again, melting into each other, Eli feeling his insides quiver and his knees threaten to give way as their tongues played off each other.

"We've got Stacy in Paris tomorrow," he panted during a pause in the action. "Tonight we should take—"

"—some time for ourselves?" Alec finished.

Eli nodded, passed the soapy loofah to Alec, and smiled as he began unbuckling his boyfriend's ruined trousers. For his part, Alec eagerly took over cleansing duties. He drew the sponge over Eli's shoulders and down his back, and then Alec smiled as he reached behind and swirled it over the firm curve of Eli's bottom, pressing it briefly between his cheeks and causing Eli to gasp and giggle at the sensation.

"I didn't expect you home so soon," Eli said. "Thought I might have time to make some dinner." Alec tossed the loofah to the floor, replacing it with several fingers, and began to massage around one of Eli's favorite places.

"Were you thinking of me before I got here?" Alec asked, glancing at Eli's erection.

"Maybe," Eli said, just as he managed to free Alec's cock. "Looks like you were thinking of me too."

"Definitely," Alec whispered before kissing him tenderly. He held Eli's hands to support him as they moved toward the bench, where Alec shed his clothes, letting them pool at his feet. Eli shoved them out of the way with his foot and carefully straddled Alec's lap.

Alec's hands ran up and down Eli's sides before coming to rest at his waist. He steadied Eli as his boyfriend positioned himself over Alec's cock. Their gazes locked as Eli slowly lowered himself onto Alec, his eyes rolling back in his head and fluttering shut as Alec stretched him, his lips parting and a crooked grin playing at his mouth. Alec watched, mesmerized by the beauty of the man on top of him. Then Eli began to rise up and down, gradually increasing his pace.

When Eli opened his eyes, he found Alec's shut tightly in concentration, his bottom lip caught between his teeth as he fought to last for him.

"Look at me," Eli said.

And Alec did. They smiled at each other, gasping and moaning to an almost simultaneous climax. Then they kissed hungrily, panting as though only the other held the oxygen they each needed desperately.

As their breathing returned to normal, Eli caressed the sides of Alec's face, looked into his eyes, and whispered, "Welcome home."

Read the beginning of Eli and Alec's story in

http://www.dreamspinnerpress.com

DAWN KIMBERLY JOHNSON is a graduate of Marshall University in Huntington, West Virginia, where she grew up and still lives. For eight years she worked as a copy editor at a daily newspaper before heading west to Oregon in search of adventure. After eight years there, five of them good, she returned home where she is trying to regain her health and still hoping for the best.

Visit her LiveJournal at http://dawnkj63.livejournal.com/. You can contact her at KimsWritingAgain@yahoo.com.